I0776953

Robert Creekmore
Prophet's Death

Published by: Cinnabar Moth Publishing LLC
Santa Fe, New Mexico

Cover Design by: Ira Geneve

ISBN-13: 978-1-962308-15-1
Library of Congress Control Number: 2024933789

Prophet's Death

ROBERT CREEKMORE

Dedication:

For Juliana.

"Long is the way and hard, that out of Hell
leads up to the light."
—John Milton

1

The winds of Tropical Storm Gabrielle punish the small dive boat. Its howling feels like the voice of nature herself crying out in lamentation at the death of Naomi Pace.

As Nate pilots the craft over each wave, there's a moment when he can hear the engines rev hard as the props come out of the water momentarily just before crashing down again. This cycle repeats every few seconds, seemingly without end.

Below deck, Rebecca and Herschel steady an unconscious Malcolm by keeping him squeezed between their bodies. It's difficult. There's nothing to hold onto since the Apostles stripped the cabin bare. The two hours it takes to get back to their dock are hell, both physically and introspectively.

Naomi was Nate's best friend. To him, she was invincible.

How could she be dead? Nate thinks to himself as he involuntarily projects images of their time together across the water.

He has successfully outrun the incoming storm wall, but a new one awaits his fractured mind when all of the chaos subsides.

Neither Herschel nor Rebecca has the same composure. They wail with grief. Reaching across Malcolm's limp body, they hold one another's hands for comfort as much as they do to keep their injured companion safe from the onslaught of the turbulent water.

Nate threads the needle at the Masonboro Inlet, just like Naomi taught him. The waves rocking the swollen bay attempt to push them easterly into the mainland. Even though it means safety, the sight of the dock fills Nate with dread. Its arrival in the foreground always meant the end of a day fishing with Naomi, until now.

He guides the boat between the two wooden bunks of the boat lift. Nate fights his way onto the dock through the sheets of rain blasting sideways into his face. He activates the hydraulics. The lift pulls the boat out of the water and level with the dock.

The three of them drag Malcolm off the boat before Nate lifts it higher to avoid the rising water.

Exhausted after moving Malcolm from the dock to the side door, the three can go no further and lie him on his side atop the sofa in front of the picture window.

"We have to call home," Nate says.

"Telling someone that their spouse is dead isn't something you do over the phone," Herschel replies.

"More urgently," Rebecca interjects, "we have to get electrolytes into Malcolm. He drank plenty of water before passing out, so he's not in imminent danger of thirsting to death. To regain some level of consciousness, we need to get something like Pedialyte in him. But, no stores will be open in this storm."

"Would powdered Gatorade work?" Nate asks.

"Yeah," she responds.

Nate gets up and begins rummaging through Naomi's kitchen junk drawer. He excavates an old plastic container, half-filled with clumpy orange Gatorade powder. Nate mixes up a batch inside a large plastic cup with a flexible straw. Malcolm mumbles and occasionally opens his eyes. When he does, they encourage him to drink. Within the hour, he's holding the cup himself. His eyes begin to regain life.

He looks around, saying, "Where is the other woman?"

"She didn't make it," Rebecca answers.

A wave of melancholy washes across his exhausted face.

"The sooner we leave, the better," Nate says.

"Will he make the week-long boat trip back to Northern Virginia?" Rebecca asks.

"No. That's why I'm going to take Tiffany's Corolla."

"They'll follow you," Herschel says to Nate.

"The HAM radio upstairs is a powerful unit. It was being used as a repeater for the weaker signal coming from the tower offshore. We turned it off before leaving. The Apostles don't even know we're here yet."

"But they do know something has gone wrong. They're bound to send someone our way to assess the situation," Rebecca replies.

"Probably not until after the storm," Herschel says. "At the moment, our best option is to get Malcolm to the local hospital."

"No. They'll look for him there once they piece together what happened. If they come, we won't be able to fight them off without Naomi," Nate says tersely to Herschel, which makes his already red eyes tear up again.

"It's not fair to invoke Naomi just to get what you want."

"This isn't an issue of want. Malcolm needs to get to a doctor, but it's safest if he sees one back home."

"Back home, Nate? This is our home, not some cookie-cutter affluent suburb full of people who wouldn't be bothered with us unless they thought we had money too."

"The semantics don't matter, Herschel. I'm taking him north, with or without you."

"We can't leave the Camille in portage right across the bay. Do you remember the nice couple, Howard and Louisa who own the marina? When the boat doesn't move for weeks, the Apostles will take note of it, since it arrived right before. Remember, Abraham isn't as stupid as his followers. When he gives the order, his minions won't have a problem kicking their door down and smacking them around until they're forced to hand over the dock rental contract. That would lead them back to my shell company, Fisher and Sons. Any private investigator worth a damn will be able to track us down."

Rebecca interjects into their argument, "Nate, you take Malcolm home in Tiff's Corolla. Herschel and I will stay behind until the storm subsides. Then, we'll pilot the Camille back."

Both Herschel and Nate's moods soften with this simple realization that they were unable to see it because of their frustration. Immediately, their bickering ceases.

"The roads are still open," Herschel says to Nate. "The sooner you leave, the better. Before that, you'll need to shower and change. You're covered in Levi's blood."

"He had it coming for what he did to Malcolm and all the other gay men he lured to their deaths," Nate says.

"In my opinion, you stabbing him in the face repeatedly was getting off easy."

"Once I'm gone, you and Rebecca need to burn my clothes."

"There's just one thing left to discuss," Rebecca says, sighing. "Who tells Tiffany that the love of her life died saving seven billion humans who will never even know her name?"

"I'll do it," Nate says, "She's one of my dearest friends. I believe I can get through it. But, like Herschel said, I won't do it until we're face to face."

"Yeah. No. I couldn't… I mean, I can't. Thank you, I mean, Nate,"

Herschel says, stumbling over words boobytrapped with emotion.

Herschel wraps his huge arms around Nate, and for a moment there is calm.

After showering, Nate mixes up more Gatorade for Malcolm to drink in the car on the way back to Tysons Corner.

The three of them hoist Malcolm onto his feet and shuffle him toward the side door. Thankfully, there's less dead weight now that he's walking some on his own.

Torrential rainfall makes the trip to the car with Malcolm even more difficult than it already is. Herschel and Nate set Malcolm in the passenger's seat. This way, while driving, Nate can keep a better eye on him and encourage Malcolm to drink fluids.

Nate quickly embraces Herschel before sliding into the car's driver's seat and heading off Wrightsville Island and toward the mainland.

Back inside, Herschel and Rebecca eat cold pizza out of the box, exhausted and hungry. Afterward, they retreat upstairs. Each takes turns showering while the other guards. Then, they remake the bed in the upstairs guest room, giving them the high ground if someone breaks in. Each is armed with a pump action shotgun and a nine-millimeter pistol.

As they slide under the covers for the evening, their day comes to an abrupt halt. Quiet sets in, and tears come as though transpired from the atmosphere around them and onto their cheeks, leaving small puddles that are quickly soaked up by their pillowcases.

"I can't believe you jumped off the Frying Pan Tower," Herschel says.

"What choice did I have? It was be eaten by a beast of lamentation or take my chances with a one hundred-foot drop into the roiling ocean."

"Most people would have frozen."

"Not Naomi."

"You learned from the best."

"Yeah," Rebecca says with a sob.

After a few seconds of silence, Rebecca continues, "I wish you could have seen her go. It's impossible to express how much of a badass she was using words and not have it be an understatement," chuckling, "The look of disbelief on Joseph's face the millisecond after she got the better of him, even after what he did to her. Even as she melted."

"Jesus Christ. I need a fucking drink."

Herschel gets out of bed. He walks into the living room, past the pool table, and heads right to the bar. All the while, he's carrying a loaded Glock nineteen in his right hand. Rebecca joins him. She sits on one of the bar stools while Herschel reaches for a full bottle of Jameson on the shelf behind him.

He places it on the counter and grabs two glasses from the cabinet overhead.

"It's a wonder that the Apostle cultists who took over Naomi's house didn't drink all of this," Herschel says while pouring two generous glassfuls.

"They're religious nuts. They aren't allowed."

"But they can smoke?"

"Don't try to make too much sense out of the philosophies of a doomsday cult, baby," Rebecca says, running her fingers through Herschel's curly red hair as he leans over the bar toward her.

The first glasses of whiskey vanish quickly, followed by a second, third, and fourth. While neither is utterly blotto, they certainly aren't sober.

Back in bed, they intertwine themselves and find dreamless sleep.

2

Blankets of rain crash onto the car with so much force that Nate can hear the sheet metal ping. He drives with the hazard lights blinking, well below the speed limit. Police cars are stationed at the bridge. They wave Nate on. They're not present to keep residents from leaving but to prevent thrill-seekers and looters from coming on.

It takes two-and-a-half hours to reach Highway Forty. Even then, the fastest Nate can safely travel is forty-five miles per hour.

Malcolm begins coming to.

"Where am I? Who are you?"

"I was with the woman who saved you."

"She died. I remember the other woman telling me.

"That was Rebecca. The woman who saved you was named Naomi.

"How did she die?"

"I'm not sure I understand how but it was Joseph Proffit who caused it."

Hearing Joseph's name makes Malcolm shudder.

"Don't worry, he can't hurt you any longer. Naomi killed him. They killed each other."

"The man I was with, Sam, he's dead isn't he?"

"Unfortunately."

"I'd say Naomi did the right thing, then."

"She usually did."

Nate realizes that this is the first time he's referred to Naomi in the past tense.

"My mom was killed by a drunk driver when I was twelve. Dad did his best with me and my younger brother, but things were never the same. There will always be a void. He died last year, leaving another. I haven't seen my brother in ten years. He won't 'tolerate my lifestyle' as he so inarticulately puts it."

There is a pause while Nate processes Malcolm's words.

"Where are we headed?"

"I'm taking you to Tysons Corner, Virginia. It's where I live. That way you can go to a hospital where the Apostles can't find you."

"Apostles?"

"They're a cult. They kept Naomi prisoner for a year-and-a-half when she was a teenager."

"It was that bastard, Levi, who kidnapped me. I met him at Legends nightclub in Raleigh. That was months ago, I think. I don't know. I was locked up for so long. What day is it?"

"September sixth, two-thousand-seven."

"He took me in June."

"Jesus," Nate says.

"When I met Levi at the club, he was nice enough and rather handsome, I thought."

"He wasn't an ugly man."

"Past tense?"

"I stabbed him in his face with my dive knife for what he did. I showered his blood off my body and out of my hair just a couple of hours ago."

"Thank you for not leaving me there," Malcolm says, tearing up.

"Why would I?"

"More people than you realize might have," Malcolm says, beginning to cry.

"It's okay," Nate says, reaching his right hand out to Malcolm's left.

They quietly hold hands for the next two hours. It's been so long since Malcolm has felt any sense of human connection. It's refreshing to feel as though his life matters to someone. The simple gesture of Nate's touch gives him that."

As they travel north, the rain begins to slack off. Nate pulls his hand away and takes the exit at the Virginia border rest station on Interstate Ninety-Five.

"I can't go in. I look like a vagrant," Malcolm says.

"I know. But, I have to go pee. After all that Gatorade, I'm assuming you do too?"

"You would have guessed correctly," Malcolm says jokingly.

"Don't worry. I won't leave you," Nate says as he encourages Malcolm to lean on him to help him walk.

Because of the oncoming storm, the parking lot is nearly empty. Besides Nate and Malcolm's Corolla, there's a white dually crew cab pickup truck and a bright red, two-door Mercedes coupe.

Five people mill around in the rest area outside the bathrooms, smoking cigarettes. Four of them are men who are filthy from a hard day's work. One is a clean-cut college-aged boy with dark hair, wearing an expensive, cornflower-blue button-up shirt, cargo shorts, and leather flip-flops. It's not difficult to ascertain who drove up on which vehicle, but what unifies them is their disapproving stares.

They see Malcolm as a transient. His clothes are ragged and filthy. His hair is unkempt and he has a long beard. Not only that, but he smells horrendous.

The stare-down Nate gives them says he will do anything it takes to protect Malcolm. Bullies are weak. They want victims who fold easily. Nate's glare is a warning that he isn't made of paper but of thick plate steel.

Luckily, the men's restroom is empty. They take adjoining stalls. Nate's is the larger one at the end, making his door ninety degrees from Malcolm's.

After a couple of minutes, they hear footsteps across the slick, tile floor. The person goes to each stall, pushing them open one by one until he gets to Malcolm's. Finding it locked, the man peers underneath to see Malcolm's legs as he sits on the toilet.

It's not one of the men from the work crew. Men like them know when they're looking at a fighter. They'll go back to their truck and entertain themselves by bad-mouthing Nate and Malcolm for a few minutes as they drive home, but nothing more. Instead, it's the college boy trying to make Malcolm's existence his business.

"It sure stinks in here," he says conspicuously, outside Malcolm's stall.

He continues, "Are you shitting out a landfill or something, bro? We don't want your nasty ass in here messing up our clean bathrooms. Get out of here and take your shit in the woods with the rest of the animals before I drag you there myself."

Malcolm doesn't say anything.

The man is pounding on his stall door now, screaming, "You don't fucking ignore me, asshole! You get out here now, or I'm coming in there to stomp your face into the goddamn floor!"

Unknown to him, Nate opens the door to his stall just behind the man. Right as the motion registers in his periphery, he feels the muzzle of Nate's pistol behind his right ear.

"It's chambered, and there's no true safety on a Glock," Nate whispers to the much taller man."

He freezes.

"I have money! I'll give you money," he says.

"I'm betting that's how you've gotten out of every snafu, paltry to felonious, of your life," Nate says as he walks behind him. "What's your name?"

"Blair."

"Do you have a last name, Blair?"

"It's not important, just tell me how much you want," Blair says as Nate forces him into the larger bathroom stall.

"Get on your fucking knees."

"What?" Blair screams in disbelief. "It'll be fine. You don't have to do this. Just let me get you the money from my wallet."

Fearful, Blair collapses to his knees. Just at this time, Malcolm makes it to the stall door behind Nate, taking in the scene.

"Please, just take my wallet. There's over a thousand dollars in there."

"I don't need your money," Nate says, painfully burying the muzzle into the back of a crying Blair's head. "I need you to die."

Nate's pointer finger tickles the Glock's minuscule safety tab protruding out of the face of the trigger. He can feel his finger wanting to pull it.

Just as he begins to squeeze, a sweet voice behind him says, "Nate, baby, don't do that."

"He deserves it," Nate says.

"Maybe. But what good is it going to do you?"

With that, Malcolm drains the lake of fire inside Nate's gut.

Regardless, Nate turns his gun around and decisively smashes the butt against Blair's right temple. He immediately falls unconscious and crashes down on his left side, leaving him between the toilet and the wall.

"You're right."

"But you just hit him."

"He's still breathing," Nate replies, as he slides his pistol into a concealed holster tucked inside the waistband of his jeans.

"Usually, I'm a stickler for washing my hands, but I think we better leave right now."

"Yeah," Nate says softly.

Outside, they find the work truck gone, only leaving Blair's red Mercedes. Malcolm is more tired than when they entered, so their escape unfolds in slow motion without the fanfare of a high-speed chase.

After getting back to the Corolla, they continue traveling on Interstate Ninety-Five, north toward Richmond.

Malcolm asks, "Do you think he'll call the cops?"

"If someone finds him before he wakes up, they will. Blair? I doubt it. A pig-headed man-child like him would be embarrassed to explain how he was forced to his knees and bargained for his life with cash while crying. Blair will say he fell, then spend the remainder of his life pretending like it never happened."

"Do you think he learned his lesson?"

"No, but I feel better."

3

Nate braces himself for blue lights at any moment. North of Richmond, his fears begin to abate. His only mission is to get Malcolm to a hospital close to their home so he can be cared for. While Malcolm isn't critical, he's malnourished and starved of electrolytes.

"You've been quiet since the rest station. Do you want to talk about it?" Malcolm says in a wispy, tired voice.

"I met Naomi almost ten years ago. She saved Herschel and my lives less than an hour later. Our cannabis business got a little bigger than we had anticipated, which drew the consternation of two brothers who fancied themselves a backwoods mafia. Had she not acted, I wouldn't be here now. Last night, I blew a man's brains out to protect her, then killed Levi. He was such a wretched man that we don't have an accurate account of how many young men he lured to their deaths. You're the lone survivor. Naomi had it right. We're done being victims."

"You wanted to kill Blair, didn't you?"

"Of course. Do you think that harassing you is the worst thing he's done? Hardly. There's a secret set of laws for young white criminals from old money. I grew up in a trailer off a dirt road. Blair got marginal justice back there. Regardless, I had to do something. He would have eventually gotten through your stall door. I'm smaller than him. My mere presence and asking nicely wouldn't have made him stop. He wouldn't have seen a second victim. However, one tends to listen intently to whoever holds a gun to their head."

"The fight you have inside, I've been unable to find for myself. I'm afraid of everything, especially now."

"Courage looks different from person to person. Being afraid now is normal. I'd worry more if you weren't."

"I work in IT. Most of the time, I'm hidden away behind the scenes making the network at BB&T run. When I have to speak in front of my coworkers, I always freeze up and stutter. They do their best to act as though they don't notice. Because of it, I feel like they feel sorry for me. I'm like a broken toy they refuse to part with. That's all I have where courage is involved."

"But you keep showing up for work?"

"Only because I'd be destitute otherwise."

"Well, you just poured water on my origami."

"Your what?"

"I thought I folded my analogy so well. Even so, it now seems soggy and limp."

"Good. You need someone to call you out on your shit."

"I have that with my best friend, Herschel. You met him earlier. Lately, I feel like our bond is fading. It's indelible, so it will never go away completely. Our relationship is like a well-worn pair of jeans. They feel right but you don't pay any mind to them after they're on. He's in love with Rebecca, the woman who survived. I understand why. She's fantastic. But, because we're not sexually compatible, I knew one day the romance disease would find him, even though it's never found me."

"I'm sorry to hear that. Everyone deserves to be loved by someone."

"Most people, not everyone. Joseph didn't, nor did Levi. Each deserved their awful outcomes."

"It was implied for brevity."

"Sorry, it is not a trait I'm known for."

"What trait are you known for?"

"Being uptight."

"Why do you say that?"

"I'm strictly regimented in what I do. I am detail-oriented, from how I press my clothes, down to eating the exact amount of calories each day. It can be difficult for people around me. But, to be in control of those small things makes me feel secure after an early life of insecurity."

"I've never met a gay man whose early life wasn't insecure. That's how you've coped with it. At least you've given it thought. A lot of people put it in a box to be forgotten until reality is unavoidable."

"I do plenty of that, but the box where I stored all of my anger has spilled open and I'm doing the best I can to close the lid again."

Nate and Malcolm interlink fingers and ride in silence to Tysons Corner.

———

Ten minutes before reaching Kaiser Permanente hospital in Tysons Corner, Nate initiates an uncomfortable conversation with Malcolm.

"The story is, you're homeless. I found you in distress and brought you to the ER. Refuse to give your name. They're still legally obligated to treat you. It's in your interest not to ping on any radars. Let the Apostles think you're dead."

Nate chooses to put his car in the parking deck and walk Malcolm in instead of dropping him off at the front. He's afraid that because of Malcolm's appearance, they may have him dragged away in handcuffs instead of treated. Nate knows his white skin will buy him advocacy for Malcolm.

The automatic double sliding doors open with a hiss. There is a small foyer before an identical set does the same, leading them into the lobby. The intake line is long. When they're finally seen, Nate has to get testy with the nurse about Malcolm not giving a name. Eventually, they're given a number and told to wait.

By the time Malcolm is called, it's already dark out. He's finally admitted to a room in the early morning hours. The two of them didn't talk much, afraid to be overheard by the staff.

Nate had to put his phone on mute. Tiffany has been dialing every hour. Likely, Rebecca and Herschel are doing the same. Letting this happen is a very raw, empty feeling for Nate. But he stands by his decision.

"I have to go home for a little while, "Nate says to Malcolm in a soft, woeful voice."

"It has to be done," Malcolm says, knowing exactly what Nate means.

Nate clasps Malcolm's hand momentarily as he turns for the door.

"I'm coming back for you."

"I believe you," Malcolm whispers, exhausted.

Minutes later, he's fast asleep.

It's Friday, September seventh, two-thousand-seven. The state of morning traffic in the DC area is in shambles. It takes Nate more than an hour to get home, even though their house is only a few miles away. Nate braces himself for the unavoidable emotional head-on collision.

When he arrives, Tiffany rushes to meet him at the door.

"Why are you alone? And why are you driving my Corolla?"

"Everyone needs to sit down at the kitchen table."

At that moment, Diane and Beverly rush out of Diane's upstairs bedroom. Less than half a minute later, Zeke walks in from the backyard wearing a tan leather welding jacket.

Nate sits down at the table. Tiffany, Beverly, Zeke, and Diane have seats across from Nate like he's a presenter at some bland corporate meeting.

Nate looks at Tiffany in her pale blue eyes and says, "Naomi is dead."

Her wails of emotional torment reverberate off the walls. It's the worst sound Nate has ever heard. They stop when she slumps over in her chair, having fainted from the emotional stress. Zeke and Diane hold her up. Everyone else's eyes are filled with tears, including Nate's.

After lying Tiffany on the sectional, Diane asks, "Herschel and Rebecca?"

"They're fine."

Diane clasps her chest and experiences relief tainted with guilt.

"They're coming home with the tugboat after the storm passes.

"Where's her body?"

"There isn't one. She disintegrated because Joseph threw indigo on her. When it became wet, Naomi turned into flakes and melted through the deck of Frying Pan Tower."

"Oh, my God."

Nate is surprised that one of Diane's infamous curse words didn't come pouring out, but she's frozen.

4

As she wakes, it takes Tiffany a moment to realize that none of this is a nightmare. This is real.

"Rebecca and Herschel," Tiffany says when her conscious mind comes back online.

"They're okay, honey," Diane assures her in a soothing voice, happy to give her some semblance of good news.

"I want to talk to Rebecca."

"I don't think that's a good idea for you."

"I need to hear about her last moments from the person she spent them with."

Nate opens his flip phone and puts it on speaker mode. When he dials, Herschel picks up immediately.

"She knows," Nate informs him.

"I need to speak to Rebecca," Tiffany says through the speakerphone.

"Are you sure, Tiff?" Herschel replies.

Subsequently, he waves to Rebecca who's playing pool by herself.

"Baby, it's for you."

Rebecca walks to the bar and takes the phone from Herchel's hand.

"Tell me exactly what happened," Tiffany requests.

"Joseph pulled out a plastic storage bag full of indigo and threw it all over Naomi. When that shit is mixed with water, it becomes highly corrosive to anything it touches. She began to disintegrate, turning into indigo flakes. It was as though the pages of the book that was Naomi were being ripped out of existence one by one. Even so, she got off a fatal shot, killing Joseph. He was the only one who knew the process for making indigo. It's over. For lack of a better phrase, she won."

"I didn't win," Tiffany says, wiping tears away.

"Imagine if Joseph created an army of beasts and let them loose. He could ask for anything from the government in return for making them stop. With that kind of power, the entire population would have been imprisoned by them, subject to the Apostle's whims. Always at risk of a massacre. Naomi knew what that was like. That's why she decided to go. Her choice saved at least one man, Malcolm. Nate took him to the hospital nearby. In my opinion, she likely saved countless lives. Naomi didn't die for nothing. She died for everything."

"I hear you're a high dive champion now."

"I wish I wasn't. I still have water in my ears and I'm sore all over," Rebecca says with an uneasy smile that only Herschel can see from across the room.

He's begun playing Rebecca's game of pool.

"I'm just glad she was with someone who cared about her at the end. And, before it was over, I'm thankful that Naomi knew Joseph had died and she wouldn't perish in vain."

"She did not."

"Thank you for your honesty, Rebecca."

"That's what family does. Love you, talk to you later," Rebecca says before hanging up the phone.

"Why have you kept this from me, Nate?"

"Because it was only right to tell you in person."

"And, letting me be eaten from the inside out from not knowing was respect?"

"I understand why you're angry. There were no good options."

"It's not so much that I'm angry at you, as I am the universe itself. Or, that the universe can exist without Naomi. I feel as though existence should vanish. Yet, here I am crying on a damn sectional sofa in a perfectly intact world."

"It wouldn't have remained intact much longer if Joseph had gotten his way."

"That doesn't mean it hurts less. No, it makes me want to go out and buy a balloon of heroin and shoot up until I can't feel anymore."

"That's not happening," Diane says sternly, crossing her arms, like a mother telling a child not to touch the stove.

"I know. It doesn't mean my body doesn't feel the draw of a simple, temporary fix."

Tiffany takes one of the pillows from the couch and places it over her head so she can block out the world.

Nate, exhausted, kicks off his shoes and crawls onto the couch with her. He wraps his arms around Tiffany and they drift off to sleep; their mutual hurt keeping one another company.

———

Neither of them wakes until ten past five in the afternoon. Diane, Beverly, and Zeke go on about their day, peeking in regularly.

Upon waking up, Nate says, "I have to go check on Malcolm."

"Y'all want some coffee?" Diane asks from inside the kitchen.

"Please," they say simultaneously.

They join Diane at the kitchen bar, still bleary-eyed.

"I didn't think to give Malcolm my phone number, and now I feel bad because I'm afraid he's worried."

"I'm going to need the Subaru. The Toyota is going to the chop shop when Herschel gets back. I wish the house had a garage.

"We bought this place for the large lot," Diane says, pointing to Zeke's workshop.

"Do you think the Apostles could have followed you?"

"No, but I got into an unrelated bind on the way here. I smashed my pistol's butt into the back of some homophobic bully's head at the Virginia Border Rest Area, knocking him out. There were no witnesses. He would have only seen the front of the car anyway. Since front plates aren't required for cars registered in North Carolina, he could have only given them the make and color. Corollas like yours are too numerous to count. Regardless, caution should be taken when it can be."

Unflinching, Tiffany says, "What you did was understandable. I'm proud of you, but glad you didn't kill him."

Nate hugs Tiffany and Diane before heading out the door with his coffee to go in a metal cup.

A reddish evening sky frames the hellish traffic. Nate weeps and he creeps along, bumper to bumper. Several people from other cars see him and seem concerned. Nate gets worried momentarily, but being sad on the Beltway isn't exactly an emergency worth calling the police over.

The hospital's parking deck is always jammed. It would seem malady doesn't operate on a schedule. Nate finds a spot on the top level.

Before the door is completely open to Malcolm's room, Nate is already apologizing for taking too long.

"It's okay," a healthier-looking, and more cognizant Malcolm says.

"I fell asleep."

"Then, you needed sleep."

"Yeah, I reckon so," Nate says as he plops down in the recliner next to Malcolm's hospital bed.

"Have they said how long before the plan on discharging you?"

"Tomorrow afternoon."

"Have they been treating you well?"

"Fairly. I can tell they're irritated with the fact that I won't give them my name. Lunch and dinner were tolerable and they kept pumping me full of fluids. That's all that really matters."

"I'm glad, but I wish you didn't have to be."

"I wouldn't be at all, without you," Malcolm says, holding his hand out to Nate.

Nate intertwines his fingers with Malcolm's.

"I lost someone close to me last to the Apostles. Claude. Knowing that I at least saved one person from them feels cathartic. Though, with them gone for good, and without Naomi, I don't truly know what to do with the rest of my life."

"Whatever's best for Nate."

"I don't know anymore."

"Baby, I can't tell you how to live. That gorgeous brain of yours already has the answer waiting in there to be stumbled upon."

"That's sweet, yet overly confident."

"Just take the compliment, honey."

5

Rebecca and Herschel maintain a holding pattern at Naomi's home in Wrightsville Beach over the next few days. On Sunday, September the ninth, the power goes off as tropical storm Gabrielle makes landfall. Though not officially a Hurricane, sixty-mile-per-hour winds easily down trees and powerlines. The area is accustomed to it and treats living with hurricanes the way people in Syracuse treat lake-effect snow: an unfortunate reality.

The pair occupy themselves playing pool and eating junk food during the outage. All the while, they keep their sidearms holstered or close by. Both assume that Abraham is likely weighing his options. If the Apostles no longer need to make deliveries to Frying Pan Tower, then perhaps he will relinquish the house. Or, Abraham could be the kind of dilletante who wastes resources on ego-driven vendettas.

––––––––––

It's Monday, September tenth and the power has been out for two days.

"We wouldn't have to worry if we got to him first," Herschel says after brooding quietly for a while, deep in thought and retrospection.

"I don't even know what that would look like. All of his men are wearing uniforms laced with that indigo shit. We can't stand against them without Naomi."

"I got the feeling Abraham's real fear was the threat Joseph posed, not us. With Joseph gone, will he be as heavily guarded?"

"For some time, I'd imagine. It will take a while for Joseph's faction to come back into the flock. Until then, Abraham deems each of them a liability and will be under twenty-four-hour protection," Rebecca says. "He's likely to be jumpy because Joseph's indigo went down with him and Abraham only has a fraction. It'll only be used in armor for himself and his security detail. His goal now is to hold onto power and stay alive until the next chance comes."

"If it comes. He only has six bodyguards, not a militia," Herschel says.

"Even so, they're impervious to conventional weapons. He probably sleeps in indigo-laced pajamas. With us and a stray faction about, I would."

"It's a problem that might never be. Even with Naomi gone, we have to keep living. What if we call it a stalemate, step aside, and just spend time with our family enjoying what good days we're given?"

"I'd like that," Rebeccas says, looking lovingly into Herschel's eyes. "How about we break out Scrabble? It works with two people. And it's getting too dark to see the pool table."

They each try to put their recent trauma out of their minds for a while and enjoy being together. After two games, both fall asleep side-by-side on the upstairs sectional.

———

At three in the morning, they hear the side door jiggle. Dozens of wooden Scrabble pieces are sent skittering across the floor, let loose by Rebecca snapping back to consciousness feet first. This startles Herschel, who wakes and places his finger over on his lips, signaling for Rebecca to stay quiet. He points toward the porch. Both gingerly walk across the wooden floor, trying to decipher cloudy memories about which spots squeak. Reaching the top floor balcony, they hear two separate sets of footsteps. Herschel delicately shuts the glass door behind them.

"We should slide down the support posts," Rebecca says to Herschel.

Both climb over the edge of the second-story balcony. Rain pelts them as they grasp the slick wood twenty feet from the ground. Herschel takes the left post, Rebecca the right. She descends with ease, while Herschel's muscular frame causes him to take it slower. At the bottom, both quietly slide into the shadows under the deck. Both are now soaking wet.

"The Apostles do not know Joseph is dead yet. Otherwise, they would have sent more than two guys," Rebecca says.

"They're going to figure it out real quick, though."

Both were fully dressed when they fell asleep on the couch, holstered Glocks and all.

Don't use your gun unless you have to. We don't want the attention," Herschel says.

"The island is practically empty."

"Yeah, but during storms there are looters. Gunshots usually mean one of them has been shot. The cops will come in multitudes."

They hear the sliding glass door above them open.

"See, there's nowhere anyone could be hiding," One of the men above them says. "They're long gone. Our job is to get on the radio and contact Joseph."

"No," the deeper of the two voices says. "They crawled over the edge."

"That's not possible. We're too high up," the other replies.

"Watch," the deeper voice says.

Rebecca and Herschel hear the wood supporting the porch creek and groan under his weight.

"No, don't…" the other voice shouts directly before Rebecca and Herschel see the rotund body of the deep-voiced man slam into the hard-packed sand chest first. The impact manifests a thud and snap, then a brief final scream before the body bounces. The flaccid shell flesh comes to rest face down.

"Bill, no!" the voice above screams.

"We have to get him before he calls someone," Rebecca says.

"Two dollars says he's coming this way. I'll post at the left corner, so I can see the side door. You go on the right in case he comes out the front and around the opposite way."

Rebecca nods quietly as she draws her pistol from its paddle holster. Seconds after reaching the corner, Rebecca hears a gunshot from the other side of the house. She turns to see Herschel with his hands up. The man coming from inside the house must have fired and missed because Herschel's pistol was still on his side.

"Who else is with you?" the man's voice shouts nervously.

"I'm by myself."

"Throw your gun down and come back inside with me."

The man begins backing up toward the side door, the house to his left. Herschel, compelled by the muzzle of his pistol, throws his Glock to the ground and follows with his hands up.

A few feet from the door, the man lets out a gasping noise as his right lung is punctured by Rebecca's meticulously sharpened knife sliding easily under his ribcage. Before he collapses, she reaches over his shoulder and pulls the gun from his hand with little effort.

Rebecca dashes toward Herschel and wraps her arms around

him, crying.

"I thought I'd lost you. I ran around the house faster than the time Naomi saved me from that mountain lion. I guess running toward something is a lot more motivating than running away."

After a pause, Herschel asks, "What should we do with them?"

"We throw them in the bay. When the storm surge returns to the sea, so will they."

Both are white men of average height. Each has brown hair and eyes. They look enough alike to be related. Only, the one who fell is larger-bodied. The man Rebecca killed is borderline emaciated, with rotting teeth.

The larger man is closer, so they begin with him. They drag his body backward by the arms. At the end of the dock, they roll him off. The slender man's body takes just as long because now they're both exhausted.

Inside, Rebecca says, "We need to leave."

"If the cops haven't come by now, they aren't."

"It's not the police I'm worried about."

"We can't take their truck to the dock where the tugboat Camille is because they'll trace it there once it's abandoned," Herschel says. "If we start walking now, we'll be picked up for suspicion of looting. We leave tomorrow morning. The rain should have subsided."

"We'll need to stay up until dawn."

"I'll go make some coffee. You reset the Scrabble board.

Just before Herschel moves toward the kitchen, Rebecca lightly kisses him on the left cheek.

6

The next morning is September eleventh, two-thousand-seven.

Looking out the sliding glass door on the second floor, Rebecca comments, "The storm surge is receding. It's only drizzling now. The water is choppy, but I think we can get out of here this afternoon."

Besides the weather, the only other thing the news stations play is footage from the terrorist attack six years earlier.

"Sometimes, I just want to see the weather forecast and not suffering," Herschel comments to himself, sighing.

"Religion is the greatest justifier of atrocity that humans ever created. You know this better than most, Herschel."

"I'm still shaken up about it all. Those men last night were so damn certain. There was a blankness about them that I can't put into words."

"I love you, but you're overthinking it. They were fucking morons who wanted to kill the world because they couldn't stand sharing it with folks who weren't like them. Abraham gave them the divine permission their hatred longed for. That's all."

"It makes me disappointed," Herschel says with sad eyes.

"I know," Rebecca replies, plopping down on the couch next to

Herschel and wrapping her arms around him.

She can't help but think about how ironic it is that a man as physically strong as Herschel could be one of the most sensitive she's ever known. It's those types of nuances that make her love him even more.

The local forecast indicates that the rain should cease around noon.

Herschel says, "When the rain lets up, we should start walking. We take next to nothing with us, making sure to wear long shirts over our holsters. It's only about three miles on foot. At a fast pace, it's only about an hour."

"That means we have a while left for me to kick your ass at pool," Rebecca jokes.

Why not? Herschel thinks to himself. Certainly, Naomi would rather them enjoy one another's company instead of cowering from the Apostles or wrenching their hearts out over her loss.

By one in the afternoon, the rain has stopped completely and there's a hint of sunlight behind the thick, gray clouds.

"I think it's time," Rebecca says, staring off at the sound from the upstairs balcony.

The cloud cover is appreciated for the duration of the hour-and-a-half walk. Once the weather clears, it will be brutally hot and humid once again.

Outside of the marina, the owner, Howard, is in the parking lot with a leaf blower shooing away errant debris left over after the storm. He turns it off when Rebecca and Herschel approach.

"Your boat took a beating, but it's no worse for wear. Where are your other friends?

"We're headed out to meet them, actually," Rebecca responds.

"Well, y'all have a good time," Howard replies in a New York accent.

This juxtaposition paints smiles across Rebecca and Herschel's faces.

Herschel unmoors the tugboat Camille while Rebecca fires up the twin diesel engines. After a few tries, they turn over and begin to clatter their mechanical tune. The dark smoke fades as the engines warm up. Rebecca guides the vessel gingerly out of the marina and into the sound proper. She points the bow north.

―――――

They throw anchor at six-thirty, giving them a half-hour of sunlight to make sure the boat is situated. Naomi was the most capable, followed by Nate. Rebecca and Herschel know enough to get by, but Herschel is awful at piloting any mechanical vehicle, including his car.

The irony of an athletic man with no coordination is something that brings loving humor to Rebecca's eyes when he trips in the living room like Dick Van Dyke. It doesn't, however, when his clumsiness is behind the helm of a sizable vessel in the confines of a narrow canal.

They share a can of Chef Boyardee for dinner.

"Tomorrow, we can dock at Ocracoke Island. We'll fill up the diesel tanks and go shopping for decent food," Herschel says.

After eating, Herschel calls Nate's cell phone and places the call on speaker.

"Are you okay?" Nate asks without saying hello.

"We're fine. Two Apostles broke in. One of them fell off the balcony of his own accord. The other one, Rebecca handled."

"How's Malcolm?" Rebecca asks.

"He's been out of the hospital for two days. Diane loves him to death. He's practically a chef, is fond of Sylvia Plath's poetry, and a wizard at Jeopardy."

"You sound a bit smitten."

"He says that I am 'dashing.'"

"That's definitely the Nate I know," Herschel chimes in.

There's a momentary silence as Rebecca builds up the courage to ask, "How's Tiff?"

The answer stumbles out of Nate's mouth, "Like a mortally wounded fawn staggering through the underbrush. She only leaves their bed to lie on the couch. She's been watching Naomi's sci-fi movies on repeat."

"She used to hate them," Rebecca says.

"I guess they make her feel close to Naomi somehow."

"Tell Tiffany that we both love her," Rebecca says.

"I will. Talk to y'all tomorrow," Nate replies before hanging up.

Games of UNO fill the evening. Some of that time is spent on an argument about the rules. It's not mean-spirited. Rather, it's flirtatious mutual antagonism.

———

It's Wednesday, September twelfth. Rebecca and Herschel begin traveling north again at daybreak. Around noon, the south end of Ocracoke Island becomes visible on the horizon. It's remote, only accessible by ferry or private craft. The northern fifteen miles of the landmass are an uninhabited, wild strip of sand. What's coming into focus to Rebecca and Herschel is the southern village, the only occupied section on the island. Full-time residence is fewer than one thousand people.

Herschel finds portage in Silver Lake. It's a well-protected cove on the southwestern side. The entirety of the infrastructure and commerce on the island sprang up around it more than two hundred years ago.

The pair walk a quarter mile to the only grocery store on the island, The Variety Store.

"This place is out of the seventies," Rebecca says.

"It reminds me of the grocery store we went to as a kid, back in Little Washington," Herschel replies, absorbing the ambiance of yellow fluorescent lighting and old compressors kicking in to keep food cool.

"I adore it."

They load up, mostly on canned and shelf-stable foods. The walk back to the boat is beleaguered due to their four heavily loaded paper bags.

After stowing it all away in the galley of the Camille, Herschel says, "Maybe we should stay here a while? What if they've sent a boat faster than ours north? If we stay out of sight, they'll never catch up because we won't be there."

Finding a little bungalow to rent for the week isn't difficult since their arrival was directly after a storm and following Labor Day weekend.

They return to the Variety Story that evening to stock their shelves with fresh food. That night, they visit a family-owned restaurant called Edward's Calabash. It overlooks the now shimmering, calm water of Silver Lake bathed in late summer moonlight. They share a large platter loaded with a healthy side of hushpuppies, fried shrimp, clams, oysters, and flounder. Most of it is consumed with cocktail or tartar sauce. The latter of which Rebecca uses to dip her hushpuppies into. None of it is recommended by the American Heart Association. All of it is delicious, especially when enjoyed alongside several PBRs.

After eating, the pair retires to their tiny cottage. It has a small bedroom attached to a slightly larger living room. It's furnished with a couch, television, a small stove, a minifridge, and a bathroom the size of a closet. All in all, it's better than sleeping on the boat.

Both settle in on the couch before calling home.

"How far did you get today," Nate asks.

"Not far. We've decided to stay on Ocracoke for five days in case they send faster boats north to intercept us," Herschel says.

"That sounds like a shit excuse. They don't know what you look like. It's okay if you need to pause for a moment. You've been fighting for too long. I get that. Just don't lie to me. You're my best friend."

"I just can't face her," Herschel says before breaking down. "We failed Naomi."

Herschel holds his right hand over his mouth, as though he'll stop the flood of emotion spilling over the cracked damn that is his broken heart. Rebecca holds him while he shatters.

After Herschel is silenced by his guttural cries for a friend lost, Rebecca talks over him through the speakerphone, "We can't today. I'm sorry, Nate." After this, she hangs up.

Rebecca takes Herschel to bed, cradling his body and soothing him as he cries himself to sleep.

Over the next few days, the pair rests, takes leisurely walks around the village, visits shops, and subsists on fried seafood.

They set off again on Tuesday, September eighteenth. Since they're down half of the original crew, it takes Rebecca and Herschel sixteen days to get home. They arrive Wednesday, October fourth, two-thousand-seven, just as the first chill of autumn drifts into Northern Virginia, making eye contact like a familiar stranger.

On a warm autumn night, a body washes up in front of the Oceanic Hotel on Wrightsville Beach, a mile north of Naomi and Tiffany's house. Large, crashing waves push the limp carcass onto the sand until they only lap at the figure's heels.

The body is wearing a black t-shirt, partially covered by body armor. On its lower half, the body wears jeans and a nice pair of boots. The corpse is long-limbed and has short, blond hair. Unexpectedly, the deceased lifts their head and gasps for air in one deep, ragged gulp, followed by a coughing fit.

"God-fucking-damnit it," the figure says as they come to their knees, dusting themselves off. After the locks are brushed back by a scarred left hand, the face it reveals is unmistakably that of Naomi Pace.

7

My name is Naomi Pace. At twenty-seven, I feel like a rotting wooden mannequin held together with baling wire and brittle epoxy.

I'm covered in sand and soaked with dirty salt water. I feel like I'm still floating out there, half-conscious, much like sleeping with your head against a moving car window. The rocking motion of the rolling waves became my only sensation, locking me away in a place where time had gone extinct. Eventually, the sea decided it finally had enough of me and spit my carcass out onto the beach.

Once on my feet, I consider removing the body armor to lighten my load for the walk home. I decide against it in case Apostle cultists are waiting for me there. Either way, I'm certain Rebecca, Herschel, and Nate are having a group meltdown. Rebecca witnessed me disintegrate on the deck of the Frying Pan Tower. Just before that, we killed Joseph Proffit. He was responsible for the abduction, torture, rape, and murder of an untold number of gay men. They were pick-up kidnappings whereupon he and accomplices lured the victims from a handful of gay-friendly establishments in Eastern North Carolina.

These unfortunate men were then taken fifty miles offshore

to the Frying Pan Tower. It was an abandoned freestanding Coast Guard station, sitting on pylons one hundred feet above the blue ocean. Along with Joseph and his men, it now sits on the ocean floor. I'm glad for the deaths of Joseph and his men. They would have never stopped, otherwise.

Buried at sea with Joseph is the knowledge of how to manufacture indigo. It's the substance that gave Joseph his abilities and fueled their false beasts of lamentation. Now, only Abraham, the Apostle's financier, has access to the ingredients used to manufacture it. They need my blood, and both water and ground-up rock from the cavern below the site of Vernon Proffit's demolished home. They have a frozen pint of my blood from the time I was kidnapped. Abraham also has some rock and water.

He'll have to be stingy with it all because besides not having continued access to my blood, the cavern is guarded by a true beast of lamentation, Svangi. He waits, pacing, desperate to feed on any human who foolishly enters. Without Joseph's magic tricks and creatures, all Abraham Proffit has is money. The problem is, where zealotry is concerned, money is often irrelevant. Without a man like Joseph who can seemingly perform miracles, interest will wane. As will their numbers.

I can't remember the last time water made me feel this uncomfortable. I've always been fascinated by it. I grew up within walking distance of a creek. But never have I been so glad to be free of it.

I feel the weight of my body as I rise to my feet. It's cumbersome initially, having floated for so long. I have nothing but the clothes on my back, boots, and body armor. I lost the gun Zeke made me, my knife, and Vincent's brass knuckles.

Standing, my back feels like it's unzipping. It plays notes from my lumbar up to my neck like someone rolling a xylophone mallet from one end to the other. On my feet, I snap my neck left then right, eliciting a similar melody and a brief tingling feeling throughout my entire body.

Even though I ache, I feel like the light inside me is stronger than ever. It beats in my chest cavity like a heart made of lumens that, if released, could melt tungsten.

But something is different. Now, instead of just the energy of the Earth underneath my feet, I can also feel the atmosphere around my body in a similar way. I don't understand why and reckon I don't care at this point. Wasting no more time pondering, I begin making my way home on foot.

I draw heat from within the Earth as I walk, raising my body temperature to accelerate drying. I find myself feeling slightly guilty, as though I'm using my abilities frivolously.

As my adopted father Al used to say, I "schlep" the mile south down an unmarked piece of blacktop running along the backside of the dunes. The few cars that pass don't seem to take notice of my appearance. They're tourists occupied with finding their rentals in the dark, unfocused and frustrated. Coming off the main drag, I scoot quietly between large condo buildings, coming out onto a parallel street. It leads sound-side, where my house is located.

In the backyard of my house, I see what looks like a small campfire. Getting closer, it's apparent that the fire is contained inside of a circular fire pit. It's the kind of thing that's purchased at a big box store back on the mainland. Why would my friends go out and buy a fire pit tonight, of all nights?

Then I realize what I'm seeing is four young men sitting in folding chairs around a poorly managed fire. Each appears to be in their mid-twenties. They're dressed like tourists, in collared shirts and khaki shorts. They could be some preppy kids from UNC-W. But it would be quite a coincidence for them to pick my house for an impromptu party.

I move forward under the assumption that they're Apostles.

In the neighbor's yard across the street, I take off my armored vest and stash it in the bushes. Then, instead of lingering from a distance, I walk right up to them.

"Think you'll see your ghost?" One of the young men says to another before noticing me.

"I believe him. She's real," the third says.

"Who's real? I say, abruptly, startling them.

I see their hands go to their sides, obviously, ready to draw pistols on me.

"What are you doing here?" the believer in ghosts asks.

"I thought y'all needed company is all," I say, purposefully trying to sound flirtatious. This play disarms them before guns even leave their holsters.

"What's your name?" The believer asks with a put-on smoothness.

"Crystal," I say, harkening back to the ploy I used against Sheriff Morton. That ended with him getting his hands ripped off. After, he was thrown into a ravine, bleeding out and screaming in terror.

"I'm on vacation with my girlfriends. I heard y'all talking and thought I'd see if you needed company. Why don't you tell me about your ghost."

"She's more of a witch," the believer says. "They call her a ghost because that's what she turns people into. They disappear, as though they never were."

"Would you like to tell me about it over by the dock?" I ask.

With little hesitation, the scrawny young man answers an unequivocal, "Yes."

"What would Abraham think?" The fourth man says to him.

"When Abraham transforms into a tall, blond woman, let me know. Then, I'll care."

Once behind my dive boat, I grab the man by his collar and twist the fabric tight enough to cut off his oxygen. I reach down for his gun with my left hand. He does the same, so I cock my neck back and bring my forehead down with as much force as I can muster. His nose rams into the corner of my right eye. I realize instantly that the impact will lead to a vicious black eye.

I speak slowly and deliberately as he struggles fruitlessly against my superior physical strength, saying, "Call them over. Say that you see the ghost. If you warn them, I'll feed you to the crabs while you're still living."

I could have easily burned each to a crisp from the ground up. However, I need answers and their screams would have woken the neighbors.

"Hey guys, come over here!" The man shouts to his three friends.

"The first man yells back, "Y'all are fucking gross. No one wants to join in."

"No. I can see the ghost," my waifish captive replies.

8

The other three see me holding their comrade's own gun to his head as they round the corner.

"Throw your pistols as far as you can into the sound!" I shout at them. The wind and crashing of waves diminish the distance my voice travels, keeping the conversation between the five of us.

I sense their internal dilemmas about drawing on me. Being that there are three, it's highly likely one will go for it. I hold my left hand out, reach into the Earth, and cause a lava tube to rise underneath their feet. The soles of their shoes immediately begin to smoke. They leap, trying to get away. I keep shifting the heat to stay beneath them at all times.

I lower the inferno and say, "Throw them now, and I'll stop. Keep it up and I'll burn you all alive."

Three kerplunks tell me they came through on their end of the bargain.

"Now, take your shoes off and swim to the end of the pier."

They move slowly, looking at one another as each pulls their footwear off.

Once they're treading water at the end of the pier, I say, "Swim out a few more feet. You're too close. Stop staring at me and start doing what I say. I'll execute him right here in front of the three of you. I've done far worse to men following false prophets."

Motioning to the man I'm holding captive with a head tilt, I say, "He wasn't lying. You can see the ghost."

The three of them begin swiveling their heads in all directions.

"No, dipshits, me. Even with a gun to your friend's head, y'all still couldn't believe it to be a flesh and blood woman."

Their blank stares tell me everything I need to know.

"Where are the people who arrived on this dive boat?" I ask.

"The second man replies, "We just got here today. It was already there. Nobody else was here."

"Why are you here?"

"The man whose head I'm holding a pistol to says, "Abraham sent us to guard the house. No matter what happens, he's never letting it go. Our instructions are to keep anyone else out, especially the two dykes who used to live here."

I turn the man around swiftly so that he's facing men and without hesitation knock his front teeth out with the butt of the pistol. This causes him to fall back into the sound. I point the muzzle at him. He struggles to tread water with one hand while using the other to cover his fractured mouth, pooling with blood.

"I have one last question. What did y'all do with the boat keys?"

"We haven't moved the boat," the third man says. "The keys were left in the ignition. I know because we were planning on taking it out fishing in the morning."

"Here's what the four of you can do, start swimming. If you make it to the other side, you get to live."

The four of them stare at me in disbelief.

"I'd start dog paddling or something if I were y'all."

With that, they take off. I wait to make sure they don't circle back. After five minutes, I'm convinced, so I head into the house through the open side door. It reeks even worse from cigarettes than I remember.

I climb the circular stairs to the second floor and then make my way to the attic door. Pulling on a chain brings down a folding, wooden ladder that I've never had much confidence in. I pull the light cord above me and peek my head up into the cluster of random boxes filled with things like old birthday cards and decorations. I count ceiling joists from the side of the house. After six, I squeeze my body into the space where the ceiling and house meet in a wedge. I slide a purposefully loosened board out of the way. Under piles of insulation is a heavy-duty bank bag holding one hundred thousand dollars. It's an insurance policy, just in case we had to run with little notice. I tuck it into my rear waistband. I don't bother putting the stairs back up as I'm trying to make it back to the boat as soon as I can.

I cross the street, backtracking to retrieve the body armor I wore, not to leave evidence.

I hustle down to the dock and lower my dive boat into the water. It only takes three attempts to start the twin outboard engines. I idle just offshore. Leaning over the portside gunwale of the boat, I begin bringing new tunnels of lava to the surface under my house. After watching it go up completely in flames, I collapsed the sand underneath it. As I throttle away, a sinkhole swallows it whole. The flames gasp one last breath before being drowned by the sea. The houses on either side now share a newly formed bay. The Apostles can never use my property again.

I catch up with the four would-be guards about halfway to the other side. I stay thirty feet away and observe them struggle as I wait for sirens.

As the night air is plunged into a cacophony, I put my left hand into the water and begin drawing heat under the intruders. Their screams are drowned out by the chaos surrounding my house's collapse. Their skin turns red and bubbles as they boil to death, leaving nothing but fatty residue and dusty bone fragments floating on the surface. I make my way to where the Camille should be docked. It's not there. That means they made it back and have escaped. Realizing they could be being pursued by other boats, I turn north.

———————

I traveled for eight days, stopping only for fuel, water, and food from marinas. I don't have my cell phone. Even if I did, I wouldn't call because it would cause Tiff to worry since I don't know where Rebecca, Nate, and Herschel are. I figured I'd call upon finding them. I never do.

It's half past midnight as I pull into a marina with open spots in the Rappahannock River, south of Tysons Corner. As I'm tying off, the harbormaster comes rushing out to shoo me away.

"You can't be here. Those slips are reserved."

He puts his hands up as I pull the bank bag out of my waistband. But instead of producing a weapon, I pull out a stack of hundred-dollar bills. Each bundle is in bank wrapping stating that it contains ten-thousand dollars.

"I'll gladly pay for the rental. That untaxed, personal bonus is for you if you can figure out how to make that happen."

I place the stack of bills in his hands. When he feels the weight of it, I know he's calculating the risk versus how much the money could change his life for the better.

"Yes ma'am. I think we can accommodate you."

"Do you mind finding me a cab that will take me all the way to

Tysons Corner for a fare and a significant bonus?"

"I know a guy."

I wait in the office for an hour, half watching a rerun of Gilligan's Island.

I give the cabbie a thousand when I greet him. It takes two-and-a-half hours to get home. As we stop in front of the house, I slip him another fifteen hundred dollars.

Alone on the sidewalk, I brace myself, afraid to approach the door knowing I can't account for the whereabouts of Rebecca, Nate, or Herschel. I pull the rusty key out of my pocket and jiggle the deadbolt until the door opens. I turn on the light to see the same house but with children's toys scattered across the living room floor.

Am I in the wrong house? I think to myself.

The guest room opens and tiny feet bobble themselves in my direction. It's a little girl with strawberry-blond hair.

Wiping her eyes, she says, "Mama-Naomi?" confused.

I say nothing, not wanting to upset her.

The door to Tiff and my bedroom, directly across from where this bundle emerged, gently opens.

"Little Milly, honey," are you up?" her familiar voice says.

"Momma-Naomi!" the excited little girl says enthusiastically, pointing up at me.

Upon seeing me, Tiffany screams in terror and disbelief.

The door to the large downstairs bedroom flies open, revealing Diane holding a black pistol-grip shotgun. She freezes, unsure of what she's seeing.

Tiffany moves quickly toward me, kissing me on the mouth as she wraps her arms around me.

She looks vaguely different, with slight hints of crinkles around the corners of her eyes.

Did Rebecca, Nate, and Herschel make it back?

"What?"

"Are they safe?"

"They returned safely, but that was seven years ago, baby!" she exclaims.

"That would mean it's..."

"Twenty-fourteen!"

9

Seven! Seven goddamn years. The realization that I missed all of that time with Tiffany makes my gut feel as though it's full of tenpenny nails. Tears drip slowly down my cheeks, but I do my best to hold it together in front of the little girl.

I wipe them away onto my sleeve as I hear Nate release a happy squeal as he bounds down the staircase toward me. Malcolm and Zeke follow. Malcolm keeps his distance, almost as if he's afraid to be struck down by a god if he ventures too close. Zeke doesn't seem as surprised as everyone else. He looks at me as though he'd been expecting my arrival for some time now.

"How?" Nate asks, holding my face to make sure I'm real.

"I was never dead. I was trapped."

"Where?" he says with tears of joy running down his face."

"Not in front of the child."

Nate nods his head as he wipes away more tears.

Then I hear a sound that frightens me almost as much as one of the Apostle's beasts: Tiff clearing her throat.

"We need to talk, outside," she says, glancing her eyes down at Little Milly.

Everyone else backs off. Tiff gently takes me by my hand. She leads me toward the back door and out onto the deck. It's late, but we have a sizable backyard considering where we live, and a six-foot privacy fence.

Tiffany throws her arms around my neck and releases seven years' worth of anguish onto my chest. Because I'm so much taller, I have to lean down toward her. I picked Tiffany up off the ground. She wraps her legs and arms around me like a sloth on its favorite tree.

"It's going to be okay. I'm here now."

This goes on for quite some time. Eventually, Tiffany's tears have been shed and she returns to her feet. We sit across from each other at the picnic table. Her eyes are bloodshot and she's still sniffling.

"I imagine you're wondering about Little Milly," Tiffany says.

"She's adorable."

"I wanted us to have a child together. I've always wanted to be a mom. I never intended to remarry. I didn't want to share her with someone who never knew you. As far as I was concerned, she already had two moms and didn't need another. And, I could never love someone else as much as you."

"What does she know?"

"I tell her child-friendly versions of your 'adventures' as I call them. That kid thinks you're Indiana Jones; her hero-mommy."

"Who's the…"

"Nate donated. I was artificially inseminated and gave birth in two thousand ten. Little Milly just turned four on October seventh. She knows Nate as her 'daddy', Diane as 'Mema', and Zeke as 'Papa'. Herschel and Malcolm are her uncles and Rebecca is her 'auntie'.

"What about Beverly?"

"She passed."

"What?" I say in shock.

"Yeah," Tiff sighs. "Breast cancer got her."

"Poor Zeke and Diane."

"It's genetic. Diane feels utterly guilty about surviving while her sister didn't. We tried to keep her suffering to a minimum. The morphine is what inevitably did her in. They called it 'comfort measures'. It was really slow euthanasia."

"Where are Rebecca and Herschel?"

They bought a smaller house half a mile away. Closer than our parents' houses when we were children.

I see a millisecond glint of happiness as Tiffany recalls our childhood together.

"Do they have—"

"No, they don't have children. Herschel had a vasectomy, so I'd say their minds are made up on the matter. Mostly, they wanted a place to be their brand of crazy in private. They eat dinner with us every night and are around all the time. Diane has no doubt already called them. They are moments away from rushing through the front door to see you."

Tiffany stops and examines my face carefully.

"You don't look any different."

"Neither do you."

"You know what I mean, Naomi. You look exactly how you did when you left the house seven years ago."

"It's not that much time," I say, shrugging my shoulders.

"No, but there should be a faint hint of its effects. Tiff puts her hands on my face as I lean my long frame over the table. "Where in the hell were you?"

"Hell would be a good way to describe it."

"You were in Hell?" Tiff says, gasping slightly as she puts a hand over her mouth.

"Something like that."

"Tell me from the beginning," Tiffany says, as she holds out both of her hands across the picnic table.

I intertwine my fingers with hers and try to gather my thoughts.

"On the platform of the Frying Pan Tower, minutes before its collapse into the Atlantic, Joseph emptied a large storage bag of indigo onto me in the soaking rain. When that shit gets wet, it returns to the Woods of Lamentation."

"Indigo is matter pulled directly out of the Woods of Lamentation. That's why it imbues abilities to people wearing clothing impregnated with it. Its existence here breaks the laws of physics on our plane. But water doesn't exist in the Woods of Lamentation, so when it's exposed to moisture, it has no choice but to return to its original state and location. Anything touching the indigo at the time goes with it. But it can't hold onto outside matter forever. When the bond inevitably breaks, matter from our universe has to return here."

"The Woods of Lamentation is where men like Vernon and Joseph go when their lives are over. Inside, they're relentlessly pursued by horrifying beasts. Once caught, they're eaten, defecated, and reformed. They experience this same fate again and again, for eternity."

"Is that what has been happening to you for the last seven years?" a frightened-sounding Tiffany asks.

"No. It was different because I didn't end up there as punishment. The light I carried within me was adequate protection. It created a perimeter, about five hundred feet equilateral from me in all directions. On the interior, the forest wasn't gray and dark. Instead, it was like a meadow on a sunny day. When I woke up there, I was confused because before, I was in a dream state, detached from my own identity. Momentarily, I believed that perhaps I'd fallen asleep while hiking, but I didn't remember going for a hike."

"As it all began coming back, the first thing I remembered was the scorching pain I felt the moments following Joseph dousing me with indigo. Then, I recalled seeing his stunned face after Rebecca and I dealt him a mortal blow. My last thoughts before completely disintegrating were about how this would be Rebecca's final memory of me and what it would do to her. Then, my mind turned to you. Afterward, there was no more Naomi."

"Self-aware again, I sat dumbfounded in an absurd state attempting to grasp what was real. It wasn't until after noticing the screams coming from beyond the perimeter that I realized where I was. As my eyes focused, I could see large figures moving through the semi-transparent border almost like frosted glass. I knew what they were doing, hunting. I had no reason to fear them, so I stepped through the barrier."

"Why?" Tiffany asks, perplexed.

"Why did I step through or why wasn't I afraid?"

"Both," she says, putting up both her hands and shrugging.

Because those beasts are like Mara or Svangi. They can't hurt me. And going through the barrier was the only way home. So that I could get to you."

Tiffany gently wipes her eyes after hearing my answer.

"Close to the edge of the dome, I could hear a faint tone, like the resonance of a wine glass. It manifested as a fragile, electrical barrier exuding pulsing waves where it touched my body. Once through, the entire structure collapsed in on itself, leaving a marble-sized ball of light floating in the air. Autonomously, it dashed in my direction and disappeared into my chest where it rejoined the larger light inside me."

"Then you were alone in the dark?" Tiffany says with wrenching concern.

"It wasn't so much dark as it was dim. Imagine nighttime out in the country, a full moon beaming through gaps in the clouds."

"The air was extremely dry. It didn't take long before I had trouble breathing. Gasping for air, I fell facedown, hands around my own throat. As I lay there, the commotion drew the attention of numerous life forms. Some were so large that I could feel the ground vibrate underneath me when they moved closer."

"Everything is gray and white there, even the skin of the beasts. Underneath, each has prominent veins pulsing with an indigo sheen. Most of them were no larger than Svangi, who is eight feet in height. A few were gargantuan. The one that sticks out the most in my mind had more tentacles than I could count, whipping furiously in every direction. Thousands of suction cups ringed with sharp tooth-like protrusions lined each slippery appendage. They're purpose-built to hook into flesh and hold on until the victim finds their way home inside a giant black beak."

"How did you get away?" Tiff asks, sobbing again.

"I couldn't run, nor would I if I had the strength. I stayed calm as the monsters encircled me. They seemed cautious, standing about fifty feet away. After an eerie quiet, the beasts uniformly charged in my direction. Instinctually, each was determined to fill their stomachs with my flesh."

"Even though I was physically weak, the light inside me was not. It ignited from my chest in a brilliant white spherical flash which knocked them back, sending even the largest tumbling through the trees."

"As my breathing returned to normal, I noticed a hazy shimmer around my skin. The light was producing a sealed environment, encasing my body to insulate me from harsh conditions. It was like the barrier I walked through minutes before. I imagine that if given enough time the shimmering film on my skin would have expanded slowly into another dome-like structure similar to the one I woke up in."

"They didn't try to come back?" Tiffany says, peering at me through her beautiful light blue eyes.

"It was strange, as though the woods themselves unilaterally stood down. The creatures all slunk away. That's okay. There's plenty for them to eat. I still heard them snorting in the brush, out of sight. They were hunting other people. There were grown men crying like infants, cowering naked behind trees. Most stayed hidden with their head in their hands. But, one of them figured out after seeing me walk past unscathed, that if he was near enough to me he'd also remain safe. He was a diminutive man with straight red hair, parted down the middle. I pretended that I didn't notice him."

"I began running, but he easily kept up. He was smaller, thus lighter and faster. Eventually, I grew tired of playing cat and mouse so I stopped and screamed at him.

––––––––––

"Come on out, you sack of shit!"

He walked slowly toward me like a scolded little boy.

"This is the longest I have gone without being ripped apart since accidentally ending up here."

"Accidentally," I replied, condescendingly. "I have delivered so many to this place that I've lost count. And nary one of them ended up here accidentally."

"My name is Mordecai," the man said, reaching his hand toward me.

"That appendage is more grotesque than any belonging to those creatures," I said, rebuffing him. "The beasts are at least honest about who they are."

He was still in the process of reforming, so his skin was raggedly trying to reach out and intertwin with corresponding patches.

It hit me, the skin's ability to repair itself has one purpose in the Woods of Lamentation, creating something for the sole purpose of destruction. It's counterintuitive while making complete sense.

"I didn't do what they said."

"And, what was that exactly?"

"Kill that little girl."

The statement made me stop and cut my eyes at him.

"What little girl?" I said with hostility.

"Alice. It was an accident. She wouldn't stop screaming."

Searing with anger, I asked, "Who were her parents?"

"They were just normal people living in the Industrial Valley of Cleveland. I rode by her bus stop every morning on the way to work. She caught my eye with her beautiful blond hair. After a while, I began waving at her. She waved back. It's like she was asking me to come talk to her."

"I waited at the bus stop in my car to meet her. But, she didn't understand and tried to run away. I put her in the backseat and locked the doors so that I could explain myself in private. She kept struggling, so I drove off and took Alice to my house. Even there, she wouldn't stop calling for help."

"I locked her in my room to get away from the sound. But it did no good. I waited for Alice to finish so that I could tell her about our love. But she didn't, so I put a pillow over her face to muffle her screams. Eventually, they did stop."

"You smothered her!" I screamed at him.

"I loved her."

"How old was Alice?"

"Eight."

And, you were how old?"

"Thirty-three."

"How did you not see the problem, you fucking pedophile?"

"Love knows no boundaries," Mordecai said, groaning as the reformation process finished. "I never touched her like that. I wasn't going to. I just needed her to tell me she loved me back."

"You murdered her," I say flatly while making direct eye contact.

Mordecai replied, "I didn't mean to."

Reaching into the Earth, I felt nothing. I realized that I didn't have access to my abilities here other than protection from beasts. But my chest felt lighter because there was no Earth for the light to be drawn to. It had been replaced with an overwhelming, heavy sense of doom that I assume was the very nature of the place itself affecting my mind.

Overcome with rage, I charged Mordecai with all of my physical strength. He was scrawny and far shorter than myself, so he toppled over backward without much resistance. I straddled him and began punching him in the face and throat, alternating between my left and right fists.

Still punching, I shouted, "You're a fucking monster. There is no way out of this place. Accept your punishment. It's eternal, just like the pain you infected an innocent with."

My grunting and growling transformed into a whimper as my energy petered out. Long-ago-healed wounds were ripped clean open. But, instead of continued fury, I found myself in a place of despair, trapped in there with wretched men like Mordecai. It made me feel sympathy for the poor beasts who are tasked with their consumption.

His badly dented face should have been dead, yet was still animated. Its grotesque form began to rebuild itself, inflating like a previously crushed plastic bottle being filled with air. The teeth Mordecai lost began to sprout anew through his gums. Soon, his eyes opened again.

Looking directly at me, he said, "It never ends. Never. Go ahead, don't stop, hit me again. You and I are trapped together forever."

"Fuck you, Mordi," I said while standing. "The worst of y'all couldn't keep me prisoner in the realm of the living. You can only imagine the monsters I've survived."

Walking away, I said, "Eternity isn't long enough for men like yourself."

Unable to hurt Mordecai in a meaningful way, I moved along at a faster pace than before. I hoped that leaving would make him vulnerable to the beasts. But, he got right up and kept pursuing me. I wanted to run, but I was exhausted. The Woods of Lamentation is more than just the beasts. It crushes your spirit like an anxiety attack. Not just in your chest, but all over your body."

I hoofed it for another two hours before I could see the woodline ahead. I didn't pay attention to which direction I was headed. There is none. It's an infinite space for those punished. No matter how far they walk, it never ends. For me, it's finite.

By the time I exited the woods, I was moving as fast as I could and was relieved to see the tracks. It's the barrier between the Woods of Lamentation and Ceraphiria. The tracks represent the human world. Our natural movement through time acts like clock gears, clicking and driving all existence forward.

My presence allowed Mordecai to exit the woods.

"Fuck off, back to the woods where you belong!" I shouted at him, still hot on my trail.

I ran across the tracks toward the Ceraphirian Woods, furiously wanting to have a word with them. But, I was engulfed in light right before breaching their woodline. I felt like the singularity of a black hole, so dense that I was sinking through the fabric of space-time. Then came the floating sensation as I drifted back to the world of the living. When I finally regained my agency, I woke up in front of the old Oceanic Hotel. I walked home believing that I would meet up with everyone. But, instead of my friends, there were four young men from the Apostles.

———————

"I assume they're… um," Tiffany says, attempting not to grin.

"Very dead. I boiled them in the sound like crabs. After, I took off north in the dive boat. Tonight, I docked it in the Rappahannock River and took a cab home."

"I'm so glad you did," Tiffany says crying, as she holds my hands across the table.

"There's one more thing," I say with trepidation, "I destroyed the house."

"What!?" she says, sharper than I expected.

"One of them said that Abraham would never give it up. That meant those little shits would have been replaced and so on. Even with the Frying Pan Tower gone, it was still a strategic location and only a short boat ride to their Fort Caswell compound."

"How did you destroy my beautiful house? Tiff asks sadly.

"I lit it on fire, then caved in the land beneath it. There's a small bay now where it once stood. I wanted to make sure they could never use any of it again."

"I understand. I'm not happy about it, but it had to be done. You showed them that you're as stubborn as they are."

"I think it's about who's more exhausted. Right now, I feel like it's me."

10

I hear a commotion inside the house. I walk over to investigate. When I open the sliding glass door, I see Rebecca rushing in my direction.

"I saw you die," she says, holding me tight, tears pouring from her eyes.

"I will someday. That day wasn't it."

"Can you die?"

"Yes. I'm mortal. Remember the large, purple bull's eye wound I got after being shot through my body armor? It took me months to recover. Had it hit my flesh, I would have certainly died."

"How can I be holding you? How is this real?" Rebecca says, squeezing even harder.

"The bad shit people like us went through growing up has inoculated us against the vicissitudes of our adult years."

"I don't believe I care how. I'm just glad to be here with you."

"Sharing the same brief flicker in the pantheon of time is all we have."

"You've become quite the philosopher."

"I wasn't completely unconscious. I'm not sure how long it

took me to come around. For some time, I had no idea who I was. That gave me time to think objectively, without being tied down to the idea of the self. I still feel a bit clumsy talking to other people. I reckon I could seem a bit strange."

"You've always had peculiar ways, but yeah, you sound like someone who has spent too much time isolated."

"My last thoughts were of how seeing what happened to me might have affected you."

"It did, but that wasn't your fault. A few months later, I started having a recurring nightmare where you had reformed after disintegrating. I wanted to take the boat back out there and search for you even though I knew you were… I spent so much time trying to put it out of my mind. But here you are," Rebecca says, laughing through tears.

After a few more minutes, Rebecca releases her grasp, and a disheveled Herschel wearing pajama pants, a t-shirt, and slippers shuffles toward me. Upon embracing, a flurry of emotions pours from deep within him, like a raw infected spot hidden under callouses. He sobs uncontrollably. I let him.

When he slows, I say, "I hear you're an uncle now."

Still in tears, he says, "Yeah. That's true. I'm the cool uncle. Don't tell Malcolm."

Malcolm rolls his eyes at Herschel.

"The only 'fun' associated with your name is followed by, 'gus'," Malcolm says back to Herschel in jest.

"You could say we are actively competing to be the uncle who can spoil Little Milly the most," Herschel says to me.

With that, the two of them have a little chuckle.

Malcolm approaches me. He doesn't know me well, so instead of hugging, he holds out his right hand and we shake.

"You pulled my bacon out of the fire bare-handed. Thank you," he says.

I grab Malcolm's hand and pull him toward me.

"Thank you," he says breathily, trying not to cry.

"Always, Malcolm."

I think back to Al and Milly, my surrogate parents. They had so much to do with this evening, even if they aren't here to see it. Their kindness and sacrifice ensured that I would live on one day to help Malcolm. In a way, they were just as responsible for saving his life as my own. Though not here, they're as much a part of our family.

I kneel, saying, "Would you like to come here, Little Milly?"

She eyes me the way Zeke did; like she expected this would happen all along. Walking slowly, she approaches me as though she anticipates me to be rigid like a statue.

After wrapping her arms around me, the first this Little Milly says is, "Momma-Naomi, you smell bad. You need a bath."

"Yes, baby girl," I say, "Mama Naomi sure does smell something awful. I think I'll take your advice and have a nice, hot shower."

"Your stuff. We packed it away," Tiff says as though she's embarrassed.

"It's understandable. I wouldn't have expected you to keep a museum to Naomi Pace in your bedroom."

Herschel asks Malcolm, "Could you help me get Naomi's stuff out of the attic?"

Both make their way up the open staircase to the second floor. The attic has an access ladder outside of Zeke's bedroom. As they judiciously begin moving boxes down, I slide into the bathroom between Tiffany and Little Milly's bedrooms. I suppose Tiff's is technically our bedroom. The concept seems foreign momentarily.

I'm so filthy that I take two washcloths to the shower. The first is just for the surface grime. The water runs off my body the color of tea for the first couple of minutes. Only after that can I take a real shower and get my body clean. Upon finishing, I changed into a blue pair of pajamas and a black t-shirt that Tiffany placed on the bathroom countertop for me. Exiting the bathroom, I see Little Milly standing in her doorway and Tiffany in ours.

"You have to come tuck me in," Little Milly says.

"Oh, do I?" I reply coyly.

"Mama said so," Little Milly says, referring to Tiffany.

Tiff looks at me smiling.

To say this child's room has a dinosaur theme would be an understatement. And, it's not just stuffed toys and anthropomorphic characters. There are detailed posters of skeletons and models filling several shelves.

"Which one is your favorite?" I ask.

Pointing to the poster over her bed, Little Milly says excitedly, "The Spinosaur!"

"Why?"

"Because it could swim."

"Do you know what animal I like best?"

"Whales, mama says."

"That's right.

"What whale?"

"I think my favorite would be the humpback. It was the first whale I ever saw in real life, back when I was in college. We took a boat way out into the ocean. I thought I was going to throw up."

Little Milly chuckles a bit, so I pause.

"Yes baby, mamas get seasick too. Luckily, I didn't. The whale jumped out of the water next to the boat. What was surprising was how loud it was. I bet your spinosaurus would have been louder."

"Mama takes me to see dinosaur bones. She said I can learn to dig them up when I go to college."

"She's right. You can. It takes a lot of hard work, but you're a smart girl."

"I'm glad you're home."

"Me too."

I pull the covers over her shoulders, then lightly tuck her in. I'm interested to see if she's like Tiffany and rolls up into a burrito before dawn.

When I turn off the overhead light, a nightlight illuminates. Instead of a dinosaur, it's a whale."

"She says it protects her," Tiffany whispers as she comes up behind me. "I think it has something to do with all the stories we've told her about you."

We leave Little Milly's door slightly ajar and head back to our bedroom. Little has changed. The only difference is that my personal belongings aren't in their usual places. I'll sort through the boxes in the morning. We lie on our respective sides of the bed, me on the left and Tiff on the right.

"I left your toothbrush and comb in the bathroom for over a year."

"All of this is my fault. I'm the one who chose to head to Frying Pan Tower that night. I wanted to save Joseph's victims and make sure that bastard didn't get away."

"I would have told you to go. You saved an innocent man. Today, that same man, Malcolm, is your best friend's husband and uncle to our daughter. You did the right thing."

"Did Nate and Malcolm marry in Massachusetts?"

"Yeah, but marriage equality lawsuits are going through the courts right now. There's a good chance our marriage could be recognized in every state very soon."

"I'll believe it when I see it. Even if that does come to pass, they'll fight to take it away again."

"I hope you're wrong."

"Me too."

"Technically, we're still married. I didn't report your death. Your identity as Al and Milly Sillman's daughter, Hannah, is still active."

"You told Little Milly my real name," I say with worry upon realizing it.

Sternly, and slowly enunciating, Tiffany says, "You were dead. There was no need for secrecy."

"The Apostles are still out there. They're weak but have a long memory."

"As do I. I haven't forgotten. But, I wanted her to know the real you, which meant your real name."

"Will you tell her all the horrible things I've done when she gets older?"

"Yes. You shouldn't feel any shame."

"I don't, but there are some things a child shouldn't know about their parents."

"She's not stupid. She'll figure it out anyway."

"No, she isn't. Little Milly is quite precocious."

"The teachers at her pre-school think she's gifted."

"They're right. And, she's curious. That's a good combination. It's amazing to see my two favorite humans mixed into one. I couldn't be happier."

"Nate refuses to use his last name because it belongs to his parents. Since I chose to give Little Milly our last name, he changed his to Pace as well. Her full name is Mildred Mia Pace."

"Mia, as in Zapata the lead singer of the Gits?"

"Yeah, you loved them. I know it's silly, but their music made you happy. That's always been a difficult emotion for you."

"I was like that before Solid Rock."

"And you don't think it somehow amplified your negative disposition?"

"I can't disagree. I spent my entire childhood dodging my father's blows and bully's punches. After that, it's difficult not to see the world in any other light than ordinarily dreary and predictably awful."

"After everything I've seen you do, I'd hardly describe you as ordinary, Naomi."

"I mean banal human behavior is excruciatingly predictable."

"We're all guilty," Tiff says.

"That's the most disappointing part."

"It is. However, there's still plenty in this world worth fighting for. That's what you do better than anyone."

"I never want to again."

"Maybe you won't."

"It feels like out there someone is winding up the clock to start this awful cycle over once more."

"You're not going to solve it here, in bed, tonight."

"You don't know that. Do you remember that time I fell asleep frustrated with one of my boat's outboards, only to have a dream that replaced a relay? The next morning, I did exactly that and the problem was solved."

"Engines are simple compared to large groups of unquestioning lunatics."

"I understand," I say softly while pulling Tiffany's back to my chest so that I can cradle her in my arms.

We lie there quietly until both of us fall asleep.

11

In the morning, I'm still exhausted from my journey home. While drifting off to sleep, I experienced a momentary flash of terror when thinking about being visited by Frieda. Instead, I was treated to a respite inside the blissful void.

When I woke, Tiff wasn't in the bed next to me. After putting on pajama pants and a t-shirt, I drag my stiff body from the bedroom to the hallway bathroom. After, Diane, on cue, presents me with a cup of coffee with too much half-and-half at the bar. There's silence while I drink the first portion. Some people thrive in the early hours. My brain comes online each morning like an ice-cold diesel engine. Hell, it's barely still morning at eleven-forty-five when I'm finally ready to talk.

"What day is it?" I ask Diane.

"Saturday, the eleventh, twenty-fourteen."

"Where is everyone else?"

"On Saturdays, Little Milly gets to pick an outing. Today, it's the Natural Aquarium. It was a last-minute request, which I believe was prompted by your arrival. She wants to understand you, and in her mind, that means your love of the ocean. It's Nate, Tiffany, and Zeke's weekend. Next weekend, it will be Rebecca, Herschel, and Malcolm. I always go."

"But, not today?"

"No. I told them I'd stay behind. We thought it was best that you have space to orient yourself and for Little Milly to keep her schedule."

"That makes sense," I reply.

"Waking up here this morning must be a real kick in the fucking pants."

"It is surreal. While I was gone, my awareness drifted through time, like a seed floating from one island to the next. Only laying down roots when the time is right. It appears that the time and place my roots were looking for is right here. That frightens me."

"Because there's a question of why?"

"It's the feeling that the equation of reality demands my presence."

"But, are you a remainder or still in play, like the queen on a chessboard."

"Either is a challenge. I'm more comfortable hunting monsters than living a normal day-to-day life. I failed with a capital 'F' last go-round. Now, there's a child involved."

"Naomi, we all fail our children somehow. You'll be no different. They'll be home at six. You can start then."

"Don't sound so certain, Diane."

"No, I'm joking in a way," she says, giggling. "The parent's curse is always second-guessing each decision, even decades later."

"Sounds terrible."

"When I had Herschel, we didn't know anything. In time, the two of us got a system together. Even if it only has the structural integrity of a balsawood model airplane, it can still fly."

"Yeah, but you have to throw a balsawood plane for it to take off."

"So what?" Diane says shrugging.

While not an oratory masterpiece, those two words convey an attitude that acknowledges that bad things are going to happen. All we can do is keep pushing forward.

I pause, drinking more coffee.

"I'm sorry about Beverly. When did she…?

"Die? Twenty-eleven. By the time she discovered the lump, it had already spread to her lungs. Eight months later, she was gone. Withered into a papier-mâché version of her former self. They told me when I was diagnosed that it was likely genetic. For years, I begged her to get a double mastectomy. Either way, I can't help but wonder why her and not me. There's always a tinge of guilt there. We had the money for treatment, but sometimes you can't buy life."

Instead of the obligatory, 'I'm sorry,' I leave space open for silence in case Diane wants to keep talking.

"She's not gone forever," I assure her.

"I know. But I miss my sister."

"The burden of death is borne by the living. We collect deaths throughout our lives. Each becomes an indelible part of our character."

"I'm full up," Diane says.

"I hope so."

I spend the rest of my day sorting through my belongings, putting back what had been tucked away in my absence.

———

At six o'clock, Nate, Tiff, Zeke, and Little Milly enter through the front door. Each looks a bit tired, especially Little Milly. Despite this, she waddles over in my direction and latches herself to my leg. When she lets go, I kneel and lift Little Milly, clutched to my chest.

Laying her head against my shoulder she says, "I missed you."

"Since last night?"

"Since always."

It's then that I see the extent of Tiffany's design to keep part of me alive. This little girl has had the story of my life mythologized to her until she feels as though she knows me. In a way, she does. Little Milly has constructed a theory of my mind based on the lore she's been told. To her, I was a very real construct before I walked through the front door last night.

"I missed you too, Little Milly," I say, squeezing her tight.

"It's time for your bath, little miss," Tiff says as she approaches.

As Little Milly begins making her way toward the bathroom, Tiffany gets up on her tippy-toes and kisses me on the lips before following behind her. Not but a few moments later, Malcolm, Herschel, and Rebecca come through the door. Like yesterday, Rebecca moves in quickly for a hug.

"I just want to make sure you're still real."

"The kink in my lower back says I'm very real."

"You need to get moving," Herschel says.

I know instantly that he wants me to go out running with him and Rebecca tomorrow.

"What time?" I ask him.

"Let's say ten in the morning. That will give the sun time to knock off the night's chill."

"Deal."

Malcolm and Diane begin to prepare dinner. It's baked chicken, asparagus, and sweet potato.

"Y'all have fallen pretty to Tiffany's ways," I say jokingly.

"All but my own daughter," Tiff says with a slightly annoyed smirk, looking down at Little Milly eating dinosaur-shaped chicken nuggets.

After dinner, it's time to tuck Little Milly into bed.

Tonight, though, she says, "Tell me a story."

"Which book would you like?" I say pointing to a well-appointed shelf of children's literature.

"A story about you, Mama Naomi."

"The Adventures of Mama Naomi, as told by the woman herself," Tiffany says, smiling from the doorway.

"What are you filling this youngin's head with?"

"True stories about you, but heavily edited for the audience. Not everything interesting about the enigmatic Naomi Pace revolves around Solid Rock and the Apostles. A lot of them are silly memories I have, so vivid, it feels as though I can still touch the moment. Other times they are stories of your experiences. For example, when you and Nate saw a really large tiger shark while y'all were spearfishing."

"Nate more than saw her."

"Tell that story if you want. It won't frighten her. She already knows it."

"Okay," I say looking at Tiffany, a bit puzzled by her tolerance for frightening tales being told to Little Milly.

"Your daddy and I spearfish, which is when you go underwater to hunt fish instead of luring them with bait. I'm sure you've been fishing."

Little Milly nods her head while saying, "Daddy takes me."

"This tiger shark was by far the largest I've ever seen. Not only that, it was really big around. That meant she was going to have babies, which would make her feel very hungry. She was so hungry, she swam up behind your daddy and bit his oxygen tank. Realizing she couldn't eat it, the shark let go. Your dad turned around and poked her right in the nose with his spear. Then, she swam away.

"Were you scared?" Little Milly asks, dozing.

"Yes. I was very afraid. I love your daddy. He's my best friend and that mama shark wanted to eat him. Not being able to see it in the cloudy water was the scariest part. But, she never came back. We got back on the boat safely and spent the rest of the day fishing with a pole instead."

When I look down, Little Milly is sound asleep.

12

A wave of exhaustion washes over me.

"I reckon it's my bedtime too," I say quietly, as I look up at Tiffany.

"Come on, then," Tiff says, reaching her hand out.

She strains, trying to pull my weight off the ground. Once I'm up, we both snicker quietly at the absurdity of Tiffany, who is nearly a foot shorter, helping me to my feet.

On my way out of Little Milly's room, I turn off the lights, causing her whale nightlight to illuminate. I pause for a moment to look at her, then walk out leaving the door a few inches ajar. I land face down on my pillow and sink through like it's made of syrup. I sense Tiffany somewhere in the background. Otherwise, I'm oblivious.

———————

I can feel the fuzzy surrealness of the place where I wake up. I know it well. It's the train tracks between worlds.

To my left are the Woods of Lamentation, where I escaped after seven years of confinement. To the right is Ceraphiria, where my presence is verboten. A familiar lantern appears in the distance on the tracks. Walking gracefully in my direction, I see a figure that soon becomes Frieda.

"Is this the part where I'm supposed to opine about my journey and how much I've grown?" I ask.

"I know who you are, Naomi. I expect nothing of the sort. I assume you are rather cross?"

"Yeah," I say with a slightly raised voice.

"You believe yourself to have been mistreated by the ambivalent being who dictates this dance we're performing?"

"Very much so."

"When you figure out how to contact her, do let us know. Because we have no clue. We only mind the time and state of the world. As you know, there are three layers to existence. Ceraphiria, The Woods of Lamentation, and the universe humans inhabit. We are all just a part of a larger whole. A stray flaw in the equation could reproduce and spread like cancer. She knows this, but continues to bide her time anyway."

"I don't care, Frieda."

"We don't know what will happen next. The Ceraphirian can't see past your decisions, because you shouldn't be here to make them.

"I should be dead, you mean?"

"Your continued existence is tenuous for the equation. Humans rarely have any real choice. None should have as much as yourself."

"I'm exhausted with your bullshit. Where's Theta?"

"Here and there. I sense a part of her in you."

"I know we're both assholes, but there's a difference between keeping a man chained to a rock for nearly two centuries and the dumb drunken shit I regret."

"No, it's a reflection of her light inside of you. I don't fully understand."

"Perhaps it's from exposure to her, like getting a sunburn."

"No, it would be something far more dramatic."

"Dramatic, as a description of my life would be an understatement. And, it's never by choice."

"You're right, but most of the decisions surrounding human lives are not their own. For now, you have stability. The Apostles have winnowed in the past seven years. Perhaps this season of peace can be permanent? We can't know until it isn't."

"So, just go home, and spend time with my wife and child, all the while praying it's all over?"

"Yes. Don't let this opportunity fly by. It all goes rather quickly."

"If I don't see you again, Frieda, just know I only hate you about ninety percent. Which is a ten percent improvement in a mere eight years."

"You were incapacitated for seven of them."

"That's not helping your case."

"You don't mean that."

"I'm ready to go home now," I say sternly to her.

Her face tells me that Frieda knows that I no longer trust her.

With that, she embraces me coldly, against my will. The world around us turns black. Her form turns to decompose into silt and I'm left in a deep, restful sleep.

———

The next morning became a mirror for the days that would follow. A wide-open child bouncing around before dawn, and us tailing after her, hoping to mitigate whatever insanity goes too far.

Out of all of my family members, I'm by far the most lenient. The first day I was alone with Little Milly, she asked if I could bury chicken eggs in the backyard so she could find them like a paleontologist would dinosaur eggs. She even knew where there were unused paintbrushes to knock off the dust. It didn't take her long to discover the freshly dug ground behind Zeke's workshop. Little Milly was able to get most of them out intact. But, the last two were so tightly packed in the dirt that they cracked.

Proud of her 'fossilized' eggs, Little Milly asked if we could make a museum display for them. The best I could do on short notice was a mixing bowl and an index card. Looking through her many illustrated books, Little Milly settles on the fact that the eggs most certainly belonged to an Oviraptor.

All went well until Malcolm and Diane began a baking project together that evening, only to find most of their eggs missing.

A year flew by. Little Milly grew in height and maturity. Our time together is less these days because she began kindergarten in late August. Her teacher is impressed with Little Milly but says she squirms too much and is often out of her seat without permission. Her intentions are noble. She is attempting to tutor her classmates who are struggling. To me, it seems to be perfectly normal behavior. However, Nate and Tiffany share a very different opinion. Regardless of what parents think of their children's behavior, it rarely has any actual sway over it.

Everything changes on Wednesday, October fourteenth, twenty-fifteen. Herschel, ever vigilant, regularly searches online for stories he believes might be related to the Apostles. Those outside our family might call it obsessive. We call it cautious. There, in an obscure blog, was a news-styled entry detailing the independent candidacy of Abraham Proffit for governor of North Carolina. He has no party, so he's running as a write-in candidate. The type who are almost assured to lose.

"He's done it," I say when presented with Herschel's findings.

"Done what, exactly?"

"He's figured out the process for making indigo. This is the preamble to something much larger."

Abraham can't possibly win. He's not affiliated with a major party or any for that matter.

"You take a population already primed to believe, then show them what could be honestly described as a miracle and they will follow without question. Joseph was able to walk through walls and control the wind. What do you reckon ol' Abraham can do?

"He's probably less powerful than Joseph. Why else would he enter into politics? If he had Joseph's power, Abraham would just seize control. Why have a vote?"

"Abraham will do exactly that if he loses. The vote isn't for him. It's to make his voters feel committed and special."

"He only has a few hundred Apostle loyalists who will vote for him."

"Abraham isn't showing his hand. He plans to build up his voting base by openly exhibiting his abilities to the world and claiming they're miracles."

"What are we supposed to do?" Herschel asks in a voice tinged with fear.

"Tell the others."

———

That evening, we hold a family meeting after Little Milly falls asleep. Herschel presents several printed copies of the article.

Once everyone is finished reading, a nervous Tiffany asks, "What are we supposed to do?"

"The Apostles are weak. But, if they're going to operate out in the open, so am I."

13

After Herschel and Rebecca head home and everyone else is in the bedrooms for the night, the argument ignition sequence begins its countdown. Three… two… one… and Tiffany's face is beet-red with anger.

"Last time, I thought you were dead for seven years!" Tiffany screams.

I'm really glad about the solid construction of this house right now. It's damn good at containing sounds.

"The time before that, they captured you. When you returned, you were well and truly fucked up. You'd been beaten to shit. If it wasn't for Diane, you'd be buried facedown next to Charles's body!"

"Maybe."

"Why?" Tiffany sobs. "Why do you have to keep doing this?" Tiff asks, almost rhetorically.

"Because, this is going to come to our doorsteps, and everyone else's, whether we want it to or not. I've seen it. Flaccid-brained morons are mesmerized by Biblical magic. It won't stop."

"I'm not stupid. But that doesn't mean I can't be furious at you for being so goddamn willing."

"Don't you get it? I'm the goat who's inevitably going to be sacrificed to set the balance back to a neutral state. I can go down fighting, perhaps doing some good in the process. Or, I can placidly wait to be murdered."

"I don't believe that."

"Then you're a fool."

I instantly regret the words that came out of my mouth. It's too late now. They've wafted through the night air and into my beloved's tender ears.

My internal dialogue turns into a cold, wordless tone as I watch her eyes widen, absorbing the insult. It had to hurt more coming from me than anyone else. I instantly yearn for forgiveness, but do I even deserve it?

"Am I a fool for loving you, Naomi?"

"No. I'm sorry. I was out of line."

"Those of us who stay behind are the reason a soldier fights Don't forget that. It's not just about the world. It's also about us. You're not some defenseless animal to be slaughtered. You are the most powerful human on the planet. Act like it and be confident that you'll come home to me."

"I don't think there's a choice. The Universe's die is cast. The equation can't stand remainders in the mix. That's what I am, the biggest of them all."

"You're a human being, not a number to be erased by a computer or some thoughtless demigod. You don't have to follow the path they've laid at your feet. I know you can't walk away, but you can use those big feet of yours to kick them right in their fucking teeth."

Tiffany collapses onto the bed, weak from the emotional effort of loving such a flawed person. I crawl into bed with her and lie with my right arm across Tiff as she cries herself to sleep.

————————

I wake to a fresh dusting of snow on the rail in front of my face. Wooden ties and gravel dig into my hip. There's no doubt that I'm in the middle ground between worlds. When I look up, Frieda is already standing over me, lantern in hand.

"Leave me alone! I just want to be with my family. I spent seven years bound inside the Woods of Lamentation before being dumped into the ocean by God knows what."

"You'd be surprised. Sometimes she doesn't."

"Who? God? But, she's omniscient."

"In a way, but not exactly."

"That shit is annoying. Stop being cryptic and just say what you mean."

"She feels and absorbs the emotions of everyone, whether it be suffering or joy. That's her lot. She's a prisoner, bound by the sentience of her own creations, awash in a sea of feeling. Before, she was a pragmatic strategist who painstakingly manufactured a nearly error-free reality. The Ceraphirian were the only cognizant beings she created. The rest of you were the result of time, biology, and evolution. We weren't there at the beginning. It wasn't until the rise of the first self-aware lifeform. Their ability to feel deeply was overwhelming. She became so wholly focused on it that she created us as a sort of maintenance crew, freeing her to explore the deeper meaning of the self that reality seems keen to give rise to. It's happened so many times in the last few billion years it would take an impractically long time to even recite the number."

"Where do I fit into all of this?"

"She rarely makes adjustments herself. But, there is one glitch, you."

"A reminder?"

"Yes."

"The equation meant to have Joseph and I destroy one another, returning things to where they were before my unexpected survival in the cavern as a girl?"

"We think so."

"We, as in the eleven of you? Including, Theta?"

"Myself and nine others. Theta has become lost. An apostate. But, her duties remain. Each of us is tasked with some aspect of reality. I, for example, am responsible for consciousness. Theta minds the weather patterns on each planetary body in our Universe. The light you have belonged to Zelia, who controlled the Earth, from the surface to the core."

"Just Earth?"

"Yes. Every other species to evolve conscious minds destroyed themselves not long after by the very weapons their brilliant minds allowed them to create. That's why you feel that tug in your chest from the core. You're bound to it, just as she was."

"When I flew, it lessened."

"The tendrils were still attached, waiting to snatch you back."

"Then, how is the Earth functioning.?"

"Earth never required Zelia's intervention. It's still plodding along the way it was intended. That's probably why Zelia assumed she could just abscond her duties. Hopefully, the planet stays in balance. You're not equipped to take over her duties."

"So, because I'm not a Ceraphirian, I have no choice? I'm going to be laid out on a cold slab when this is all over. Why bother?"

"Humanity. The further up the political ladder you climb, the more weapons they allow you to control. Get to the top and you can make the world go 'poof' in a matter of minutes."

Frieda pauses, then says, "The planet Little Milly lives on."

Stepping closer to Frieda, I say, in an intimidating voice, "Don't you ever mention her name again."

It felt like the ground trembled under my feet as I spoke the words. As it resonates, the Woods of Lamentation, off to my left, begins to rustle. The movement was caused by the heft of every creature within it being drawn in our direction by my anger. Frieda locks her eyes on the woodline, then on me.

"They listen to me," I say.

"Why?"

"The beasts see me as an equal monster. When they converged on me, Zelia's light created a lumen explosion that saturated everything in sight. After, the beasts stepped aside, realizing I was more powerful. I can call them if you want. Once they cross outside the woodline, they're mine for the taking. Just like Svangi."

"No, that's perfectly fine."

"Are you having a difficult time remembering your lesson in fear? Knowing that you expect me to die, leaving Tiffany and my daughter behind, is an equivalent fear to me, that the beasts are to you."

"Your death is a sacrifice for all humans."

"No, Frieda, I can win."

"It doesn't matter. You're not supposed to be here."

"You can't stop me from trying."

"I don't have to, inevitability will."

The following day, Thursday, October fifteenth, I wake up at four in the morning. I lie there for half an hour with my eyes shut, trying to fall back asleep, hoping to rest instead of dealing with Frieda's horseshit.

After a leisurely cup of coffee at the kitchen bar, I put on shorts, a T-shirt, and my running shoes. I'm out the door at four-forty. The brisk autumn air has me missing Wilmington. After the first mile, I don't feel the cold any longer. At the three-mile mark, I see a figure running in the opposing direction, on the opposite side of the street. The stride is familiar. Herschel. When I wave at him, he has the same epiphany and comes to a stop.

"Can't sleep either?"

"Nope. She's so damn mad at me, and I'm exhausted with the Ceraphirian. Frieda has it in her head that to neutralize the Apostles, I have to die."

"Fuck that. How do you even begin to tell someone something like that so casually?"

"They see the world more pragmatically. I'm only a minuscule part of something unfathomably large. I'm not worried about myself. Being dead isn't a big deal. It's Tiffany and Little Milly. How can they ask me to do something like that to people I love? I refuse to accept it."

"What if she's right? Is she God?" Herschel asks.

"Not remotely. Hell, she intimated that God herself isn't aware of everything."

"That sounds about right. If God were paying attention, she'd do something. Earth is like an unsupervised daycare filled with sharp objects."

"Not all the time."

"If you were an alien species observing us from a distance, what do you think you'd notice more, the moving moments between individuals or the constant dropping of ordinances upon innocents?"

"There are none left."

"Aliens?"

"There's not a single sentient species remaining in the Universe besides ourselves. Self-awareness breeds acrimony, cruelty, and extinction."

"But, it also leads to empathy," Herschel says.

"Sadly, I can't use empathy to stop the Apostles. Violence is the only language they comprehend."

"Luckily, you're more than fluent."

"But, I'm going to need your help. Nate and Rebecca, too."

"You know we'll always be here when you call. Each person in our family would have died without you. Nate and I would have been killed by the Mace brothers. Rebecca would have been eaten by a mountain lion. Your skills helped us secure the money needed for my mom's cancer treatment. Malcolm would be at the bottom of the ocean, and Tiff would have overdosed. If Frieda thinks you should have died in that cave when you were a girl, she means that we should all be dead. I can't abide that kind of obtuseness."

"The Ceraphirians have always said that they can't see past my choices even though they view time all at once. Let's give them some more choices that will obscure their vision."

Together, we jog back to Rebecca and Herschel's house. We're careful to enter quietly because Rebecca is still asleep. Usually, they run together mid-morning. Rebecca isn't even aware that Herschel's not in bed.

They own a house much smaller than the primary family home. It's a three-bedroom ranch built in the nineteen-fifties. When walking through the front door, there's a hallway to the left leading to the three bedrooms and one full bath. To the right, they've had the house remodeled into a modern, open-space design. The kitchen is set against the wall closest to the road. It blends into the dining room on the opposing wall. There's a small, fenced-in backyard with a generous deck.

It's a quarter-till six. We sit at the bar, the only thing separating the kitchen space from everything else. As I drink my second cup of coffee of the day, I hear the bathroom door shut. Rebecca is up. The toilet flushes, followed by the sink running for a while. She doesn't realize I'm here until this moment.

"Are you okay?" she asks intently.

"I couldn't sleep is all. I ran into Herschel while I was out jogging. It seems he had the same idea."

"Can I get you a cup of that?" Herschel asks Rebecca, pointing at the coffee pot.

She drinks it black and without sugar. I have no idea how.

Over breakfast, I explain what Frieda told me. Herschel expresses his anger, yet again. It makes me wish I could put him in a room with Frieda to give her an earful. At six-forty-five in the morning, I begin slowly jogging home with a stomach full of eggs, sausage, and grits.

I arrive with five minutes left before Little Milly's school bus arrives. I begin walking when I get to the sidewalk in front of our house. I place my hands on my head for a few seconds as I make my way toward the front door. Nate stands on the front porch holding Little Milly's hand as they await the imminent sound of a large diesel engine, signaling the beginning of a long day for such a small girl.

I worry about her. She's quiet and rather shy with her peers. I believe she is the shortest student in her Kindergarten class. She's also the most gifted. That carries with it the baggage of expectation. It's already been suggested that she might skip grades at some point, making the size differential between Little Milly and her classmates even more awkward. I know what it feels like, though from the other end of the height spectrum.

Tiffany wasn't much taller than Little Milly when I met her in first grade. We were identically opposite. I was the tallest in class. Tiffany was tied with another girl for the shortest. We both knew what it was like to be different on the outside while trying to contain what would have us ostracized on the inside.

I lean down, pick Little Milly up, and hold her tight for a few minutes. One day, she'll be a teenager. I'm going to absorb as much of this as I can.

"I want you to tell me the most interesting thing you learned today when you get home."

"I will, Mama-Naomi," she says.

I put her down when I heard the hiss of air brakes. Nate and I escort Little Milly to the bus door. She takes her assigned seat, the second from the front, on the right-hand side. This allows us to wave goodbye as they pull away.

"Alright. Something's obviously up," Nate says to me sternly.

"It is. Frieda visited."

"Those bastards simply refuse to allow you to live in peace."

"That's a bit reductive."

"Regardless, no good fortune ever comes out of one of their visits."

Tiff is still fast asleep when we go back into the house. Malcolm, Nate, and Zeke left early for the farmer's market. After a proper shower, I sit down at the kitchen table with Nate and lay it all out. His face turns red with anger.

"Herschel has likely already said everything you're thinking right now, Nate."

"For an entity tasked with overseeing sentient thought, she's failing miserably," Nate replies. "The reason they fear you," Herschel says, "is that they can't see past your decisions. You're the marionette that ripped off her strings and ran away."

"If I had truly torn loose my strings, I wouldn't keep getting pulled back in."

"No strings doesn't mean the puppeteer won't chase after their wayward puppet. In the Ceraphirian's case, they know you're uncatchable. They're trying to lure you in, hoping you'll willingly tie yourself back to their cross brace."

"Fuck that."

15

By noon, I have everyone at our large kitchen table.

"It won't be long until Abraham publicly demonstrates his newly acquired abilities. Instead of waiting, I'm going to make a public spectacle first, just on a smaller scale," I say.

"What?" Tiffany asks, infuriated, pounding her hands on the table."

"I have to officially lay claim to Al and Milly's land so I can embed myself right on top of them."

"Why?" Diane asks, utterly confused.

"Marine animals fleeing predators, where no cover is in sight, will attempt to stay directly atop the attacking animal's head. The pursuer turns and turns, trying to sink their teeth in, only to be outmaneuvered. Their meal, staying painfully out of range. Even though I'm more powerful than any of them individually, I won't be able to fend them off alone. For that reason, I have to do something entirely unholy. Make indigo."

"But you don't need it," Malcolm says.

"The indigo isn't for me. It's for Nate, Herschel, and Rebecca. They're going to need protection."

"From beasts?" Rebecca asks.

"Yes, and from God literally doesn't know what else."

"It would appear so," Nate replies, half chuckling at my commentary.

"You're in charge," Diane says. "What's the first step?"

"I need to find an experienced glass blower who can keep their mouth shut. After that, I require a vehicle that can safely transport fragile cargo up mountainous switchbacks while under fire. And Zeke, I'm going to need another gun."

"It'll take me a few weeks," he replies.

"It's early. Hopefully, we still have time. I doubt Abraham has a lot of indigo. Likely, just enough to become a walking bamboozle machine."

"Why do you need to drive there? Can't you just open a doorway anywhere you want?" Diane asks, confused. "I pulled you through one after firing off several rounds of double-aught buck into that bastard, Joseph Proffit."

"It doesn't work that way. In fact, it hasn't worked at all since I returned. Even before, I could only do it when prompted by desperation. The surge in emotion amplifies it. Frieda said, years ago, that on Earth I can only cast a portal to a place where someone I love is, and only if I'd been there before. Other planes of reality, like the Woods of Lamentation, are different. Regardless, even then, I can't pass through myself."

"I don't understand. Why not?" Diane asks.

"Frieda said it's because I don't love myself."

"Oh, honey, but we do," Diane says sympathetically.

"That's why y'all could pull me through when I escaped from Joseph."

"I need to know what you're going to tell our daughter about where Mama-Naomi, her dad, Uncle Herschel, and Autie Rebecca are going and whether or not they'll ever come back,"

Tiffany says in a shaky voice.

"I'll tell her we're leaving because we want her to have a world to grow up in. To do that, Mama-Naomi has to stop some bad men. That's no less the truth than the stories you told her about me while I was gone."

"Those were stories of the past. This story is unwritten. I can't be sure it has a happy ending yet."

"Neither can I," I say, reaching my hands across the table to intertwine my fingers with Tiffany's. "But this must end."

"Why a glass blower?" Malcolm asks.

"Because to make indigo, I have to use a condenser of sorts. I saw Joseph's setup while attempting to save Claude. He drained Claude's blood because Claude was in the direct vicinity of a portal I'd opened. Being around me, especially when I use my abilities, is much like being exposed to radiation. While my light isn't physically dangerous, the effects are absorbed by nearby human cells. The minuscule reflection remaining in Claude's blood allowed them to make enough for Joseph to become a nightmare."

"When my blood, or blood from someone exposed to me, is combined with water from the stalactites and dust from the cavern below, it emits a plume of indigo steam. The steam rises into what looks like a three-foot diameter, upside-down martini glass. At the top is a glass cone pointing downward. It's there that the steam bursts and becomes indigo. Below, they hang a petri dish by four wires affixed to four glass loops. I have to build that and drain my own blood so we can make a version of the protective uniforms Abraham's men have."

"But it doesn't work for you," Herschel says.

"No, it doesn't. The light I carry inside me cancels it out. I'll be as vulnerable as ever."

"That doesn't sit right with me," he replies.

"It doesn't matter. It's the best thing we have going at the moment."

"You need to wear body armor," Nate says.

"After being shot at close range through Kevlar, I might rather be killed outright."

"You're wearing it," Tiffany says sternly.

"For Little Milly," I reply.

Preparation begins the next morning.

The glassblower we find is four hours into West Virginia. He doesn't have a webpage or use social media. Despite this, the telephone book from the nearest town, Belington, is online. It lists, "Gary P. Sloan's, glass-blowing classes." It's a landline.

He picks up after the second ring. "Gary P. Sloan," he announces, proudly.

It take a while to convince him I was serious. To demonstrate my sincerity, I wire him fifteen hundred dollars as a deposit.

This is after he hangs up on me twice. Tiffany is able to put together a rough illustration of what we needed. Gary doesn't have an email address, so we fax the black-and-white schematics to the closest library for him to pick up. He estimates that it will take four to six weeks.

During that time, Herschel got in contact with a car dealership that specializes in creating armored Hummer-H-ones. They advertise them as 'bulletproof'. In my experience, that kind of claim depends on the size of the bullet. The Hummer has to be equipped with a gigantic, turbocharged diesel engine because of the armor's weight. It roars with a low rumble and whines when taking off and shifting gears. The outside is OD green. Surprisingly, it comes appointed with seats encased in the finest leather and modern electronics. There's even a backup camera encased in a clear, bulletproof housing. Its materialization in my driveway doesn't cause a second look. Washington D.C.'s adjacent suburbs are populated with enough arrogant, monied fools to make something like this more common than it should be.

We take it on our trip to West Virginia. The Hummer has two large fuel tanks, so we don't have to worry about not being able to find diesel fuel.

I feel utterly obnoxious as I pull the behemoth away from our driveway with Rebecca, Nate, and Herschel in tow. Nate rides shotgun, Herschel is behind me, and Rebecca is in the rear passenger side seat. The further west we go, the more at home I feel. The mountains remind me of my time with Al and Milly, my surrogate parents. I roll down the window so I can get a whiff of the air. It's clean and wet with wisps of fog. Then, I'm hit with the familiar stink of skunk. Ironically, I now associate that smell more with cannabis after years of growing it as a cash crop. It's not an uncommon smell to have your olfactory system violated by when driving through backcountry Appalachian roads. During the summer and fall, the source can be difficult to parse out. Though since it's November Thirteenth, I assume it's a critter and not a plant.

Gary P. Sloan's glass-blowing shop is on the corner of a thickly forested crossroad. The hardwoods are bare this time of year. Luckily, this stupid Hummer has heated seats.

On the corner across from the glassblower's shop is a feed and hardware store. Diagonally, there's an apiary shuttered for the winter. Both establishments are constructed of old, gray wood. The shop looks like a repurposed mechanic's garage, mostly built with cinderblocks.

"Stay back for a few minutes," I instruct Herschel and Nate.

"Rebecca and I will go in first."

Gary is a rotund man of average height with a slightly olive skin tone and small features. He appears to be in his mid-forties. Gary's long hair is being held back with a red bandanna. He's wearing a leather apron and equally thick leather gloves. He slips them off his hands as he walks toward the two of us and slides them into his apron's left pocket.

"I've been looking forward to meeting you'uns. This isn't nearly the weirdest thing I've ever been commissioned to create, but it sure has been the hardest."

"He leads us over to a wooden crate. Inside rests the three-foot diameter, upside-down martini glass, sitting openside down, half covered in styrofoam peanuts.

"The object, as I've been referring to it, is nine-millimeter thick borosilicate glass and weighs seventy-five pounds. It's difficult to manage but is quite fracture-resistant. The thick loop at the top should easily hold the weight."

"Thank you," I say, as I pull the fifteen thousand dollars in cash I owe Gary out of my pocket, ready to end this conversation.

"So, you'uns not going to tell me what it's for?" Gary says.

"It's classified," Rebecca replies, coyly.

"That's cool, man," an obviously stoned Gary says. "Art is like that. Even if commissioned, it's always personal."

Rebecca smiles at his response, finding it humorous, knowing full well what we intend to do with it.

Nate backs the Hummer up inside, through the rollup garage doors. The four of us lift the crate into the cargo area, where two ratcheting straps are used across the top, affixing it to a set of tie-down points in the front and back. This keeps it held firmly in place.

I wonder quietly to myself if I'll ever get to use the tie-down points to restrain a human.

Putting the thought out of my mind, I thank Gary.

Shaking my hand, he says, "It was a pleasure helping create something so bizarre."

"You're welcome... I guess?"

Scatter-brained as he seems, to look at his work, you'd think it had been created by a machine. It's completely clear, thick, perfect glass. I can't help but wonder how much of Gary's business is bongs. Probably most of it.

Watching the forest recede as we drive home is depressing. It disappears, bit by bit until trees only exist sparsely between strip malls.

Herschel brought a travel edition of Scrabble. The juxtaposition of their playing a harmless game while riding down the road in a vehicle created for war isn't lost on me.

16

It's Monday, November sixteenth. Neither myself, Rebecca, Herschel, nor Nate woke up in time to see Little Milly off to school. That duty fell to Uncle Malcolm and her Mema, Diane. Tiffany has been too much of a wreck to do anything. The crescendo of her tension has passed. She's beginning to descend slowly back to a somewhat more relaxed state, or what passes for it.

She's been that way since we were in first grade together. Tiffany feels her emotions with an inordinate level of intensity. The uncertainty and fear of the unknown get the best of her. She has every right to feel that way. At fourteen, we were ripped apart for eleven years. The two years we spent together after, I was a sloppy drunken mess. Then I was 'dead' for seven. What if I'm gone for twenty next time, or never return?

Frieda seems to think my death is necessary. However, I have no intention of walking sublimely into their slaughterhouse.

It's five-after-ten before everyone roused from their slumbers and gathers in the main part of the house. In Rebecca and Herschel's case, a brief drive through the neighborhood. The eight of us sit around our huge rectangular dining room table and begin our plot.

"How long are you planning on staying here until driving yourselves straight into a hornet's nest brimming with irrational lunatics?" Tiffany poignantly asks.

"Early January," I say flatly. "That will give Zeke time to get all the kinks out of my new gun and us to get together supplies for a prolonged siege."

"A siege?" Diane repeats with concern.

"The audacity of my plan should allow us to get the jump on them and lay claim to the deed with little bloodshed. But, if we're going to occupy my land, they're going to have a static target to take aim at."

"What's the point of all of this?" Diane asks. "Fighting surrounded is a hell of a lot worse than striking, then retreating. When I was a kid, the Vietnam War was on television every night. The news anchors talked a lot about asymmetric warfare. That's when a much smaller force strikes in an unexpected way without warning. Unable to plan for the fight, defend its position, or pursue the fleeing attackers the more powerful force becomes entrenched, no longer able to move forward. Why not do that?"

"To what end?" I ask rhetorically. "I've been fighting them one small battle at a time since I was fourteen. Even if I can keep their expansion at a minimum, what happens when I die of old age and am no longer here to stop them? Then, my only accomplishment was to stave off the inevitable, dropping it straight into the next generation's lap. Without someone who can strike through their indigo-lined armor and defeat their beasts, the population will eventually fall in line due to fear. The lurking incarnate horror will drive the true believers to out-zealot one another. Their unwavering certainty and inability to feel basic empathy will be the preamble to the extinction of our species."

All sit quietly with the profound reality I've just laid out slinking like venomous centipedes deep into the gyri of their brains.

"My plan isn't to wait and defend myself. It's to grow stronger."

"Grow stronger, how?" Diane asks.

"The closer I am to the cavern, the greater my strength. It wants to teach me and pulls on me incessantly to return. So, I'm going to do exactly what it wants, return home."

"Satellite imagery shows the Apostles have rebuilt the church. They're not exactly going to let you in the front door," Herschel says.

"Al taught me that when you build a log cabin, you cut out the door with a chainsaw after the logs have been laid. I can do the same with the cavern. I'll dig a side tunnel and cut out a new door. We don't even need excavation tools. I can move the Earth around enough to create a five-mile-long tunnel, bolstered with millennia-old granite. I'm figuring it'll take three months. This won't be a large passage, just enough for us to walk through in a single file. Otherwise, I'd have to remove debris."

"You don't have any kind of survey. How can you know which direction to dig in," Malcolm asks.

"Svangi. I left him there to protect the only place they could harvest the stone and water they needed for the ritual. That was nearly nine years ago, right after fighting off Joseph's men. He's massive, relentless, impervious to man-made weapons, and always feels as though he's starving. He's likely eaten everyone the Apostles have sent down there since. Regardless, Abraham already has an unknown amount of rock and water from before. It's not enough to rule with force. But, he can build political consensus behind himself because he speaks their religious language and can perform what they'll perceive to be miracles. The rest will fall in line through fear of violence."

"He's no politician," Herschel comments.

"Religion is politics in this country."

We spend the next few weeks in preparation. I have Zeke fabricate a truck-holster for the lamentation gun. He creates it with his 3D printer. It's a paddle-style holster. He bolts it into the inside console, accessible to the driver's right hand. The gun is identical to the one I lost on Frying Pan Tower after taking Joseph down.

The only way I could kill the beasts Joseph created was with a lamentation blade, which I can create with any type of metal. But, the charge ceases once I'm no longer touching it. This seemingly made shooting a bullet with a lamentation charge impossible. Zeke, the brilliant engineer he is, found a way.

It's constructed from a single-shot .410 shotgun with a wooden stock. The barrel is removed from the firing mechanism and stock. Zeke machines a revolver cylinder four times the size of a .357 and ten inches long. It's positioned between the barrel and the stock.

Each round is a specialty load. They're custom-made, ten-inch long .410 shells. Inside each one is a six-inch-long stainless-steel spear, tack welded to a thin, twenty-foot-long braided wire, attached at the metal base of the shell. This way, the lamentation charge reaches the projectile after it's been fired for at least twenty feet, before breaking off and becoming ineffective. After the cylinder rotates, a permanent titanium blade severs the previous round's wire before advancing the next.

The firing mechanism is double-action, meaning the shooter can cock the hammer or pull the trigger hard enough for the hammer to go all the way back by itself before coming down. That way, I can shoot six times in a row.

Getting it reloaded quickly is essential, so Zeke machines four speed loaders, which are round devices that hold yet-to-be-loaded shells in the same pattern as the shotgun's cylinder. Once the empty shells are ejected, six can be loaded simultaneously. A knurled nob at the top releases all of the shells into the cylinder with one quick turn to the left.

Constructing it took less time than before since we only needed to follow old diagrams instead of having to invent the gun all over again. Preparing for the worst, Zeke makes one hundred loads. We also have four Glock-nineteens, two twelve-gauge pump shotguns, and my thirty-aught-six scoped rifle.

We pack an extensive toolset, two axes, shovels, tents, sleeping bags, inflatable mats, as much clothing as we can, sewing supplies, extra cloth, and some cooking utensils. I estimate we'll have enough food to last us four months. After that, we're going to have to figure something out.

Our plan is to leave home mid-day on January third, twenty-sixteen, and stay overnight at a Greensboro hotel. We'll depart early the next morning so we can arrive at the Yancey County Register of Deeds at eight in the morning, on Monday the fourth. It's the first day the office reopens after Christmas break. Meaning, it will likely be sparsely manned.

We meticulously review satellite imagery of the region. The Apostles have clearly rebuilt their megachurch and expanded their facilities beyond their original borders. Much of what I knew from my time there as a child in the nineties has been razed and replaced with modern buildings.

What's most troublesome is what appear to be checkpoints set up at the county line of each road. What terrifies me is that they don't seem to be hiding their blatant disregard for state and federal laws. Rather, their presumption of autonomy has caused surrounding municipalities to quietly capitulate due to fear.

17

Zeke and I spend three days at the gun range in Warrenton Virginia between Monday, November twenty-third, and Wednesday, November, twenty-fifth. We pay an absurd sum to rent it out, no questions asked. For the first two days, we task ourselves with fine-tuning the lamentation gun. Mostly, I practice creating the indigo charge for the first time in years, then forcing it through the gun itself. After two dozen shells, I'm confident I can do it on command.

The morning of the second day is dedicated to practicing my reloading. While my hands are rusty, they're lightyears from unlearned. I cut my time in half by mid-day. Even though I'm not technically firing, it's not something I could do at the house. I never want Little Milly to see this gun. But, I'm not naive. I know one day she'll grow up to learn all of this, if there is a future for her to live in. For now, I want her to be a child concerned with dinosaurs, not existential threats.

Handling the lamentation gun while thinking of her, I blurt out to Zeke, "I may not come back."

"Why would you say something like that?"

"Because it's true."

"I could easily say, I might not come home because a sinkhole may open up underneath me. Could it happen? Sure. Will it? It's unlikely. You've bested them at every turn since you were a girl. Why would this time be different? They've already killed you. What else could they possibly do?"

"Kill the people I love instead," I say, a tear flowing from each eye.

"We'll keep Little Milly safe."

"I know," I say breathily, exhausted from the emotional exertion.

There's silence for the remainder of the day while I alternate between reloading the lamentation gun and accuracy training with the Glock. My groupings are okay, but nothing like Nate's. When he shoots a pistol, the holes in the bullseye have holes.

On day three, Zeke, myself, Rebecca, Herschel, and Nate put hundreds of rounds through our various firearms.

After Little Milly goes to sleep that night, we sit outside on the deck cleaning all of our guns around the firepit. Each of us pointlessly hopes that we'll never have to use them. At least that's what I'm supposed to think. I want nothing more than to kill some fuck who has it coming. Not just to take him off the board, but for my enjoyment.

I've begun to worry that I'm a serial killer. But, if I'm worried about it, wouldn't that by default mean I'm not? How do I balance the image I have of myself as a caring mother and wife, with that of the woman who longs to use the four tie-downs in her Hummer to restrain an evil motherfucker while he screams impotently for his life?

We meticulously pack the firearms away inside the tall, biometric safe Diane had installed in her walk-in closet years before I came home as a way to keep Little Milly safe. Also inside is three million dollars in cash stuffed into a duffle bag, in case we have to run.

Herschel has made more money than any of us could spend in our lifetimes from tech stocks he bought more than a decade ago.

Because of his experience with the Apostles, Zeke keeps a pistol on him at all times. While he sleeps or when he visits somewhere firearms are prohibited, it's locked away in a small biometric safe in his bedroom.

After locking Diane's safe, the five of us go back to our seats outside with drinks and a large joint for Herschel and Zeke to share. It's cold but the fire keeps us cozy. Diane, Malcolm, and Tiffany are inside watching a romantic comedy involving the ocean or something. Little Milly snoozes away in her bedroom, the door closed over with a six-inch gap.

It's a brown liquor kind of night for me. Nate has a vodka tonic, Herschel and Zeke, beer. We get drunk but hold back from getting plastered.

"We've all been here before," I say. "But nothing is guaranteed.

"We know," Nate says confidently.

"To me, it looks like a cycle," Rebecca says.

"It is," I respond. "The Universe is doing long division. Each time around, there's always a remainder, me."

There's quiet for a few minutes while we all stare into the crackling flames turning wood into ash.

"There won't be a fourth," Nate says after draining his vodka tonic. Joseph told you that there were a dozen safe keeps. You destroyed Frying Pan Tower, taking the number down to eleven. Before that, you flattened half of their Fort Caswell keep, and Solid Rock as well. That leaves nine more. If we can find them, maybe we could become disruptive to the point of forcing a quagmire."

"It won't matter if he continues to gain followers. He'll be able to replace his dead members, put up new structures, and buy new property. We have to take away their motivation, central propaganda machine, and stores of remaining indigo. All of those things orbit Abraham as though he's a large celestial object."

"At least his campaign for governor is running woefully behind," Rebecca comments.

"It's not a normal campaign. Abraham is about to shock the entire world. Soon he will be all anyone can talk about. Some will be dismissive at first, then fear. Others will embrace him immediately because his policies will be about hurting people they loathe. I watched this kind of fervent hatemongering bring people together in churches growing up. So did you Nate. They'll never stop. Even if they were to kill all of us queer folk and non-believers, they would eventually turn on themselves. Anger, hatred, and false piety are all they have. Without an enemy, who are they?"

"I reckon I'm done," Nate says abruptly. "I want to be up in the morning with Little Milly. It's Thanksgiving, after all."

From the look on Nate's face, I can tell that he knew the four of us completely forgot. To the outside observer, it might seem as though he's angry with me. He's exhausted and terrified for his daughter's future. So am I.

The logs have burned down to embers. Zeke douses them with water. After, we lock the sliding glass door and go our separate ways. Too fucked up to drive, Herschel and Rebecca go upstairs and sleep in Beverly's old room. After showering, I slide into bed with Tiffany who is already wrapped up like a red-headed burrito. I steal some covers back and wrap myself around her, knowing soon this will all go away, perhaps forever.

18

I try to absorb every morsel of this time. If I had the arrogance to pray, I'd appeal to God to let me pause this moment and live here for eternity. That way, I could wake up every morning a mother instead of a murderer.

But that doesn't happen. Christmas comes and goes. We continue the festivities for Little Milly's sake, all the while preparing to slip into a whole other reality in a matter of days. One where monsters are real and savagery is the only response toward those who'd harm us. We slowly load up the Hummer bit by bit the week between Christmas and New Year's Day.

In Zeke's workshop, there's an entire pallet of freeze-dried camp cuisine waiting to be gagged down, water, stoves, individual packs, tents, sewing kits, fabric, and sleeping bags.

Technology-wise, we have a laptop, a satellite phone, and a reliable inverter to charge them.

The crate housing the condenser we commissioned from Gary P. Sloan in West Virginia, has remained exactly where we loaded it.

With luck, Little Milly will never catch on.

At six years old, Little Milly is getting close to an age where she's going to expect more details from us. But for now, simplicity is the rule of the day.

We break the news of our trip at dinner on January, third, twenty-sixteen. The only explanation we could come up with for our absence was calling it a 'business trip'. That way, if she repeats it in school, nothing seems out of the ordinary. Even so, the result manifests an immediate waterfall of tears.

"Please don't leave me," she levels at us through her tears.

I don't have a response because I can't bear to tell her the awful truth, but lying is even worse. Nate picks up Little Milly, still wailing. He places her against his chest, allowing her to cry on his shoulder. He walks her around the house like that for five minutes, rubbing her back, and tells her that it will be okay.

Her sobs slow, but they're not yet completely gone. Nate turns on one of her favorite dinosaur specials. They sit together and watch as Little Milly gradually settles down. After we clean up the dishes, the rest of us join. Lost in the love of paleontology, she soon forgets to cry. Eventually, Little Milly smiles involuntarily at the appearance of a computer-generated Spinosaurus.

After it's over, Mema-Diane bathes Little Milly and gets her ready for bed. We wait around quietly for her to drift off to sleep. Once Tiffany confirms her slumber, Diane unlocks the safe. Each firearm is housed in its own rugged, polymer container, lined with form-fitting foam inserts. Our body armor is the last thing we pack away.

Herschel and Rebecca go home to spend one more night in their own bed. Everyone is emotionally exhausted. The idea of going to sleep sounds utterly delightful.

———————

The first thing I feel when I'm conscious again is a metal collar around my neck. As I move, the sound of a chain clinks across the wet rock underneath me. The walls above and the surroundings shimmer with an indigo glow that barely lifts the veil of darkness.

I hear water dripping. I'm on a small, flat, stone island, surrounded by clear, cold mountain water. I know exactly where I am. This is where Theta kept Frederick Severe prisoner for one hundred eighty-one years. The last time I was in this space, I entered through a small cave on a steep ridge.

At that time, neither Rebecca nor Ezra could follow me into this smaller cave opening. To them, it appeared to be a rock wall. Yet, I could pass through.

I reach down into the Earth and bring up searing heat in an attempt to melt the chain and release myself. Nothing happens, despite my hand glowing white-hot. It feels as though there's a pliable force field around the metal. Then I see the indigo flecks within it shimmering in the light emitted by my glowing left hand.

I think back to what Frederick described happening to him when he was in my place. He called the man who tortured him, "Not a shadow, but the void where space should be. Pure emptiness." He appeared in indeterminable intervals to crush his bones with a maul hammer. Only, his injuries healed unnaturally, just to have it done again and again for two lifetimes.

I've done nothing to deserve this, but neither did Frederick. The Ceraphirian, Theta, was furious at him for defiling what they consider a holy site, the cavern under the Apostle's compound. He was a miner trying to make his way in this world, ignorant of the offense he caused.

Theta, knowing full well that being a kind person, he'd never be confined to the Woods of Lamentation, took it upon herself to create an off-grid prison between worlds to administer an unjust punishment.

I freed Frederick in two thousand six. He was a fragile, broken man who turned to dust upon exiting the cave. Am I receiving the same treatment?

A staircase, shimmering with indigo rises from the water on my left side. As a walkway begins to form from the bridge to the island, I brace for eight pounds of steel to strike my ankles and shins. To my relief and irritation, the figure I see is Theta.

As Theta opens her mouth to speak, I hear the faint sound of wind howling in a veiled, distant place.

I interrupt her before her words hit the cool atmosphere of the cavern, "Goddamn it, Theta!" I scream. "I'm sick of all your bullshit pageantry. I don't have the patience for flashbacks or to watch you turn into a miniature weather phenomenon. It's tacky and boring."

"When I did those things, I was showing you something you needed to see. You must understand that I don't have you here to treat you the way I did Frederick. I feel unbearable remorse for my actions. You're here to make a choice about how all of this is going to end."

"How can I make a choice with an indigo collar around my neck?"

"Once the choice is made, it will come off."

"I need rest. We leave in the morning."

"You're no longer at home."

"What did you do?" I seethe.

"I pulled your molecular structure into this place because it's a neutral spot between worlds. It's not something I've done to a person before because it would have killed anyone else. Anyone except you."

"How could you have been so sure?" I snap.

"Because, you disintegrated into the Woods of Lamentation,

only to reform and walk out."

"I wasn't just walking out. I was making a bee-line to get my hands on the lot of you."

"Yes, and in your carelessness, you brought someone back with you."

"Mordecai," I exclaim.

"Yes, that little bastard."

"We can't have him running loose. Point me in his direction."

"You're already headed in the right direction. While those in the Woods of Lamentation are under constant predation, they briefly speak from time to time. Your bubble became a legend to the tortured, a faint glimmer of hope because it was something different. Curiosity grew, leading its location to be heavily prowled by beasts. Its existence acted like bait. Mordecai just happened to be the one with a line in the water when the big fish struck. Otherwise, there's nothing special about him."

"How long has Mordecai been in my world?"

"He washed ashore a few miles north of you back in twenty-fourteen. After finding his way to a homeless shelter, the first thing he did was seek out a minister to speak with. The pastor was a member of the Apostles of the Cloven Hand who served undercover at First Baptist in downtown Wilmington."

"The one with all the hateful signs across from the nightclub, Spectrum. I'm familiar with it."

"Their conversation piqued the interest of the pastor, who in turn, informed the Apostle's higher-ups. Since then, Mordecai has become a trusted advisor because of his experiences in the Woods of Lamentation."

"Let me go so I can kill him."

"It's more complicated than that, Naomi."

"Send me back to my bed, then," I say with anger building behind my eyes.

"Which brings us to the choice. Your first option is to return to your bed. However, tomorrow morning, you will wake up with the knowledge that the four of you are walking into certain death. But, with your deaths comes survival for Tiffany and Little Milly. Unfortunately, they, like most of humanity, will live out their days in a grayer, diminished world."

"Or?"

"Or, I let you out of this cave, with all of your gear, to do what you do best."

"And what's that?"

"Create mayhem directed at those who deserve it."

"Do you really consider this a choice? I won't have my little girl survive in a world like that."

"You don't want Little Milly to survive?" Theta says, puzzled.

"No. I want her to truly live."

"I see," Theta says, pausing. "Naomi, my dearest, you are the only human I have ever admired."

"Let me go so I can get to work before the sun comes up."

"Before your decision is final, remember, doing this means I can't guarantee your daughter or Tiffany's survival. This is one of those choices we Ceraphirian cannot see beyond."

"And if they survive."

"The world they will inherit will be utterly horrifying. The Apostles will have free reign. Just imagine what they will do."

"No, imagine what I'm going to do."

Theta smiles as the collar around my neck falls to the granite floor.

Standing, I examine my clothes. I have on a green flannel, jeans, a hat, and a nice pair of hiking boots. I walk across the bridge to meet Theta. She's so much taller than me that I have to look up to talk to her. It's a strange sensation for a woman who is six feet tall.

"Why are you here?" I ask.

"To nudge the equation in your favor."

"But, not too much, or the fabric of space-time basically dissolves, or something like that, right?"

"That's simplifying it, but yes." I'm here because I believe in you."

I feel the need to diminish her compliment, but abstain.

"Thank you," I say, walking across the bridge, toward the cave entrance. There, my pack awaits.

Lying next to it are my camouflage coveralls and body armor. The back has a heavily padded rifle insert. The long gun is slid in through the top, muzzle down, and rests directly against the wearer's back.

I unzip the compartment to see my thirty-aught six's black polymer stock. Inside a padded insert within the compartment, I see the suppressor, which has to be removed before packing the gun away.

My Glock Nineteen rests on the ground, protected by a left-handed paddle holster.

I make sure to put the body armor on before my coveralls, to conceal it. It would look odd if someone were to see me.

"Where's the lamentation gun Zeke built?"

"There's no room for it in your pack, and they haven't made any beasts yet. Momentarily, Abraham and his guards are at For Caswell overseeing the construction of new homes. After you collapsed their fortified battery, the space was no longer zoned as a historical site. Abraham took the opportunity to build more homes to boost Fort Caswell's population."

"So, just regular ol' bags of flesh and water, then?"

"Technically, yes they are mostly… Oh, you mean they're easy to kill?"

"Yeah. I reckon sarcasm and innuendo is a human thing, not a Ceraphirian one."

"I'm working on it," Theta says, half smiling. "But your assessment is correct. They have no indigo armor, and no beasts to accompany them. But they have countless M16s. It took them five years to replace all the ones you locked away in the cavern with Svangi. Abraham's men have spent most of their lives roaming these mountains and can shoot well because missing here means going hungry. So, don't get too self-assured.

"I won't, Theta. Thank you."

"The final thing I can tell you is this: they have checkpoints everywhere. Each has a single rocket-propelled grenade launcher. That's what would have ended your lives."

I look into Theta's eyes with deep admiration. She's gone right up to the line. Telling me anything else could be cataclysmic."

The pack is the same one I put away in the Jeep. It has plenty of food, a stove, a headlamp, a flashlight, a sleeping bag, a water bottle, toiletries, and my GPS. But something is there I didn't pack, the satellite phone.

"Call them," she says."

"Do I have to?" I say stubbornly.

"Yes, Naomi, you have to. Blame it on me. But I know part of you is excited for your solo hunt."

The cave leading to the outside is twenty feet long and much narrower than the main cavern. The entrance is peculiar. When Rebecca, Ezra, and I were here ten years ago, the opening appeared to be made of rock to them, but I perceived it as an open passage.

The light I carry has changed my body and allows me to see what

Theta built, because she carries the same. When Rebecca or Ezra touched the opening it acted like solid granite, preventing them from going further. But I could walk through. On the other side, I could see their hands against what looked like dense glass molded into the shape of the exterior rock. Regardless, I could walk right back through to the outside. But now, all I see is darkness, which means it's still nighttime.

Outside, the temperature is well below freezing and the sky is clear. I grew accustomed to the cold years ago. But I still haven't gotten used to letting Tiffany down.

19

Tiffany spent an entire week obsessing over satellite phones. Multiple tabs of reviews and videos populated her open browser. The one she bought looks like a long, skinny, black brick. There's a huge flat antenna that extends by folding out, doubling the already ridiculous length. Inputting numbers is achieved on a backlit, monochrome screen. It costs more per minute than a late-night, one-nine-hundred number in the nineties. Other than phones like this one, there is no other mobile service out here because mountains absorb tower signals. It works, but the technology is so finicky that even leaves can interrupt the connection. But, being that it's one of the long dark nights of winter, the leaves are underfoot, rather than hanging from stems overhead.

I find a small boulder under a patchy outcrop of trees, take a seat, and unfold the stupid antenna. It takes about thirty seconds to boot up. With a satellite phone, you have to dial a three-digit country code first, no matter where you are. That makes the call even more frustrating because it takes me ten minutes to remember that North America's calling prefix is zero-zero-one. After hitting send, it doesn't dial right away. It takes another half a minute to get the call through the network. I should be calling Tiffany, but I'm ringing Rebecca and Herschel's landline instead.

Their old phone was left over by the previous owner. It has a real bell inside that cuts through silence like a guillotine does the aristocracy. The phone rings only once before Rebecca picks up the handset next to her side of the bed. She installed an aftermarket caller ID display.

"Yes?" she says matter of factly.

"It's Naomi."

"Are you okay? I don't recognize the number. It says, No caller ID - Unknown."

"It's the satellite phone. I'm already in the field."

"Wait, what? Holy hell, how fast did you drive?"

"That's the thing, I didn't. Theta pulled me through somehow. I woke up in the cave where I found Frederick Severe."

"How did you get away?"

"Theta let me go," I say.

"How in the hell do you have the phone with you?"

"She pulled my pack through with me, along with the phone, my rifle, and sidearm."

"She said coming here tomorrow together was going to end in our certain deaths. I believe Theta is genuinely attempting to nudge the equation in my favor."

"Are you sure you can trust her? She's a Ceraphirian, like Frieda," Rebecca asks.

"Yes, strangely I do. They're individuals, not a hivemind."

"I trust your judgment. What's the task?"

"To take one of their checkpoints over so they can't fire a rocket-propelled grenade into our Hummer. That's what Theta said would have killed us."

"I reckon I owe her a drink."

"She's not the greatest company," I reply jokingly.

"Where are you now?"

"Not far from the cave entrance. Being here again gives me the surreal feeling of walking through an abandoned theme park. My surroundings tell my conditioned brain that there should be fighting going on all around, but there isn't. The conflicting stimuli have created an eerie feeling."

"What should we do?"

"It's going to take a few days. But once I capture the checkpoint, I'm going to need y'all to make it there quickly. You'll need to be stationed nearby. Book accommodations in Morganton, North Carolina for two weeks starting tomorrow night. I think two counties east should be enough of a head start if this whole thing blows up in my face. But, please stay vigilant. They have operatives all over this area."

"That won't be a problem. I'll start booking it the moment we get off the phone. And we'll keep our sidearms on us at all times," Rebecca says cooly, despite knowing what they're facing."

"Make sure to tell Little Milly that Mama-Naomi left early for the business trip and that she loves her. I need to go so I can preserve the battery."

"Happy hunting, sister."

With that, the line goes dead.

The ridge is at most, half a mile wide. It rises in elevation like a ramp, leaving two steep edges on each side. Ten years ago, when I was here with Rebecca and Ezra chasing after Joseph, we camped five miles uphill. There, it comes to a cliff with an overhanging rock. Rebecca and I rained down hell on the Apostles with the very thirty-aught-six I carry in my pack now.

Using a series of incendiary and traditional rounds, we destroyed the trucks they were using to haul away rock and water they hoped to use for the manufacture of indigo. We also put quite a few of their men in the ground.

We had a few good days but were eventually made. Rebecca escaped. I was captured and ended up in a hospital bed underground where they kept me drugged while they drained my blood. That was a mistake. Svangi killed what I estimate to be forty of their men during my exodus. It's difficult to give an exact number because their bodies were shredded into bite-size pieces by a Beast of Lamentation.

Heading in that direction would be fruitless. I collapsed that entrance during my escape, leaving only a small section underneath the Apostle's compound intact.

I'll head downhill. The drop-off is too high on either side of the ridge.

Digging around in my pack, it doesn't take long to locate my National Geographic map of Pisgah Forest. The trees block enough wind that I'm able to open it completely and lay it on the boulder. I use small stones on all four corners as paper weights.

There are three ways into town. Highway Nineteen runs north to south. Highway Eighty, which climbs two thousand feet through nauseating switchbacks. And, Highway One-Nintey-Seven North, which boasts an equally curvy two-lane road.

The north and south entrances on Highway Ninteen will be heavily guarded, as will the two more remote roads. Just slightly less so. No. I need something that's been overlooked.

With my headlamp on, I scan back and forth for the inevitable prize. It takes an hour before the words *Mill Creek Road* grace my vision. It appears to end at a parking lot connected to an old

National Park road. Based on the change in elevation and lack of paved surface, it's going to be the kind of place you'd need a capable four-wheel-drive vehicle to traverse.

Tucked away in the front pocket of my pack is a new handheld GPS. Unlike my old monochrome unit, it has a crisp, detailed screen with preloaded maps of North America. Within a few minutes, I'm able to pin a waypoint where I believe the trail intersects with the old parking lot, high up in Yancey County backcountry.

Strangely, it runs directly behind the golf course I ran through when I escaped Vernon Proffit as a child in nineteen-ninety-five.

From that point, it's only a few minutes to Highway Eighty. That places us just two miles south of the old Solid Rock compound where; now overseen by their offshoot, Apostles of the Cloven hand. Same shitty smell with a new name.

From that point, it's only five miles from the Register of Deeds Office in Burnsville. There'll likely be patrol cars posted at Seven Mile Ridge because it intersects directly in front of the Apostle's primary keep. Looking at the satellite data, it's obvious that the church I caused to collapse was rebuilt even larger. Hubris is the crux of their movement.

I won't be able to get to the site until at least tomorrow night. I wouldn't dare travel in broad daylight, especially with trees bare of foliage. I keep my rifle stuffed away in its case and my nine-millimeter tucked in my coveralls. The only weapon I have immediate access to is a large, green-handled, drop-point auto knife I keep clipped inside my lefthand pocket. Just in case Theta is wrong about beasts and I need to charge it into a lamentation blade. Otherwise, I'd be defenseless against them. Either way, I'm still the most terrifying creature in the forest, which is the way I like it.

I stash my GPS away to save the battery. The route is strictly downhill for five miles. There's no getting lost without falling to my death.

It's Monday, January fourth, twenty-sixteen. I should be able to get to the bottom of the ridge before daybreak. The climb down at the end is steep enough that I will have to go hand-over-hand. Luckily, there's a small shelf right before. It should provide me with a place to camp during the day. I keep my headlamp extinguished as I head out. There's enough moonlight to see several feet in front of me.

As the miles tick by slowly, my legs begin to wobble a little. Even though I keep a fairly rigorous exercise routine, walking downhill for long distances isn't one of them. And it's things like this that lay my mortal nature on open display. No matter how powerful my abilities are, they won't lighten my pack or give me legs that never get tired.

At five-thirty in the morning, I reach my destination.

I pull a granite dome over myself for protection and concealment. I make sure to draw up the Earth's warmth underneath my shelter. Even so, I double down and crawl into my sleeping bag just before the morning. Not long afterward, my conscious mind is set adrift.

20

The moment I feel the railroad ties underneath my back, I become uncontrollably pissed off. Once on my feet, I see Frieda's outline coming out of the distance. She walks on the tracks in my direction. The same old lantern precedes her.

In a whisper, I say, "Theta, if you can hear me, I need you."

I'm certain it will do nothing. Regardless, I've released it into the complex architecture of this place. Maybe the message will worm itself where it belongs. I begin to wonder: if I kill Frieda, will I inherit her light? Or is she like Mordecai, able to heal and reform?

When she is within speaking distance, Frieda says, "If you had only died in the Hummer, as planned, everything would have been resolved."

"Do you call allowing an insane cult to become the ruling body of this country solved? It won't just be us. Their sickness will spread across our borders, infecting the rest of the world."

"It's a solution we're willing to accept."

"Because you don't have to live with the consequences."

"It resolves in less than two hundred years."

"You're dooming generations to live without hope. And, I'm

assuming there will be much bloodshed."

"We're trying to calculate our way out of the mess you created."

"You're plotting to doom billions to save yourselves from the difficulty of actually solving a problem without harming someone else in the process. I can't abide that."

"It has to end somehow."

"I'm aware, Frieda. But, are you sure you've picked the right side?"

"We've chosen the simplest route, with the fewest variables for failure."

"Then you've chosen the most direct route to collide with me because I will not get out of your way. Doing so would mean letting you run over my little girl's life as though she's nothing but a possum under a semi."

I try to calm myself, but it's pointless. This isn't the rage I felt at the indignation of my abuse, but that of a mother. I close the distance between myself and Frieda.

"I think you and I should visit the Woods of Lamentation," I say before grabbing Frieda violently by her hair and dragging her off the tracks.

I may not have the use of my abilities here, but Frieda is small and physically weak. Snow crunches softly underfoot, between Frieda's screams. A low cacophony of growls hisses, and snarls rattle through trees in hungry anticipation.

A stone arch doorway opens in front of us. It doesn't appear to lead anywhere. Only a blank space is contained within its edges. Then, as though emerging from nothingness, steps Theta's immensely tall frame.

"Stop right there, Naomi," Theta says holding out her palm. "Taking her in there, no matter how much she deserves it, is only going to make things worse."

"I'm about to make myself feel a lot better by handing out pieces of Frieda to Beasts of Lamentation like they're dog treats."

"And what about her light, Naomi?"

I cock my head and coyly say, "Aren't you just a little bit curious to find out?"

"Theta. Stop her!" Frieda screams.

"This is long overdue," I say.

"Have you gone soft for them because of that stupid man, Frederick Severe?" Frieda says. "Or is that only reserved for her?"

"What you've been doing is extremely risky, Frieda," Theta says. "It's their world that winds our reality. And like a real watch, it can be overwound. Their species has grown smart enough to destroy themselves but are too stupid to realize that doing so isn't a valid solution. And you want to introduce the chaos of a fanatical death-cult revolution to the mix? Have you considered that the end-result of your actions might be extinction?"

"There was a slight uptick in the probability," Frieda responds.

"And you're risking all our existences on it?"

"All?" I ask. "You don't live on Earth. Humanity could destroy itself and your coven of cosmic-psycho-witches would be just fine."

"Not without your kind," Theta replies.

"They're the last ones," Theta says to Frieda.

"Last what?" I intrude. "Sentient life? I already know."

"Without a sentient species to observe the universe, everything ceases to exist, including the Ceraphirian."

"You were willing to do what? Risk everything, Frieda?" I say in disgust. "You're not allowed to gamble using other people's lives like they're gameboard pieces."

"More like an abacus," Frieda responds.

I twist Frieda's hair tighter at that statement. She grimaces in pain.

"Bring her through," Theta says, pointing to the still-open portal.

"Where does it go?"

"Frederick's old place."

I drag Frieda through the doorway by her hair, breaking the stark film of nothingness beyond its edges. I'm struck with the brief sensation of falling that abruptly stops. The following moment, I find myself on the ladder Theta uses to travel to the space she creates between worlds.

Theta is already waiting on the rock island in the middle of a deep, cold mountain aquifer. I look to my right to see Frieda standing next to me, her hair now untangled from my fingers.

Theta sees the look on my face and says, "Don't bother. She can't get out that way without my permission. If she decides to leave through the cave door, her fate will be that of Zelia, mortality.

"What would happen if I walked out the door?"

"I haven't pulled your molecular structure through. If you walk out of the cave's exit, you'll wake up back in your sleeping bag. I could pull you through, but there would be no point. You'd have to trek all the way back to your camp."

Frieda slowly begins inching away from me. I cut my eyes at her. She only has one place to run, out of the cave entrance. I feel her clumsily paw at my mind, attempting to influence me.

"That won't work on me, asshole," I say to her.

Then, I look up to see Theta staring off, in a daze. I realize Frieda is working her way into Theta's mind. Frieda takes two quick steps away from me before I'm on her. I wrap my right arm around her neck and begin to squeeze. I pull my green auto knife from my left pocket and ignite it into a lamentation blade. The indigo-charged metal's crackle echoes inside the enclosed space.

Holding it in front of Frieda's eyes, I say, "You know I'll fucking do it, fear of what happens to your light be damned."

When she doesn't comply, I squeeze harder. Cutting off her air seems to have no effect. Soon, however, the vertebrae in her neck begin to pop. Still nothing. I look up to see that Theta's eyes have turned white, crackling with indigo lighting flashing within them. Desperate, I place the broad side of the knife blade against Frieda's right cheek. There's a searing noise, like steak on a griddle. She screams in pain. This coincides with a dazed Theta shaking her head, regaining control over her own body. I release Frieda, and she falls to the ground. Spitefully, I burn her left cheek with a matching knife blade-shaped burn. Frieda covers her face, wailing in pain.

Knife back in my pocket, I grab Frieda by the throat, with my left hand and lift her torso with my right. I throw her across the water, onto the stone island. A dull thud resonates underneath Frieda's sharp scream. Theta quickly wraps the metal collar around Frieda's neck, dulling her abilities.

"Was all of that necessary, Naomi?" Theta asks.

"No. Some of it I wanted to do because she deserved it. And because I enjoyed causing her pain. Won't she heal like the men in the Woods of Lamentation?"

"We're in the space between worlds. Here, the rules are a mixture of both. Once she's back home, the damage you've done to her face will quickly fade. Until then, she will heal at the pace of a mortal. Like Frederick, her wounds will eventually vanish."

"How could you side with this sack of meat, sister?" Frieda moans at Theta.

"How could you risk our reality, sister?" Theta says condescendingly."

As Frieda continues to groan in pain, I ask Theta, "If the continuation of existence relies on the observation of sentient species, who was there to watch when God created the Universe?"

"At the time, she was the observer. However, once enough sentient life emerged within all the universes she spawned, God became overwhelmed by her own design. It's her nature to absorb the emotions of all self-aware beings across ever-increasing infinite realities. That's why she created the Ceraphirian, to oversee this one. I assume she did something similar with all the other Universes. But, we are isolated here by design, to stand in her stead as she mainlines the essence of all thinking beings and resides within every elementary particle. Her state is nearly trance-like. Some of us think it was part of her plan all along."

"Maybe that's why humans seem to be designed to feel everything so profoundly, so she can benefit?"

"She would say, share."

"And I would tell her to kiss my ass."

"I'd like that," Theta says, trying not to smirk.

"Ceraphirian don't count as observers?"

"No, we're a part of the fabric of this reality. So, when the last human is gone, that's it. All of our existence will disperse into nothingness. I assume there are near-infinite self-contained realities. But this one is ours. None of us can escape into another."

"Have you lost your fucking mind, Frieda?" I say, looking down at her.

"We have only taken extreme measures because of extreme circumstances."

"And sister, what happened to the last two sentient species?" Theta asks rhetorically, so Frieda can explain it to me.

"They destroyed each other using weapons that harness the energy of entire stars."

"Their once great societies have been reduced to minute particles floating in the icy vacuum of space. And now you want to risk all we have left in the spirit of streamlining history, instead of making an effort?"

"Efforts have been made. She's obtuse and incorrigible," Frieda says to Theta, referring to me. "She doesn't care about anything but her family, especially the little girl, Milly."

My left knuckles catch a glancing blow across the bridge of Frieda's nose from above, eliciting a sickening cracking noise."

Frieda no longer knows whether to cover her profusely bleeding nose or burnt cheeks.

"Don't worry Frieda, it'll heal. It won't even take two hundred years," I say as she grimaces.

"You didn't have to—"

"It's time she learns what being human feels like. She has a harder head than you. All you needed was a dash of empathy. This one can't see past her obtuse calculations."

"I understand anger, Naomi."

"This is a mother's rage, an entirely different species unto itself."

21

I don't wake up until noon. That's not unexpected. I plan on staying concealed for the remainder of the day and begin moving after nightfall.

This iteration of the Apostles is much weaker than when Joseph was in charge because he had a substantial supply of indigo. He was impulsive and, quite frankly, he was viewed as charismatic by all the wrong people.

Abraham, on the other hand, is a lumbering sloth in comparison.

Although their numbers are down, those who remain are the truest believers. The kind who are prepared to fight to the death because they know, with juvenile certainty, that paradise awaits.

But, to my reticence, there's the incongruency of Abraham's expansion. Their megachurch was rebuilt even larger this time. The entirety of Solid Rock was razed and then refashioned with modern buildings and amenities.

While Joseph played his role as a young visionary, Abraham, thirty years his senior, went the executive route. He's meticulously crafting a plan and will execute it on his own schedule. This frightens me. I could always count on Joseph to be erratic. That inevitability is what got him killed. Abraham is playing a hand I cannot see. Otherwise, he wouldn't be overseeing a period of expansion.

After a cup of coffee, I place my hand on the ground to feel for the vibrations of human footsteps. After a few minutes, I'm satisfied that there is no one nearby. I open a small doorway facing away from the ledge's sharp overlook. It's not sheer, but it's steep.

I venture out and have a look over the field where Rebecca, Ezra, and I hid in the waist-high grass, preparing to dart across the road, ten years ago. It feels like the legend of a person I was once upon a time. That past is very much still real. Here I am, the result of it.

I sit with my feet dangling over the edge of the drop-off and take in the severity of the dim winter sky cutting across the unchanged landscape of sorrowful yesterdays.

Though I dread it, I need to call home and speak with Tiffany. I love her, but Tiff is such an idealist. As much as I disagree with such notions, it's something I love about her. Futilely, she longs for a simple right versus wrong, rather than bad versus less bad.

My being cast into the wilderness on a solo hunt is far better than all of us being dead. Now, I just have to convince her of that. It's not that she would want us dead. She's of the mind that for every dreadful choice, there is always an unseen third option. There isn't.

I return to the interior of my dome hideaway, pour another cup of coffee, and retrieve the satellite phone. Back at the overlook, I begin dialing Tiffany's cellphone number. It's half past noon. Little Milly should be at school.

Tiffany answers directly after the first ring.

"Naomi?"

"Yes, baby. It's me."

"I spoke to Rebecca. Where are you? I'm so scared."

"I know. This wasn't my decision. Theta brought me here. In doing so, she saved my, Rebecca, Nate, and Herschel's lives."

"Years ago, you took it upon yourself to hunt them alone. Here you are again, in the same place, but this time you were never given a choice. It's as though you have to be there, no matter how it occurs."

"Some version of that. Hopefully, this is the least shitty one."

"How much more can we all give? How much can you?"

"If Frieda has her way, I'm to give everything."

"I wish you could—"

"It's done. I fucked her up pretty good. She's locked away where Theta kept Frederick Severe."

"Is Theta going to do to her what she did to Frederick?"

"No one is going to be crushing Frieda's bones with a sledgehammer for the foreseeable future. Theta's experience with Frederick left her permanently changed. She seems almost human now and less logistical. However, it was Theta's anger that got her into that spot to begin with. But, what's more human than anger?"

"Maybe. But, it seems you must participate willingly or not, so it goes with Theta."

"I'd rather not think about it right now. How's Little Milly?"

"Confused."

"She thought everyone was leaving, yet the only person missing was one of her mothers. All of the 'whys' she asks are beyond my understanding, so I'm not sure how to explain all of this to a scared little girl.

"Did you tell her I left for the business trip early?"

"Yes. But she wants to know why you didn't come to say goodbye."

"What did you tell her?"

"That you didn't want to wake her up. That's satiated her line of inquiry momentarily. Little Milly is clever. She'll find another inconsistency quicker than I'd prefer."

"In a couple of years, she'll be too smart to lie to, but too innocent to hear the truth. Preserve Little Milly's childhood as long as her naivete will allow."

"So, what's your plan, hero-Mommy?"

"There's an overland, four-wheel drive trail that creeps up through the Pisgah National Forest. It climbs up to the ridge. Once over the top, you're in Yancey County. From there, it continues down into the valley. There should be a checkpoint at the top of the ridge. It's likely sparsely manned. Communication is difficult up here. They won't be missed for quite a while."

"So, you take their camp and make their checkpoint yours?"

"I reckon so. For a while, anyhow. Hopefully, they have better food that I can steal."

"And when you're done eating it all, you're going to call Rebecca. Then she, Herschel, and Nate head to your location?" Tiff nervously jokes.

"They should be okay to make it there. McDowell County isn't under the Apostle's control. If there's going to be a party, it'll be at the top of the hill."

"You have it all under control, then?"

"If all goes as planned, they won't see us coming until we want them to."

"I believe in you."

"I've gotten this far."

Further than anyone I've ever known. From that lanky tow-headed girl in my first-grade class to the hero the world will never know, but to whom they owe everything."

"I only need appreciation from you and Little Milly. I relish the days to come when the world can mind its own business."

"It'll be soon."

"I have to get off the line so that I can save the battery."

"I understand."

"Tell Little Milly that I love her and her mama."

"I will. Be sure to tell Mama-Naomi that we love her back," Tiffany says.

"If I see her," I say wryly.

The line goes dead.

I return to the interior of my small dome shelter and close the doorway behind me. Inside, it's much warmer than out in the slicing-cold wind. For some reason, I begin to cry.

At five in the evening, I peel back a doorway through the dome once more. Nightfall is almost complete. It's time to break camp. I return the granite used to create the dome back to its natural state, within the ground.

With my pack on, I start descending the hill slowly. I may have climbed this before, but I've never descended it. I think to modify the gradient of the slope with my abilities, but I fear that the change would be so extreme Apostle patrols passing in their trucks might spot the difference. For now, their guard is relaxed. I don't want to do anything to change that.

A quarter of the way from the top, my right foot slips when a rock about the size of a softball pops loose and tumbles down the hill, making a loud 'click, click' noise as it descends.

The sound becomes the only thing I hear as I realize my body is floating in thin air. Panic sets in.

I'm falling!

I instinctually place my hands behind me in an attempt to catch myself. But, instead of rocks perforating my organs and shattering my bones, I feel a strong gust of wind at my back. It keeps me suspended, cradling my body. I'm able to command it to turn me upright, and gently grab hold of the sloping surface again.

Did I do that myself? It felt similar to when I cause the Earth to shift, like a shape in my mind. I'm shaken up and don't understand what's going on, so I focus on the task at hand, descending.

Theta, what did you do? I think to myself.

It takes another forty-five minutes to get to the bottom. I'm pouring sweat. Partially because of the exertion, but also from terror. I've been afraid for my own life, and those of my family on too many occasions. I've learned to control it so I can move forward. But this is a new fear, not being there for my daughter. Or worse, the world she will inherit if I fail.

I take a few deep breaths and try to put it out of my mind.

There isn't a lot of cover. I head east, in the direction of Burnsville, shielded by a thin layer of small hardwood trees. I know that in a mile, I'll reach the edge of the ridge I just descended. I cover the distance easily, only having to duck down when a pickup passes. There's no reaction, so I feel safe assuming they didn't see me. I mean, I am covered head-to-toe in camouflage.

Once I'm safely inside the forest, I turn on my GPS to orient myself. Afterward, I activate the dim setting on my headlamp and begin to navigate the pitch-black valley.

22

I'd prefer not to have my headlamp illuminated. However, under the heavy tree cover of Pisgah National Forest, moonlight fades quickly. Luckily, I'm far away from any kind of trails or houses. It's nothing but backcountry.

The sound of trickling water surrounds me. Despite the frigid temperatures, moving water takes longer to freeze, if at all. The wall of the continually rising ridgeline has multitudes of icicles the size of baseball bats hanging off of them. There are multitudes because water weeps out of these rocks year-round. During the winter, it freezes to the rock walls and continues to grow downward in the form of sharp spikes.

Still, some of the water gathers into small streams, winding their way down to the Toe River. Which, of course, passes directly in front of Solid Rock; the Apostle's headquarters.

A thick fog flows from both sides of the valley, converging into a soup bowl at the bottom. I can sense my surroundings through the Earth as my feet touch the ground. But, my ability to do so is not as sensitive as if I were barefoot. I have no desire to reach down and touch the ground, though. I'd rather keep my hands gloved and boots on.

For now, everything seems safe enough. However, the further down I drop into the valley, the more occluded my vision becomes by the fog, which has slowed my progression significantly. By five in the morning, January fifth, twenty-sixteen, I conclude that I won't be making it past the former Solid Rock compound by dawn.

I'll have to bed down for the day about a mile directly across the river from their newly built megachurch, which rests on the location of Vernon Prophet's old home. Below are his riches; guns, ammunition, and two of the three ingredients needed to create indigo. Unfortunately for them, I left Svangi behind to roam the void of what remains of the cavern, cutting off their access to it in two thousand-seven.

Since then, a spot on my left palm has had a constant, small, sharp tingle. A speck of the light within me animates Svangi. When he hurts, I feel it. Poor Svangi has been starving for the entirety of that time. He can't die from hunger, but he is cognizant of the discomfort. I feel plenty guilty about it.

I won't be able to get back to him today, but I hope to soon. As strange as it sounds, he's the only pet I've ever had. My mother hates dogs and my father was allergic to cats. Today, my chosen family has none in case we have to drop everything and run again.

The sun comes up soon and I'm exhausted. I'll make camp right here.

There are no Apostles left alive who have seen me create a granite shelter, making its stealth level extremely high. I have my suspicions that Joseph was telling Abraham next to nothing. It's taken him a decade to create indigo. So, it's likely that most of their knowledge of my abilities quite literally died with him.

I settle on a spot next to an old-growth oak tree. When I

create the granite dome, I make sure to wrap it halfway around the tree, giving the effect that the tree grew into the rock. That gives the illusion that the rock is a part of the long-term, natural environment. The bark of the tree even pokes through the wall on the inside. It's like having a silent visitor.

I pull heat up from deep underground, create a privy, and a spring to collect fresh water. There's nothing I can do at this point other than stay warm, wait, and rest.

———————

The day goes by quietly. I sleep off and on. I never sense anyone walking near my shelter. After having a warm meal, I return my camp to its original state, leaving no evidence behind.

At six in the evening, I get going. My headlamp is off for now. There are too many Apostle eyes in this vicinity. This makes for slow going. However, I'm closer to Highway Eighty, so there is some spillover moonlight from the opening in the tree canopy.

After a couple of miles, the Toe River turns and drifts away from the road and toward the opposite wall of the valley. The terrain flattens and the river morphs from a rushing torrent to a calm and meandering flow. A person could easily walk across it in warm weather. Or, more enjoyably, stand in the middle and fish.

The forest is quiet this time of year. Bears are hibernating, and breeding season is ending for whitetail deer. The blankness in my ear isn't a foreign sensation, but one from a distant past. Much like the feeling you have when you find a toy you haven't seen since childhood. I've spent the last two years living in the Washington Metropolitan Area. Even under my current circumstances, it's liberating to look up at a clear night sky partially obscured by a forest canopy.

At midnight, I make it to the golf course. There, the trail splits. Going right would lead me up to the Mount Mitchell backcountry, toward where Al and Milly's home used to be.

I stay on the main path, which allows me to travel behind the golf course. It should dead end at a gravel parking lot. It's a leftover from the National Park Service before Solid Rock took over and drove them out. How? I don't know. I've wondered that for years. I've come to two conclusions. One, having another Ruby Ridge on their hands was not advantageous for the ATF or the FBI. Or two, they just don't care who the people of Solid Rock or the Apostles hurt. To them, they're poor hillbillies and not worth their time. Honestly, it's likely both.

An eighth of a mile from the trail's end, I stop and prepare to make camp. It's too far to climb to the top of the ridge and still have the energy to fight. And, it will be daylight by then, which removes the element of surprise. I need my kills to be clean and silent if I'm to avoid having them radio for backup. That is, if the radio signal will even reach the next Apostle location because of the thick granite.

I walk fifteen feet into the woods and form a protective dome, just like yesterday. After eating, I pass out, face first on my sleeping bag.

———————

It's the evening of January fifth. After wiping away the geological evidence of my presence, I begin my ascent of the trail. It was originally intended for four-wheel-drive vehicles. It's mostly dirt, rock, roots, and ruts. I'm at a disadvantage because I have to keep my headlamp off to avoid a sniper's bullet. The trail winds up over one thousand feet in elevation, twisting into pretzels the entire way.

It's a grueling ascent after all I've already been through. My pack is beginning to dig into my shoulders. I'm almost relieved to spot a light up ahead after hours of walking. It's a campfire.

I want to strike now. But they're too far away. It will be daylight before I get into position. Begrudgingly, I hunker down for the night just as I did both days prior.

———————

I wake at two in the afternoon on Wednesday, January sixth. I take time to eat because, after that, all I can do is lie and wait until the clock on my GPS says it's past six in the evening. I wish I had a book with me.

Mostly, I stare into the granite above and contemplate what will come after all of this is over. I can't yet fathom a life without war. But this time, I think I'm ready to learn how.

I unexpectedly fall asleep again, waking just before nightfall.

———————

I create a doorway in my dome shelter so that I can exit and have a look up the trail.

The fire is burning brighter now since it's the beginning of the evening. I wonder if some of them fell asleep last night, or did they just run out of wood? I decide that it is time to break camp.

After getting within a mile of their checkpoint, I step into the woods and begin ascending off-trail, toward their location.

I count at least three people. I'm too far away to feel their movement through the Earth, but I can see their figures around the unkempt blaze.

23

It becomes apparent, the closer I get, that the peak is near a very large rock overhand that the Apostle guards are using as shelter.

Within five hundred feet, my only choices are to step back onto the path or begin climbing the long, sloping granite shelf leading to the rock overhang suspended above the unsuspecting men.

Just as I begin my upward trajectory, I hear an engine turn over, releasing a low rumble. Swiftly, I step off the rock and duck back into the wood line, placing me only eight feet from the offroad trail. I lie face-down, allowing the camouflage pattern of my coveralls and pack to do what they were designed to.

Peeking out, I watch a late nineteen-seventies model white Chevrolet S10 growl past. In its wake, the truck leaves behind a thick, greasy smell.

There were two men in the cab. I couldn't see if there was anything in the bed.

It dawns on me that those two guys were returning to Burnsville from their shifts. The two replacements must have arrived while I was sleeping. Of course, that doesn't mean there aren't more than two. Who's to say how long Abraham is keeping them posted? It's no likely less than twelve hours, probably more like twenty-four. I'll be long gone by then.

I lie in place for another half an hour, just in case another vehicle leaves or arrives. But there is nothing.

Back on my feet, I return to the sloping granite leading to the top of the overhand. It's not a strenuous gradient, but I'm judicious not to make too much noise. Near the top, I begin to semi-crawl due to the incline. I take off my left glove and place my hand directly on the rock for a moment. I don't feel anyone up ahead of me, but below are three men sheltering next to the fire.

If they're being replaced in teams of two, why isn't there an even number of guards beneath the overhand? To me, this says that someone is out in the woods, too far away for me to sense their location.

As I approach the top of the overhand, I crawl in a prone position, as flat against the rock as I can be.

I visually scan across the trail, searching through the granite and soil with my mind. I find nothing. There's a gnawing feeling inside of me that says the phantom guard is real, not paranoia.

Then I notice something out of place. It looks like a ladder. *A deer stand,* I think.

The mystery sentry is on an equally high ridge directly across from me. It looks to be twenty-five feet tall, topped with a small platform. There's only enough room for one person. Hunters use them to keep their scent and movement concealed from their prey. The thing is, most hunters only carry bolt-action rifles. This motherfucker has a rocket-propelled grenade.

The deer stand is positioned so the shooter has a direct line of sight down the trail. Because the trail curves off to the left, as it enters McDowell County, I can only see trees.

Even with my rifle's suppressor installed, I can't shoot the man in the tree stand without the ones below noticing. And what happens to the RPG if it falls from such a great height? My surrogate father, Al, didn't teach me about those. He had a twelve-gauge double barrel and a Mauser. That's all he ever needed. The rifle he used to harvest deer. The shotgun was for hunting fowl and home defense.

I'll have to wait for a shift change. It seems to me that they are taking turns in the tower and sitting by the fire between shifts.

But why are they doing this? Maybe they're afraid of the government? In two-thousand-seven, they illegally occupied the decommissioned Coast Guard station, Frying Pan Tower, leading to its destruction. Perhaps they believe the Feds are watching. Or, they suspect I'm back and are afraid of what I might do.

Abraham must. What are the chances that a sinkhole would destroy only my coastal property? His men vanished, never to be heard from again. Not that he gives a shit about them. It's practically impossible. But, he knows I'm what I'm capable of.

With my left glove still off, I place my hand onto the rock and send my mind into the Earth. I reach out, but the man in the tree stand is too far away. I can do whatever I want to the three men sheltering underneath the overhang, below where I'm perched. However, if tree-stand-man sees me, he'll likely shoot at me with his rifle. Hell, if he's scared enough, he might just fire off his RPG.

I hear faint voices, interrupted occasionally by static. They're talking over the radio. I can't tell what's being said.

Have I been made?

I lie perfectly still. After a couple of minutes, I see one of the men from below walking toward the other side of the ridge. After an exchange of words at the bottom of the ladder, the man who had been on duty walks back toward their camp. Within a few minutes, I can sense the man's footsteps as he grows closer to joining the other two.

I'm not in a rush. It's only eight o'clock in the evening.

An hour later, I hear the radio, just like before. A few minutes later, like Deja Vu, there's an identical exchange. It's ten-past-nine. That gives me just under fifty minutes to come up with a plan for exploiting the next shift change.

I slowly retrieve my rifle and install the suppressor. This takes a lot of deliberate movement and is frustratingly slow.

With the task finally completed, I gently chamber a round into the breech.

As ten o'clock rolls around, I prepare to take the shot by sighting where the two men met prior through my scope. I aim at where I imagine they will stand again in just a few minutes.

Moments later, one of the men from the camp begins walking toward the deer stand. As that happens, the man stationed in the tree stand begins to descend the ladder. Impatiently, he begins walking downhill toward his replacement. They stand facing one another, apparently arguing. Then I see the perfect shot and flip down the safety.

Exhaling, I pull the trigger. I aim for and hit the left side of the man's neck facing away from me. Because he was at a lower elevation than the man facing him, the bullet, unimpeded by slicing open a soft carotid artery, strikes him center-mass.

Both are dead instantaneously. The RPG falls to the ground beside them without exploding.

I hear static. One of the two men below me has picked up the radio.

Still lying prone, I force the shelf underneath me to let go. It falls like a pancake, down upon the two remaining Apostle guards.

I don't fall at the same rate. Instead. I call the atmosphere toward me, creating a mighty updraft, like the one before when I fell off the embankment. This allows me to lower myself to my feet, gently, rifle still in hand. My bag, however, took a bit of a tumble.

There are boulders in the path where some of the overhang broke off after hitting the ground. Most of it remained intact and was stacked neatly on top of the flat rock below.

While it was loud, we're so far away it's unlikely anyone else heard.

I no longer need to take the path to get down to their campsite. I shimmy down off the rock instead.

There's a lot of blood, bits of viscera, and flesh flung about. One of their legs is sticking out. I can't help but think of the Wicked Witch in *The Wizard of Oz*.

"No ruby slippers for me, it seems," I say aloud to myself.

The first order of business is to neutralize that damn shoulder-bomb so it can't ever be used again. As I walk toward the direction of the two men I downed minutes earlier, I stumble across my backpack on the trail. It's a bit scuffed and dusty but relatively unscathed.

The two men are lying atop one another. The one on top still has the RPG strapped to his back. Instead of attempting to take it off, I begin forcing their bodies and the weapon into the ground where it will become useless. After, I get to work clearing the road of boulders. I have the Earth below each deform downward, allowing gravity to roll them off the trail and into the nearby ravine for me. By the time I'm finished, it's been an hour since the overhang collapsed. I figure that if anyone was going to pay a visit, they would have by now.

I pull the satellite phone from my case. It's hardened and was cushioned by the sleeping bag during the fall. It boots up without a problem. I put in Rebecca's number and hit send.

24

"Yes," Rebecca answers through her cell phone.

In the background, I can hear Nate and Herschel arguing about taking loans from other players in Monopoly.

"Whose side are you on?" I ask, facetiously.

"Nate's. There are no rules against it, technically."

"How long do you reckon it will take you guys to load up and get to my location?"

"Where are you on the trail?"

"Right at the top, on the Yancey County border."

"How many?"

"Four; two with one bullet. The other two were flattened under a slab of granite."

"No one heard the collapse?"

"It's been more than an hour ago. Not one Apostle has shown up."

"I've been over the map repeatedly. I'm certain I can navigate us to the trail off Mill Creek Road. Beyond that, getting us up the mountain is up to Nate. He'll navigate by the Hummer's onboard night vision, so it'll probably take a while. I'd say we'll be there in three hours, give or take."

"You've got plenty of time. The Register of Deeds office doesn't open until eight in the morning."

"We'll be underway in fewer than ten minutes. Leave your phone on, in case we need to our satellite phone to call yours."

"I should have enough power for that."

"Stay safe. I'll see you soon," Rebecca says before hanging up.

"Phone call over, my world reverts back to the whispers of the dormant winter forest. When the green backlight of the screen extinguishes, I'm enveloped in darkness. I leave it that way. Why risk having my headlamp spotted? Despite my heavy layers of clothing, the cold is beginning to wear on me. I can't enclose myself in a granite dome, because it would block the phone's signal. However, I can create a heating system.

I lie atop the collapsed overhang and bring up copious amounts of thermal energy from beneath. It spreads evenly through the granite slab. Every few minutes, I roll myself because one side gets too hot, the other too cold. I feel like a hotdog spinning on a convenience store display. I don't care. Being cold sucks worse than feeling stupid.

———

Nate and Herschel cease their argument over the finer points of sanctioned Monopoly rules and begin packing before Rebecca hangs up the phone with Naomi. Like Naomi, each dons body armor, concealed by camouflage coveralls.

Unlike her, each dons a high holster for their sidearms, making them readily available.

Driving from their rental cabin in Morganton to the Old Fort exit at the base of the mountain takes close to an hour. Nate never pushes the Hummer too hard on the highway. The dealer said it could reach ninety-five miles per hour with the modified engine, but he keeps it at the posted speed limit of sixty-five.

The large, knobby tires release a deep droning sound as they plow over the cold asphalt. Loud as it is, it's not drowning out a conversation. Little is said. Everyone is collecting themselves for what will come when they reach the trail and beyond.

Nate leaves Highway Forty, one exit before it begins the winding ascent toward Black Mountain, and Ashville beyond that. They take a left onto Old US Seventy West, which switchbacks its way through a section of thickly forested road, parallel to the base of the mountain range. The tire noise takes on a deeper tone now that they're turning slower. Churching through nauseating, deep twists in the road makes five miles seem to take forever.

Breaking the silence, Rebecca shouts, "Slow down," to Nate from the passenger seat. "The turn is coming up on the right."

"I figured it would be on the side with the gigantic mountains," Nate replies, sarcastically.

Rebecca rolls her eyes as a way to release some of the steam built up in her brain, a result of being trapped in a cabin with her husband and his best friend for days.

There's no sign pointing toward Mill Creek Road, but it's there, regardless. Nate slowly turns. The blacktop is unmarked, its width thinner than a modern road. It continues into the woods, but there's a steel, dual-swing-gate, with a giant padlock, securing both arms together.

Danger. Keep out. The rusty metal sign on the right side says.

"By the looks of that sign, you can't say that the people down here haven't known something nefarious has been afoot on the other side of this ridge for some time now," Nate says.

"'Afoot' Who are you right now, Sherlock Holmes?" Herschel says chuckling.

"I'm pretty sure this vehicle will go forward whether the gate is present or not," Nate says aloud to everyone, including himself.

He pulls up the lever to his right, which causes the transfer case to engage itself into four-wheel-drive mode. He gingerly feathers the accelerator, moving ahead slowly until the tubular steel police bumper on the front barely touches the opening of the gate. The turbocharger forcing pressurized air into the throttle body whines as it assists the diesel engine's build-up of torque. Nate pushes the pedal down harder.

There's a momentary chirp from the tires, then a high-pitched breaking sound as several of the chain links give way, scattering in bits onto the road ahead of them. The gates swing free.

Nate turns off his headlights and engages the terrain through the large screen built into the Hummer's dash. It shows a detailed forward view as seen through an overpriced night vision camera. When put in reverse, the view changes to the one mounted on the bumper. The tech is fascinating, but nothing compared to sunlight. The images are stark, greenish-white hues. The absurd, two-dimensional world on the screen is all Nate has to go by to get them to Naomi.

The trail quickly transitions from asphalt to gravel. Despite the night vision and terrain, Nate is able to maintain a speed of twenty miles per hour for a short while; until the climb.

Through the twists of the switchbacks, he can barely keep the speedometer above two miles per hour. No one is complaining. Often, they're wedged between a wall on one side and a drop-off on the other. Nate's head-sensing camera finally picks up what looks like the body of a tall person lying on top of a granite slab. The thing that gives it away as being Naomi is the heat signature from the rocks themselves. Every granite surface shows up gray on the screen, other than the one underneath the bright red and orange humanoid shape. There appear to be threads of bright red and white rising from the ground beneath the glowing rock.

"She's keeping warm, at least," Nate says, pointing down at the screen.

"Stop here. I'm going to call her," Rebecca says to Nate.

Rebecca opens the front passenger door into the bitter cold and extends the antenna on the phone identical to Naomi's.

Tiffany had it overnighted the morning after Naomi disappeared from their bed.

In half a minute, Rebecca hears the trill of electronic ringing through the receiver. After four rings, she hears her friend's voice chimes in over the earpiece.

"Hey," Naomi answers casually.

"Are you okay?" Rebecca asks.

"I'm fine. Just trying to keep warm."

"It looks like you're rolling on top of a hot rock, through the heat-sensitive night vision."

"Like a six-foot-long hotdog stuffed into several layers of her finest winter apparel?"

"That's very specific."

"I've had time to think about it. It's almost four in the morning."

"I know. It's been rough going for Nate, driving through all of this only using a small screen."

"I'll take over when y'all get to the top of the hill. I'm sure he's exhausted."

"See you in a minute," Rebecca says, just before hanging up.

25

I stand up on the rock and listen for the Hummer's tires under the judicious command of Nate. I sense the Hummer's vibrations through the ground. It's more of a droning hum, unlike the rhythmic percussions of footsteps.

They come to a stop directly at the top of the hill, in front of the two pancakes of granite I'm standing on. I slide off to the ground to meet them.

I'm facing the passenger side, so I meet Rebecca and Herschel first when they open their doors.

Rebecca embraces me, saying, "I thought I lost you again."

"Not if I can stop it," I reply.

As the two of us pull apart, I hear Herschel say, "It smells like a pig pickin'."

I take a deep whiff.

"Oh, shit," I say, covering my mouth. "I must have cooked them."

"Who?"

"Them," I say pointing at the guard's leg sticking out from underneath the slab of collapsed rock.

"Oh, fucking gross, Naomi," Herschel balks.

"I was cold. I forgot."

"I understand, but it's still disgusting."

"Yeah. It must have come on so slowly that I became nose-blind to it."

I lift up the collars on my coveralls and sniff. Herschel and Rebecca glare at me.

"Yeah, I smell like my grandpa's pig cooker cranking full force."

I turn to see Nate dazed, staring at the leg sticking out between the collapsed rocks.

"Wow, I'm kind of sorry I missed this," Nate says, rubbing his chin, as though he's in deep contemplation over the mechanics of what happened. "Well, fuck them anyhow."

"Are you going to do something with their bodies?" Herschel asks, with his nose jammed into his elbow, uselessly attempting to breathe through the fabric of his coveralls.

"No. I want them found. It's a warning of what we are willing to do. I'll sink this entire town into hell if have to."

"Could you do that?" Rebecca asks.

"Yes. With enough time."

"I'd like to see that," Nate says, opening the driver's side door before climbing in."

I walk around and take a seat behind the wheel. Nate rides shotgun. Rebecca and Herschel take the backseat.

I look to my right. Attached to the inside of the driver's side center console is a thick polymer holster holding my new lamentation gun. I run my hand across its wooden stock. *I've missed you, old friend.* I think.

Once all four doors are shut and locked behind us, I catch a glimpse of everyone's faces as the stench of my clothes permeates the interior. Herschel now has his undershirt permanently pulled over his nose and mouth.

"I'm sorry that I've made the Hummer smell like slow-roasted Apostle," I remark with genuine remorse because it really is starting to reek.

I put my foot down on the accelerator. I'm a far more aggressive driver than Nate. Even so, I'm going no faster than eight miles per hour. But, under these conditions, it feels like I'm driving in the Daytona 500. It takes another hour to wind our way down the zig-zagging trail. Eventually, it bottoms out and becomes a flat, dirt road running behind the golf course.

We stop just inside the wood line, out of sight from the main road. It's Thursday, January seventh, twenty-sixteen.

"I figure we shouldn't show up until eight thirty," I say. "I want to make sure everyone's in their offices. That gives the stragglers time."

"What's the plan?" Nate asks.

"The three of you file in behind me, guns drawn. Close off the hallways so I can have a chat with the Registrar of Deeds."

"What's their name?"

"Travis Mills."

"If you need to take a piss, now is the time."

Herschel and Nate traipse behind a couple of trees while Rebecca and I stay with the Hummer. After their return, we do the same. Then, the four of us eat a light snack.

"We'll pass by the location of the former Solid Rock Compound, where I watched Patty Proffit shoot Daisy Chambers in the back for the crime of being raped. It was so cold when it happened that I could see mist coming from the exit wound in her chest. Almost like her spirit was set free."

It's quiet for a minute When I become more aware, I turn to see everyone silently looking at me.

"You stared off there for a minute, Naomi," Herschel says with concern.

"I was just—"

"Seeing it all over again in your mind's eye, unable to turn it off?" Rebecca says.

"Yeah," I say meekly.

"I do the same with my fall from the cliff. I wake up jumping, reaching into the empty space above me, frantically feeling for your hands. Then I hit the boulders. I don't die instantly. Instead, I suffer helplessly for hours."

"The *could-have-been?*"

"Definitely."

"Frieda seems to believe my fate is inexorable. No matter my choices, each path leads to the same ending. Me dead, then the exponential rise of the Apostles of the Cloven Hand. If that happens, we live under their theocracy for two hundred years. Then, there will be a bloody revolution for Little Milly's Great-Great-Grandchildren to experience. Only after, do we exit a mini-Dark Ages."

"But, I don't believe in the inevitable. The choices we make today will set the precedent for our victory. Don't hesitate to shoot first if cornered. Every cop in this town is part of a private militia run directly by Abraham Proffit. They are rogues, not legitimate police officers. After, they'll sweep everything under the rug, embarrassed. They won't dare ask for outside help."

There's silence as our long-thought-out plans come to fruition. And with it, a present sort of anxiety as though what we're seeing isn't real when the Hummer exits the forest's sanctuary.

The gravel road brings us to a parking lot not dissimilar to the entrance at the bottom of the mountain. It shows early signs of being reclaimed by nature. Roots run heavily above the dirt and gravel and there are small trees growing any place a seed's embryonic roots can gain access to nutrient-rich soil. While the trail is rarely accessed by anyone but the white Chevy truck from earlier, the lot was designed to be used by fifteen or sixteen cars.

The trail leading away from the abandoned parking lot will lead us directly to Highway Eighty, possibly making our unwanted presence known. If that occurs our only defense will be to roll down the windows and shoot. As we make our way to downtown Burnsville.

While inside a vehicle, I'm somewhat insulated from the Earth. My abilities become far more limited. At high speed, they're essentially useless.

There are steep hills on both sides of the trail that gradually give way to lots where the occasional house sits. One after another we take note of the moss and vines growing on them.

"They didn't want anyone near the trail entrance. Maybe they're not just keeping people out, but others in?" Rebecca says.

"I thought they worshiped that son-of-a-bitch?" Herschel replies, confused.

"The world is changing," I say. "In the marketplace of ideas, the Apostles' kind of fucking sucks. That's why Abraham is going public. His abilities will garner him unyielding attention from local and national media outlets. That will firm up what remains of his base, and quickly build a new one."

The sun is freshly up when the blacktop of Highway Eighty comes into sight.

26

The blacktop of the two-lane highway is framed by stark, bare hardwoods. A heavy blanket of fog that appeared overnight meanders around them. In the thick of it, the heavy mist makes the sun seem like a fuzzy yellowish spot in the sky.

The graying of the morning may give us an advantage. Most of the non-government jobs around here revolve around agriculture. During the winter months, that means fewer people in the fields and vehicles on the road. Even if we encounter others, they may not realize we're out of place because we'll be heavily obscured.

Fifty feet from the highway, the gravel road transitions into an unmarked paved road. Directly in our path is a gate, like the one my friends encountered at the beginning of the trail.

"Can you melt it from inside the Hummer?" Rebecca asks.

"If we're not moving. But, I don't want to run over molten metal. It won't destroy the tires, but it will do damage to them that could come back to bite us in the future.

"What we did before worked. Butt the police bumper up to the gate, put it in four-wheel drive, and push the peddle down. It's not fancy, but brute force works."

The chain around the gate is no competition for a large displacement, turbo-charged diesel engine. Metal scatters across the faded road surface.

Before turning left I slip the Hummer from four-wheel-drive to all-wheel, which will give me better traction on the blacktop. Four-wheel is only meant for slippery surfaces. Using it on a firm road will cause the axles to bind and skip, eventually causing permanent damage.

It's not long before we begin crossing in front of the Mount Mitchel Golf Club. Records indicate that it belongs to Abraham Proffit now. I assume it'll be a draw for like-minded politicians and wealthy donors after his brand gains traction.

Across the road from the golf course is a large granite outcrop. Beneath it is what deceivingly looks like a small puddle. It's actually an underwater cave that surfaces into Vernon's former sarcophagus, where he kept his trophies. I found a small passage only a child could have squeezed through, which allowed me to gain access. After, I crawled out of that very puddle on the side of the road and ran into the night for my life and freedom.

I try not to zone out before, like I did while discussing Daisy's murder.

I know what happened. I don't have to force myself to relive it, I think.

Instead, I try to calmly keep my eyes focused on the winding road ahead of us. In fewer than five minutes, we begin rolling past the newly rebuilt Solid Rock Campus. On our right, the old church still sits at the south end of the campus. Everything else has been replaced by modern buildings. Even through the trees, I can see their new mega-church at the northern tip of the compound. It looks like Abraham had portions of the mountainside blown away to fit his new monstrosity.

When I was a child, in the nineties, this was the same lot where

Vernon Proffit's house sat; where I was kept prisoner. After I killed him in two-thousand-four, a slightly more modest mega-church was built on the same spot. Bizarrely, it was built around the Proffit's old house, where it was kept as a sort of memorial.

Inside their house was a safe concealing a manhole, which led down to the cavern. I destroyed the former church and the house inside by collapsing the entire structure. The entrance is still inside there, hidden from all but their inner circle. Regardless, anyone who's entered since has quickly been eaten by Svangi. What a good boy.

We'll cross in front of the dreadful bridge where Daisy's last breaths were drawn in seconds. As we get closer, I see that it's gated now. Two guards in Apostles of the Cloven Hand uniforms stand watch. Directly after I get a visual lock on them, I push the accelerator to the floor. The errant whooshing sound of the turbo winding up the massive diesel engine causes their heads to whip around in our direction. They were likely expecting a farmer's pickup. Instead, they both collect faces full of bent tubular steel.

Both bodies end up underneath the tall vehicle. There are several thuds, bony parts slapping against the underside of the Hummer. I come to a complete stop five hundred feet down the road from the bridge.

"They barely saw it coming," Nate says with calm curiosity.

"Too bad," I reply. "They got off too easy."

I turn the wheel left, complete a one-hundred-eighty-degree turn, and head back toward the bridge. Along the way, we roll over what's left of the two guard's remains, which are scattered over a large portion of the roadway. I catch a glimpse of Herschel covering his eyes. Out of the four of us, he's the most squeamish but, blessedly, the best adjusted to normal life. That doesn't mean he won't do anything necessary, but only because it's necessary. Rebecca and I, on the other hand, crave this kind of hyperstimulation. And the violence. Nate does as well, but has a cooler head about him and is far more calculating.

"Why are you stopping?" Herschel asks.

"The bridge," I say, as I turn the Hummer around again, pointing it back in the direction of Burnsville.

I step out into the fog and slowly shut the driver's side door easily, so as to not make a sound.

In front of the gate, I kneel down, touching the road surface. I reach into the slabs of granite below the river. They've been sliding past one another for multitudes of millennia; dance partners in geologic time. I plan on upping the tempo. As the rhythm crescendos, the ground begins to shake, causing the two-lane bridge to ripple slightly. The flexing of the structure swiftly extends beyond its limitations, causing it to break up into large pieces and fall into the river. I begin to focus on the church, but it's out of my grasp for now. Not wanting to waste any more time, I run back to the driver's side door, pull myself in, and take off.

"That should slow down any reinforcements that might get called in," I say while running over the two guard's body parts for a third time.

I expect some kind of pursuit, but all I see behind me is fog.

"I don't think they know," Rebecca says from behind me.

"The guards didn't have time to radio. We had several small earthquakes during the time I lived here. They likely mistook what I just did for one. Nothing of concern, just a peculiarity of living on top of an old mountain range."

When we reach Micaville Loop Road, I go left. Both short roads end at Highway Nineteen, but going this way puts me out on the highway closer to the Burnsville side. I snake past a few small houses and trailers set directly against the river, then come to a T-junction with the two-lane highway. A quick left puts me five miles from downtown.

We've risen slightly in elevation along the way, which has seen a lot of the fog dissipate. Now, it hangs around in small, dense patches. In ten minutes, the small hamlet of Burnsville comes into view. I haven't visited since two-thousand-seven when I administered justice to Sheriff Alton Morton and subsequently stole his patrol Jeep. I used it as a ruse to draw Vernon Proffit out of his house, which is the mistake that ultimately led to his death.

We turn right off the highway, taking us toward downtown. The narrow road turns into Main Street, which runs the length of the town, then reconnects to Highway Nineteen.

We pass directly by the lot where Maddie Bellew's house once stood. When I was eighteen, I laid a trap that burned her alive inside of its chambers of horror, where so many like myself had suffered at her hand. Now, a cottage sits in its place, not dissimilar to Maddie's former home.

Downtown, the road splits into a one-lane loop that goes around the town square. The county's administrative office and police headquarters are on the left. I follow the traffic pattern, which loops me back around. I turn my attention briefly toward the statue at the center of the town square, which should be of Captain Otway Burns. Instead, to my fury, I recognize the alternate visage right away, Vernon Proffit; right down to the Coke bottle glasses.

"They replaced the statue," I say, pointing.

"Is that him?" Nate asks.

"Yes, I'm afraid it is."

I pull into a spot directly in front of the Register of Deeds office.

"Stay close to the building," I say. "I'm about to make this structure an island."

27

My three accomplices take refuge on the Yancey County administrative building's front steps. Nate has his Glock drawn. Herschel and Rebecca both hold black Mossberg 590 pump action shotguns with eight plus-one shell capacities in their hands. They also have holstered pistols identical to Nate's.

Main Street is lined with the cars of those who work inside, along with several police cruisers. Their headquarters is one small town block to our right, on the same side of the Town Square.

I begin to bring lava up from deep within the Earth until it bursts forth, encircling the entire building. The pit created is roughly ten feet across. Even getting close to it would cause one's skin to burn.

"We're alone for a while now," I say looking up at my flabbergasted companions.

Confused onlookers begin to assemble in the square, then there are police sirens. We duck inside and immediately head right toward the office at the end of the hall. As heads poke out in curiosity, they immediately disappear behind their doors. Locks click like a wave as we move forward.

The lights flicker as the heat melts the powerlines over the scorching moat. When they split in two, there's a bright electric-blue flash of light outside accompanied by a loud crackling explosion. There's a low rumble as the enormous generator on the roof kicks in, returning power to the building.

At the end of the hall, we come to a door that has "Travis Miller, Register of Deeds" inscribed on a gold-colored nameplate. I put my right hand on the handle and push down, only to feel the resistance of a locking mechanism. At that moment, a bullet bursts through the door, inches from my head.

In shock, the four of us take several steps back. Rebecca and I on the left, Herschel and Nate, on the right.

There are five more shots, then nothing.

"He's reloading a revolver," I say to the three of them as I approach the door again.

Knowing I only have a few seconds before more bullet holes are punched through the wood, I reach out and begin wriggling my consciousness into the atmosphere. I channel it through my left hand, pushing the air around me toward the door at a great velocity.

Wind rushes down the hallway behind us. Windows break inside offices because of the low pressure caused by the sudden vacuum. Travis Miller's door flies off the hinges, striking a desk sitting a dozen feet directly behind it. This pushes the occupant of the ornate piece of office furniture toward the back wall, pinning him underneath the heavy door.

From underneath, six more shots pierce the already bullet-riddled wood, hitting nothing but the now still air.

Instinctively, we all dive to the floor. When the spent brass cartridges clink in unison on the antique oak floor, I stand and snatch the door off of his body.

"Travis, I believe we have some business to discuss," I say to him just before slapping the revolver from his hand as though he were a child.

Travis appears to be in his mid-fifties, with a bald crown and salt-and-pepper hair.

Blood is pouring from his nose and mouth as he whispers, "What do you want?"

"I want what's mine. I want my goddamn inheritance."

"You'll have to get the laptop from the bag on the chair in the corner. You've ruined my desktop. You could have just made an appointment instead of setting off explosives outside of my door."

"That wasn't an explosion," I say, as I hold my scarred left hand up, charged white hot. "My name is Hannah Sillman."

"You're not Hannah. She died. No. You're Naomi, the reprobate. Every true believer knows of your wicked deeds."

I reach into the left breast pocket of my coveralls and produce Hannah's birth certificate, Social Security card, and my North Carolina license, which states that I'm Hannah Sillman.

Her identity was Al's eighteenth birthday present to me. Months later, he would sacrifice himself by jumping on top of Vernon Proffit as I ran for my life while his deputies raided his home. Vernon murdered him and burned everything he'd built to the ground.

"That's right, I rose straight out of hell this morning. Come have a look," I say grabbing Travis by his collar and dragging him to the front window of the office so he can see the boiling lava encircling the building.

"Is that real?"

"Yes, Travis, it's very real. And it's true, I was sent from hell. You can either do what I ask or I can drag you back down with me. Well, not all of you. Just enough to keep you alive."

"All you need is the deed transferred to your name?"

"Yes. To Hannah Sillman, daughter of Al and Milly Sillman."

"It usually takes a couple of—"

"Shut up right there, Travis. I think if you work real hard, you can make it happen."

"But—"

"The first thing I'll burn off won't be your fingers or toes. It will be your cock and balls. Ask yourself, what do you actually believe? Is your love for Abraham cock-and-balls worthy, or just kind of convenient?"

"I'll do it," Travis says nodding, slinging his blood everywhere with the action.

Rebecca, Herschel, and Nate stand guard as I keep my eyes on Travis, making sure he keeps his word.

Twenty minutes later, a printer warms up and pushes out several pages of a document. I return my birth certificate, Social Security card, and license to my coverall's pocket, along with the deed.

"There was a time, a man like you would be heading for your eternal punishment. Even though you deserve it, you're more useful alive. What you have to understand is, you're no longer a county official. You're my employee. Your only job duty will be to inform them that this deed is legitimate and enforceable by state and federal jurisdiction. Abraham isn't going to want to hear it. So, you'll just have to keep repeating it. If not, I'll fucking get you when you least expect it, and it won't be over quickly. Do you understand?"

"I understand," Travis Miller, Registrar of Deeds, replies, shaking.

Before he can get any ideas, I pick up his revolver and toss it through the pan-glass window facing out to the square.

The crowd's low murmur and slow splats of lava bubbling sonically invade the office. Blue lights now flash across the building.

At that moment, Travis's desk phone, now on the floor, rings.

"Right on time," I say.

Slowly, I raise the receiver to my ear, "Hello."

"Who is this!?" the frustrated man responds on the other end of the line.

"I'm the one who all this hell seems to follow."

"Whoever you are, this is Police Chief Ray. You have five minutes to exit the building."

"Carry any gas cans lately, Deputy Ray?"

"No. Is this some kind of joke?"

"This is Hannah Sillman. Vernon Proffit killed my father nearly twenty years ago during a raid. You were there, young Deputy Ray, carrying the gas can that Vernon used to burn down Al's barn. He'd locked me inside the feed room to burn to death. Do you remember now?"

"Your real name isn't Hannah Sillman, and we all know it."

"Names be damned! I am the daughter of Al and Milly Sillman," I scream, "and I'm taking back what is ours. Unlike in nineteen-ninety-seven, you're the helpless ones now."

"If you come out without much fuss, I'll put in a good word for you with the judge."

"Now why in the hell would I go and do something stupid like that?"

"Because, otherwise, we're coming in."

"How do you reckon that will work? There's a river of lava between the two of us."

"We have a helicopter overhead. Our SWAT team is about to drop onto the roof. Once they do, you won't make it out alive."

"How did you get a fucking helicopter? This is Burnsville-nowhere-North-Carolina."

"From military surplus. The War on Terror has been kind to us."

"Look, you don't want to do this. The updraft caused by the heat will destabilize the helicopter's lift."

"You have five minutes," Chief Ray says.

"Wait! You need to push the crowd back."

The line goes dead.

28

Looking up, I say to everyone else in the room, "The asshole just hung up on me."

"Chief Ray can be like that," Travis says, seemingly forgetting his former allegiances.

"Do they really have a helicopter?" I ask Travis.

"Yeah, they do. Uncle Sam was giving the damn things away," Travis says, as a matter of fact, with seemingly no confidence that they'd rescue him.

Then comes the sound of rotor blades slicing through the atmosphere. *Thunk, thunk, thunk.*

"I'm going up to the roof to greet them," Rebecca says.

"Don't move," I say. "They're going to crash. If you're up there, it might be onto your head."

A few seconds later we hear a series of hard bangs as the team breaches the roof door with a small, handheld battering ram. It only takes three hits. We're on the first floor of a three-story building. It won't take them long to get to us.

The rhythm of the helicopter rotors noticeably changes. It becomes slow and uneven. A high-pitched whine follows. Then the sound shifts toward the broken window. Just coming into my field of view overhead is the failing helicopter. Spinning out of control, it ejects two men into empty space. One falls into the lava, the other hangs limp in the branches of a large hickory tree.

"The crowd!" I shout, panicked.

I hold my left hand toward the window and release a fast gust of wind, blowing out the glass along with the frame. The helicopter is hit by a hurricane-force burst of air, causing it to grab more lift and fly over the onlookers. Instead of landing on them, it drifts into the empty town square. Then gravity has its way with it, pulling it to the ground on top of the statue of Vernon Proffit.

The crowd scatters as the woosh from the igniting fuel sends a blast of heat out in all directions. I won't lie, seeing the statue demolished brings a smile to my face.

"I hear boots. They're coming down the stairs," Nate says.

"Get away from the door," I whisper.

Even Travis listens. He knows they'll kill him to get to me.

We split ourselves into two groups, taking positions on either side of the door. It's myself, Travis, and Rebecca on the left. Herschel and Nate are on the right. I kneel and place my left hand on the old wood floor.

"They'll be the only ones moving," I say.

"What?" Travis replies.

Frustrated, Rebecca puts the muzzle of her shotgun against Travis's head saying, "You need to shut your goddamn mouth, Travis. She made a promise not to kill you. I didn't."

With that, Travis shrinks away and leans against the wall.

"There are four," I mouth while holding up four fingers on my right hand.

I don't want to use anything hot inside this kindling box. Instead,

I'll make the box itself my weapon. They're in the stairwell between the second and third floors, which puts them within my reach.

I command the long fibers of the old-growth lumber to shear away from the floors and walls inside the stairwell. I pinpoint each man's location. Hundreds of wood spears impale them before they can react. Their bodies are immobilized.

They scream. Automatic gunfire rings out as each tries in desperation to escape. Ignorant men often find out all too late that bullets won't solve every problem.

The sharp fibers continue to weave their way through their legs, into their torsos, and eventually shred apart their brains. The screams turn to groans, then silence, over two minutes. An eternity when your insides are being woven like a basket.

"Don't you even think about moving, Travis," I say just before peeking around the door frame."

A significant portion of the old plaster on the wall above the entrance had cracked and fallen to the floor. The lathe hiding beneath had all been stripped away, leaving a hole six feet wide.

Touching the floor again, I feel for movement. I only sense the people in their offices lying prone on the floor quivering, attempting to avoid the stray bullets whizzing overhead. The stairwell has gone quiet.

On my way out the door, I say to Herschel, "Stay with him."

He immediately looks at Travis and asks, almost nicely, "Are you going to behave?"

Travis nods his head. The blood from his nose has dried on the lower half of his face where it bled profusely earlier.

Nate flanks my right and Rebecca my left. She has her shotgun in her hands, and Nate has his pistol drawn.

We see the first SWAT team member, no more than two steps

from the bottom of the staircase. The filaments of wood suspend him in a standing position.

On his uniform is an Apostles of the Cloven Hand patch. The other three men directly behind him are propped up in the same fashion, allowing me to see the same insignia on their uniforms. Their skin is bulging with the shapes of the wood strands going to and fro inside them. Blood is pouring out of the mouths, noses, and ears.

"It's going to take limb pruners just to get them to the morgue," Rebecca comments snarkily.

Cautiously, we retreat back to Travis's office.

"They're very dead and the helicopter is burning in the courtyard. I think we should show ourselves out," I say.

Rebecca grabs Travis by the collar, drags him into the hallway, and forces him to look at the gruesome fate of the four men in the stairwell.

"She can and will do worse things to you. Do you understand?"

"Yes," Travis whispers, defeated.

Rebecca releases him, saying, "Now go back to your office and wait to be rescued, you sad little man."

Travis does as he's told.

It's like a circle of hell outside. Smoke from the burning fuel darkens the sky. Lava bubbles and pops from the ground surrounding the building. The crowd is long gone, and the Apostle's police force has taken positions further back.

I place my hand on the ground and cause flames to billow up, effectively hiding our movement as we make our egress from the front door to the Hummer. It's a winter's day, but it feels like Death Valley in July.

We return to the same positions. I'm the driver, Nate rides

shotgun; Rebecca behind him, and Herschel behind me. I back up and turn the vehicle one hundred eighty degrees, putting the front of the Hummer toward the soaring flames.

I try to fill the moat back in from inside the car, but it becomes apparent that won't work. I'm too far away. But, I don't want to get any closer and risk damaging the tires.

I crack open the door and gingerly step back outside I kneel on the ground. The Hummer's bulletproof door guards my head and torso but leaves my lower extremities exposed. A flash of Charles's death dances across my mind. He bled to death from a cut to the femoral artery on the inside of his leg.

I place my left hand on the ground and ask the Earth to return its subterranean fury back home, deep within the planet. The road surface in front of the administrative building is gone, leaving blackened soil in its place. I make sure to keep my body covered as I crawl head-first back into the driver's seat.

At that moment, a sniper's bullet ricochets off the hood of the Hummer. After being deflected, the fragments leave at an angle to my left. I pull my feet up quickly. Seconds later, a bullet strikes the ground where I just knelt.

With the door shut and seatbelts on, I put the behemoth into gear and pulled out to the left. This takes me north, into the high country. Home.

29

Once I'm far enough from the building, we hit pavement again. I'm currently heading down the wrong way on a one-way street. Not that anyone's coming. I look to the right to get a glimpse of the helicopter crash. It's as though the statue of Vernon has been erased. The bronze likely melted in the blaze.

At the end of Main Street, two police cars are parked nose to nose, in an attempt to keep us from leaving. The entire front end of the Hummer is covered with a robust, tubular-steel police bumper. The exterior is bullet-proof and it weighs nine thousand pounds, more than twice that of a police cruiser.

"Not a chance, assholes," I say aloud.

I press the accelerator to the floorboard and aim right between the cruisers. Realizing that I'm not bluffing, the two officers begin firing their service pistols in our direction. Most go wide. Three strike the metal of the Hummer's body, causing no damage.

I'm going fifty-five miles per hour on impact. The two officers narrowly escape, both diving in opposite directions. The four of us take a hard jar. However, the significant advantage we have in mass easily pushes their cars in opposite directions while barely slowing us down.

A single bullet strikes our bumper impotently as we speed away.

There's no one else waiting ahead. Most of the officers, like the crowd, had to scatter on foot. The two at the end of Main Street must have been away from town when everything started. They won't be chasing us, either, unless they can run sixty miles per hour.

We find our way up into the hills, across one-way bridges, dirt roads, and plenty of switchbacks until eventually arriving at the lot where Al and Milly, my adoptive parents, lived most of their lives. It's the place I consider my childhood home.

Upon seeing the property, I think, *Has it really been that long?*

Nothing has changed up here. The cult faded for a while. But, all they needed was an overconfident leader to give them direction and permission to commit atrocities in the name of divinity.

We pull into what remains of the driveway. I haven't been here since two-thousand-seven. Nine years later, a lot of brush has grown up along with a few small trees. The foundation of their cabin still remains, as do the barns. Al's burnt-out tractor has begun to crumble, its rusted-out frame resting on the ground.

"This is where you grew up?" Nate asks.

"Yeah. It's a goddamn shame. Al and Milly were such kind folks. Solid Rock consumed them like a black hole that pulled in anyone or anything decent. The two years I spent in their house were the best of my life. If I'd had Tiffany with me, it would have been perfect."

"They're going to catch up with us, eventually," Herschel says nervously.

"Yeah, I know," I say driving the Hummer between the house and barn.

We come to a stop in the upper left quadrant of the sizeable property. We're about fifty feet from a small but rather steep hill leading to the creek behind the lot. Its cold water marks the edge of the property line.

I shut off the ignition, saying, "Lock the doors," to everyone before closing mine and handing Nate the keys. If I die, the bulletproof exterior of the Hummer will be all they have left to protect them.

Nate clicks the lock behind me. He trusts implicitly that I can handle myself. I kneel, place my left hand on the ground, and begin pulling up tons and tons of granite sheaths from below. Five-foot-thick walls begin rising up all around us, forming a circle fifty feet in diameter. They continue growing, rounding inward the higher they reach, until a hole thirty feet overhead closes slowly like a giant camera aperture.

Moss rapidly grows on the surface, even though it's winter. Tree roots burst free of the ground and wrap themselves across the dome. This might camouflage the structure for those unfamiliar with the property, but I'm certain that there are plenty of men like Chief Ray who were around in the nineteen-nineties and will recognize the peculiar shift in terrain.

Once I'm certain that our new home is stable, I knock on the driver's side window. Two seconds later, I hear the lock's audible click. I turn on the Hummer's low beams. All of the passenger doors open and my friends step out.

"This is like the small dome you made for the two of us when we fled from Joseph and the Apostles back in two-thousand-seven, but on an epic scale," Rebecca says in astonishment.

Neither Nate nor Herschel, my two oldest friends, have ever seen me do anything like this. I rarely use my abilities in day-to-day life. It seems undignified, flippant, and disrespectful to do so. Perhaps I should have trained? Maybe then I wouldn't be in this situation.

In my head, I hear Tiffany's voice say, "What you should do is stop blaming yourself for not being able to see into the future."

Even the Ceraphirians can't prognosticate when it comes to my path. I think that's why Frieda has grown to hate me.

They all stare off into the distance of the artificial dark while I walk over to the wall closest to the hill, directly across from the driver's side door. I place my hand upon the rock and cause the space to light up gradually as bioluminescent lichen grows rapidly across the interior of the dome's entire surface. Soon, everything is bathed in an ambient bluish glow. After, I walk back to the Hummer and turn off its light to preserve the batteries.

Herschel and Nate seem almost dumbfounded, but Rebecca is giddy with excitement.

"I've missed this," she says.

"What, living our lives on a razor's edge?"

"Maybe. Don't act like you didn't feel a rush from besting those assholes."

"I won't. You're not wrong. I feel more alive than I have in a long time. Sometimes, I think back to those times and wonder if I'm the same person any longer."

"You are. We are. Even more so than before. Despite everything, we never shifted our mores. We held true."

"Regardless, I long for a day when this is over. Simultaneously, I fear it. Will I devolve into a minivan-driving mom whose only excitement comes from watching banal reality television?"

"Even after the Apostles are gone, do you really think your work will be over?" Rebecca says. "Perhaps it won't be as existential, but there will always be someone out there who has it coming, whom no one else can touch but you."

"When that time comes, I want you to be the one who explains it to Tiffany."

"That's fair. Frightening, but fair," Rebecca says, smirking.

I cause lava tubes to gradually rise, then reroute into a grid several feet below us, generating heat from the ground up. Quickly, the soil below us softens as the frost layer melts. The humidity rises slightly, making breathing more pleasant. Within fifteen minutes, the ambient temperature, according to the Hummer's display, is seventy-four degrees. Lovely.

On the eastern side of the dome, directly across from the Hummer's hood, I bring forth a cold spring about three feet by three feet. On the southern wall, I created a small shower room out of granite walls. There, I increase the temperature of the lava tubes around the spring. The water is forced up between two vertical rock slabs until it runs over the slightly lower one, on the inside. I form a chunk of granite around it like a long 'U'. It acts as a showerhead, depositing the water onto the granite stall's occupant. Upon reaching the shower floor, the water is channeled into a hole leading it far back into the Earth.

About ten feet away, for makeshift privies, I create two granite seats with holes in them that lead deep into the ground I make sure the distance the waste will fall keeps the stench from our noses.

Afterward, I am exhausted. But, for the moment I believe we have everything we need. Yes, we will be sleeping on the ground and eating freeze-dried food, but we will be warm, clean, and healthy.

30

It doesn't take long before I sense vehicles moving in our direction. There are seven, maybe eight police cruisers. All that likely remains of their fleet. They come to a stop all in a row on the road directly in front of the property.

Twenty minutes go by with no action. Then I feel five sets of footsteps. They're heading in our direction, judiciously. They're terrified of me. Each of them knows the legend of Naomi to be true now.

They're a cult without mooring. When they were only Solid Rock, faith was steadfast. To question it was heresy. Then, Vernon Proffit fell by my hand. Now, anything is up for grabs. Cults don't run on prophecies fulfilled, only those *in potentia*. What they need is the stability of an endless crest on the hill to peddle toward like a bike on a treadmill. Before, everything was preordained. Now, there's fear instead of arrogant confidence.

We hear the sound of a muffled explosion impacting the exterior of the dome, toward the road. The resonance of their first rocket-propelled grenade strike causes our ears to ring. But it can't breach five feet of Appalachian granite.

I walk up to the wall near the impact site. I weave my mind into the stone, feeling for the fracture. Easily, I pull more slabs out of the ground. The fresh sheaths push the existing upward, covering the damage. They fire at the same spot again to see if the integrity has been weakened. I repair it within seconds.

Thirty minutes go by, then suddenly there are four blasts in close succession. In under a minute, I have the exterior surface back to normal. Five minutes pass, then there are two more. Frustratingly for them, I easily reverse the damage. Afterward, all the men return to their vehicles, yet no one drives away.

"They're just standing next to their vehicles. I think they're talking, but I don't know about what," I say.

"Their egos are smarting and they're running low on grenades," Rebecca says.

"Yeah, you're probably right. I doubt they want to use all of them at once. They're likely to hold some back in case they get a better opportunity," Nate replies.

The remainder of the day is consumed with gauging and monitoring the Apostle's response to today's incursion. Thankfully, all remains quiet. By seven in the evening, half the police cruisers have left.

"I reckon they've been reduced to surveillance," I say chuckling.

We're all able to wash off the day's horrors with a warm spring shower and a mediocre rehydrated meal. And of course, they brought board games. I try not to roll my eyes or groan.

"Okay, I'm in," I say as they look at me, pulling the boxes out of the Hummer.

"Monopoly? Yeah, that's a great idea," I say sarcastically. "Let's all strangle each other, then Rebecca and Herschel can file for divorce."

"We're not that bad," Herschel says.

"I reckon not. Most of the time, anyway."

I ask the Earth to grow a large patch of fluffy moss underneath our four sleeping bags, making the mats we brought with us unnecessary.

We clear out a spot in the center, get comfy, and play.

I wake up at seven the next morning in a panic that I'm late getting Little Milly ready for the bus. Considering the previous day's events, it's humorous that's what I'm worried about.

It's Friday, January, eighth, twenty-sixteen. Little Milly has a spelling test each Friday morning. I hope the turmoil of our absence hasn't messed that up.

As we all settle in for breakfast, I say, "I believe we're eating in Milly's old chicken pen. Or, where it once was. I spent a lot of time collecting eggs from those broody damn hens."

"I wish we had some of those eggs right now," Herschel says jokingly.

"My grandfather often said, 'People in hell want ice water'. It's ironic since he's most certainly running through the Woods of Lamentation as we speak."

"And while he runs, the same beasts serve you," Rebecca says. "I see you beginning to stare off. Don't forget who you are."

"And who is that?"

"The most powerful person alive."

For some reason, that makes me cry.

"What's wrong?" Rebecca asks, reaching out and holding my hand.

"Probably because, once, I was a very meek girl. I would hunch my tall frame over, hoping futilely not to be noticed. My grandfather would purposefully home in on my vulnerability. The bastard used to tell me he wished I had been born a boy. At least he didn't do to me what he did to my mother."

"Poor Dotty," Rebecca says.

"Yes. But, it's still no excuse. Plenty of people are abused, yet don't become abusers themselves."

"That abused little girl threw a helicopter yesterday, saving dozens of people, despite the fact they were all likely Apostle cultists. Any of them would have cheered your death."

"I didn't want to kill anyone who wasn't a direct threat to our safety."

"It's commendable, because I couldn't have held back," Rebecca says.

"I understand that feeling."

After eating, the four of us walk the perimeter. As we do, I glide my hand along the smooth granite surface of the dome searching for damage. There is none.

"We need to call home," Nate says. "That means somehow we have to find a clear patch of sky. Right now, all of those come with a chance of intermittent bullets."

"Y'all, stand behind me, I have an idea," I say, walking toward the North wall.

I stop three-quarters of the way to the eastern side of the dome. I place my left hand on the wall in front of me. I pull ten-inch sheaths of granite, eight feet wide, from the ground. They climb up the wall in a zig-zag pattern forming a stone staircase reaching nearly to the top of the dome. They're firmly embedded into the rock. Despite this, I form four, equidistant columns underneath them for added support.

After, I create a large center column. It's ten feet in diameter, supporting a flat top with a diameter twice as large. It's reminiscent of a giant wood screw. The circular deck slides into place next to the top stair, five feet from the peak of the dome.

"It's an observation deck," Rebecca says.

"Exactly," I reply while filling the void around the base of the deck's column. "I should be able to climb to the top and pull back an opening wide enough that we can get a signal while sitting. If we stay seated, we'll be out of their line of sight. Hell, they probably won't even notice."

"Are we ready to head up?" Herschel asks, nervously.

"I'll go first," I reply.

"We trust you," Rebecca says.

"I don't trust me."

"The rest of us disagree."

"I can't stop you. Do what you want. But, you're under no obligation to ameliorate my feelings."

As I ascend, Rebecca, Herschel, and Nate follow behind me. The trip takes forty-five seconds at a moderate pace.

We sit in a circle directly under the peak. I pull back a perfectly round hole in the ceiling ten feet in diameter, allowing bright light and cold air to rush in. I turn on the satellite phone as our eyes adjust. After it's booted, I pass it off to Rebecca. Rebecca can soften Tiff's mood far better than I. She's under a tremendous level of stress. It's not knowing that's the worst for her.

I watch Rebecca as she goes through the phone's ridiculous dialing procedure. The still winter forest and insulation of the thick dome stand in stark contrast to the abrupt sounds coming from the speaker, making it seem louder than usual.

Then I hear it, the muffled sound of Tiff's high-pitched voice resonating from the speaker pressed up against Rebecca's ear saying, "Hello?"

When receiving phone calls from a satellite phone, the caller ID only says, 'No caller ID - Unknown' so she can never be certain who's calling, unlike individual cell phones.

"Hi, Tiff," Rebecca says.

She becomes so loud that everyone becomes privy to the conversation.

"Is she…?"

"Dead? Not at all. Naomi is doing what she does best."

"Manslaughter and mayhem? Yeah, I've met my wife."

Rebecca chuckles a little before saying, "She's more 'Naomi' than I've seen her since our night at the top of the Frying Pan Tower when she killed Joseph.

"We," I interject, sitting across from Rebecca.

"We," Rebecca says.

"You did aim the gun, Rebecca," Tiffany says to her.

"I suppose I will take partial credit."

"One day, I'll get you to commit to half," Tiff says.

"Maybe. Would you like to speak with the woman in question?"

"I'd love to," she says.

Rebecca hands the phone over.

"Hey baby," I say to Tiffany.

"Hi," she responds, almost coquettishly.

"I'm sorry about what Theta did. I didn't have any say in her choice."

"I know. But, I think I might be in the early stages of trusting her."

"Why would you want to trust a Ceraphirian?"

"Because it would have been easier for Theta if she'd just let the four of you die. Theta had no reason to save you other than the conviction to do right by humanity."

"We'll see. Though, I am leaning in your direction," I say.

"In the meantime, what do you have planned?"

"I'm going to start digging a hole."

"How long do you think it will take you to reach the cavern?"

"Three months. It's five miles away, to the southwest."

"That's still really fast."

"All I'm doing is pushing dirt out of the way and compacting the Earth around it tighter. That way we won't have to haul any out."

"Oh, that's all?" she says sarcastically.

"Yeah," I respond flatly.

"The rest of us already believe in Naomi. Perhaps you should give it a try."

"One day. Probably my last one."

"Don't say that," Tiff's voice strains.

"I'm sorry. It was a bad joke."

"I know. But never joke about your death around me. I can't bear it."

"You seem a bit more at ease than I expected."

"You have your team with you now. And Theta."

"Don't get too infatuated. They're not gods," I say.

"But, one could be a friend."

"Maybe."

31

Nate and Malcolm speak for a few minutes, then Herschel and his mom, Diane. Zeke doesn't come to the phone. He's doing what Zeke does when he's worried, working in his shop.

While this goes on, I look over the edge of the platform at the northwestern section, where the hillside was absorbed into the dome, breaking up the otherwise smooth interior walls. It's there that I'll begin excavation. It should provide good initial structural integrity and allow me to create an entrance we walk into instead of crawling down a hole.

After Herschel hangs up the satellite phone, he opens the laptop he brought. It's connected to the phone with a USB cable. The internet connection is slow but usable. Herschel begins searching for stories about yesterday's incident at the Register of Deeds office.

After a few minutes, Herschel comments, "Not a goddamn thing. Just a report of two minor earthquakes near Burnsville. Seismographs must have picked up the bridge collapse and helicopter explosion. Normally, I'd expect to see videos of something like that all over the web. However, yesterday I didn't see one civilian carrying a cellphone."

I say, "They won't work up here, and the Apostles don't allow the flock to have cellphones or computers. The folks running the town have computers, but only in their offices, where their activity is extensively monitored. Like most cults, they have to quell outside influence. By now, nearly every person in the county has either fully committed to the Apostles or is remaining quietly out of their way."

"You'd think someone would take an interest," Nate says.

"Nearby locals are afraid of the Apostles. Rumors about Joseph's abilities still echo through these hollers. Monied city folks simply don't care. To many of them, this is a throwaway part of the world. A pretty postcard and a story about that time you passed through one afternoon thirty years ago."

"Are you finished, Herschel?" I ask.

"Yes, but I'll want to check again tonight."

"That's a good idea. For now, I've got work to do."

I close the large hole at the peak of the dome. Daylight recedes until it's just a pinprick. Then we're back to the dim, bluish glow of bioluminescent lichen.

As we descend the stairs, Rebecca says, "I've known Tiff a long time. I've never seen her so calm when it comes to this kind of shit."

"It's Theta. Tiffany is trying to convince herself that Theta saving us means she has our best interest at heart. That might be true. But, the Ceraphirian see further than we do. It could be one giant ruse."

Nate interjects sharply, "Or, Tiffany actually believes in you and doesn't find it absurd that an ancient demigod might as well."

That smarts, coming from my best friend, but it's deserved.

Back on ground level, Rebecca asks, "How can we help you?"

"The only thing the rest of y'all can do right now is keep me company and bring water. This is going to be tiring."

Headlamp on, and a bottle of water from the spring in hand, I head over to the northwestern corner of the dome.

"How are you going to do it?" Herschel asks.

"The rocks jutting out mark the site of the hill near the creek on the backside of the property. I'll start here, descend, and then begin a gradual curve until I'm headed southwest."

"Then what?"

"The cavern is where it all began. The pull in my chest I've told you about, that's where it's tethered. It wants me to return so that I can understand. And, I made Svangi a promise."

"Just make sure he doesn't eat us," Herschel says.

"I've taken your suggestion into consideration," I reply sarcastically.

The spot I've chosen for the entry has two weathered, flat boulders lying diagonally on top of one another. I cause them to rise vertically, then separate them by five feet. This creates two door jambs. Above their six-and-one-half-foot peaks, I slide another smaller boulder atop the two vertical ones. This establishes a primitive stone doorway.

The rocks and dirt inside my new passageway begin to recede inward as I force them out and away from the dome. There are groans and cracks as they slide against one another. Within thirty minutes, I've created a hallway ten feet in length. I'm drenched in sweat. After catching my breath, I ask the surrounding trees to grow their roots in a crisscross along the inside wall and ceiling of the new passageway. Once hardened, they brace what best could be described as a new mineshaft.

I rest, then repeat the process. By lunchtime, the tunnel has descended twenty feet. I've already begun changing the direction incrementally. I keep going until quarter-to-seven. At that point, I'm too exhausted to continue. It dawns on me that eventually, we will have to start bunking in the passageway. I don't relish the thought.

We eat high above, on the observation deck while Herschel scrolls through the dark reaches of the internet for any new information. Nothing.

We don't want to call home yet because Little Milly may not be in bed. When she asked about calling us to speak on the phone, Diane brilliantly said, "They're in another time zone." I don't want her asking too many questions or sensing the stress in our voices.

Once we're strong enough, I plan to fight the Apostles head-on, hopefully before Abraham makes his next move.

———

We keep this cycle up for two months. Each day, our crew rises at seven, eats, and then heads into the tunnel around eight. As time passes, returning to the dome each evening becomes a heavy burden. After digging more than three miles of tunnel, we decide to move our camp permanently into the mineshaft. This means our communication will go silent.

Before leaving the dome for the last time, I open the observatory and have Nate start the Hummer. We let it run for half an hour. This way, the alternator can bring the onboard batteries back to a full charge, ensuring it will start when needed.

When the air has cleared, we gather on top of the observatory platform to make one last call home in what will likely be five weeks. It's a somber affair. Tiff and Malcolm both cry. It's good they're together right now. They've become quite good friends over the years. Diane plays tough, as usual. And Zeke valiantly asks me to put the lamentation gun he made to good use.

When we make camp each night, I have the Earth create a deep hole for waste and a spring uphill for drinking water. I make a hot spring large enough to bathe and wash our clothes in. With different water, of course. Morale and progress run on full stomachs, rest, and cleanliness. Herschel even brought their travel Scrabble game. I'm so tired of their insistence that I play.

The closer we get, the worse the itch on my left hand becomes. Svangi is nearby.

We break through on Saturday morning, April second, twenty-sixteen. The shriek released by Svangi is deafening and, frankly, terrifying. But he can only make that one wretched noise, so I can't be sure what it means. Then, I feel our connection again. We're tethered by the speck of light I put into him nearly a decade ago. It's what gives him awareness. His character is not unlike that of a dog, a very protective one.

Half of the fluorescent bulbs have completely burned out. Their flickers illuminate old, deep crimson blood stains spattered across the walls. Below them, countless rifles and spent casings rest; turned green by time and oxygen.

All of this is a result of the Apostles sending what I estimate to be forty men down here during my escape. Foolishly, they allowed themselves to become trapped. Traditional weapons do not affect Svangi, only a lamentation blade or being submerged completely in water can kill him.

The false Beasts of Lamentation the Apostles create technically could hurt him. However, true beasts are multitudes more formidable than the imitations. On the day the cave was painted in blood, I witnessed Svangi kill three in less than a minute. Beneath the unnatural blue tint, Svangi appears.

He does not age, or tire, but he's felt an uncontrollable hunger for the past nine years. Beasts of Lamentation do not actually need to eat, but regardless, their stomachs growl constantly for sustenance. In the Woods of Lamentation, loathsome men fill their diet. Their hunger is motivation, thus plays a vital role in keeping the equation balanced.

I feel guilty for asking Svangi to stay on guard in the cavern for all these years. It's too much, even for him.

I try to imagine what finally seeing him is like for Rebecca, Herschel, and Nate. No matter how graphic, a verbal description of his visage is hardly preparation at all.

Svangi's skin is muted-bright white. A shimmering, indigo-colored substance pumps through large, bulging veins. He has no eyes. There are holes in his skull where they should have been. It would be a misnomer to call them dark. They are voids capable of swallowing time and whatever hope remains within his victims. Regardless, Svangi can see. He walks on four long, spindly legs with large spear-like tips, making him eight feet tall. His body is small, round, and plump. His head is oblong. A mismatch of randomly arranged, human-like teeth populate Svangi's upper jaw. He doesn't have a lower. All that remains is a hole with loose skin around the opening. He's intractably hideous by human standards, but I have an extraordinary affection for him.

I fan my arms back to warn my three companions to take several steps backward. While they do, I walk into that damn cavern for the third time in my life.

I hear Herschel say, "H-O-L-Y S-H-I-T, Naomi, that's Svangi?!"

"Yeah," I reply, almost contrite. "It's not Svangi's fault he looks like that."

"Speaking of looking, he's staring at us like food," Herschel says.

"Whatever you do, don't run. He's just confused. Even so, don't give him something to chase."

Svangi charges, screaming in our direction.

I step further inside. In my left hand, I produce a ball of light the size of a grapefruit. It's a small piece of the larger sphere inside my chest. Its brilliance fills the cavern. I hold my palm out, allowing it to float in front of me. Instantly, Svangi transforms from a vicious predator to a docile helpmate. He kneels in front of me, getting as low to the ground as he can.

"No, Svangi, rise. You have protected what is sacred for nine years. You're not my servant. You are my friend and always have been."

Svangi approaches me. He eyes my companions, fifteen feet behind me, still inside the mineshaft.

"Svangi, don't eat them, protect them," I say sternly, pointing over my back.

"That's not making me feel any better," Herschel says.

A brief, high-pitched shriek comes out of Svangi.

"He understands," I say.

"Are you sure?" Herschel asks.

"Yeah."

"Like, really, really sure?"

"I'll play Scrabble with you tonight if you come over here

and meet him."

Nate begins to step forward.

"No, I mean Herschel specifically. Otherwise, no deal."

"Didn't you say that he eats people whole?"

"Not always. Sometimes he dismembers them beforehand."

Herschel lets out a frustrated groan.

"I can stop him, but I won't need to. I'm close enough that we're linked. I can feel his intentions and influence them. Svangi is the best bodyguard you could have. Believe me, he's on our side."

"If he eats me, you get to be the one who explains it to my mother."

"That's fair."

With trepidation, Herschel stiffly walks toward me. He pauses at the entrance.

I say, "Watch," as I command Svangi to walk toward me and lean his head in my direction. I pet him like I would an old Labrador Retriever. His skin feels like ultra-fine sandpaper, very sleek, but dry. I keep scratching his head as Herschel bravely starts to do the same. With Herschel still in one piece, Nate and Rebecca walk around my left side and join in.

"This is it, then? Where it all started?" Nate asks.

"It started in first grade when I met Tiff. Everything else has been a result of others' reactions to the development of our relationship. But, this is where that journey took its most drastic turn."

The three of them begin widening their visual curiosity beyond Svangi.

"The cavern is nothing like it was the first time I was down here. Besides the high ceilings, it's small now. No more than fifty feet from one end to the other, and no wider than thirty. The rubble to our left is from a collapse in two-thousand-seven. Before, there were miles of winding passages."

"Oh, I wonder how that happened," Rebecca jokes.

"A simple chain reaction."

"Yeah, so simple," Herschel says, looking toward the weapons room. "Is the ladder you used to escape in there."

"Yeah. It leads up into their megachurch now. I destroyed their last one."

"Maybe you should drop the new one on Abraham's head," Nate says.

"He, his guards, and church elders would survive. All I'd be doing is killing everyone who wasn't important enough to be given clothing with indigo sewn into the fabric. They're the same ones who are most likely to turn on him in the future. Hurting them will only push those like them to insulate themselves further out of fear. They know I'm in the dome. But I don't want them to know I've made it down here. They're still waiting for the other shoe to drop. They don't know from which direction yet."

"Now what?" Rebecca asks.

"It wants me to understand, whatever that means. Before, though, we need to make camp."

I create amenities similar to the dome. On the western wall, across from the newly formed mineshaft entrance, I have soft moss grow in a patch large enough for us to sleep on. Five feet north, toward the weapons room, I form a small spring for drinking water.

Behind a large boulder, in front of the collapsed cavern, I create two closed-in privies. I pull up a flat rock wall between the privies and create two enclosed showers on the other side.

This takes most of the day. At nine, I'm forced to pay up when Herschel breaks out the Scrabble board. I come in dead last three times in a goddamn row.

———

The next morning is Sunday, April third. We wake up at nine, which is two hours later than usual. We've earned the extra sleep.

The first thing I see is Svangi patrolling the cavern, as he's done for the past nine years. I realize that his service has finally come to an end. I need to send him home. I can protect the cavern for now. When he notices that I'm awake, he makes his way toward me. This horrid, giant beast sits by my side waiting to see what interesting things I have planned for the day ahead. I pat him on the head as I pull my lower body out of my sleeping bag. I head toward the bathroom and Svangi follows. How do you explain to a nightmare creature that you like going pee by yourself? Luckily, he stops before getting to the stall, likely sensing my feelings about the matter.

At breakfast, Nate asks, "Shouldn't we head back today so we can call home and let them know we've made it through?"

"We can head back this evening so we can call first thing Monday, once Little Milly is off to school."

"What do you need to do this morning, then?" Herschel asks.

"I need to figure out how to send Svangi home. I haven't opened a door to the Woods of Lamentation for nearly a decade. I have before, so there's no reason I can't again."

The pull on my chest from the spot on the cavern floor, a mere twenty-five feet from us, has become overwhelming. I'm usually able to ignore it, but not down here.

"I think the light wants me to return to the spot where Charles died. Just over there," I say, pointing toward the metal weapons room door.

Nate says, "You haven't been on that side of the cavern yet. And none of us have been more than a few feet behind you. I know you're afraid, but we're here with you now. You're not alone

like you were then. It's the path you chose. I think it was a good
one. Now it's time to complete it."

"Can I at least finish my coffee first?"

After procrastinating for another half-hour, I begin getting dressed for the day. All the while eyeing a singular spot on the cavern floor with ominous dread.

Standing, I say, "I want you all to stay right here. That includes you, Svangi."

"What's going to happen," Rebecca asks, with concern.

"I don't know. That's why I want you to stay back."

Trepidation spikes as I move away from my friends. Though only a few feet, the distance feels like lightyears. It's as though somehow I've been isolated from everyone. When I'm almost there, I experience a sensation as though a strong hand reaches into my chest. It takes a firm grasp on the light within me and is drawing me toward it. I realize that I'm no longer walking. My feet are levitating six inches off the ground, while my body is gently being pulled toward the place where Charles bled to death. I try to turn around to see my friend's faces, but there's nothing.

When I adjust my vision forward again, I perceive only darkness. My feet still aren't touching a solid surface. I dangle in a void, waiting. Then there's a speck of light in the distance. It becomes overwhelmingly bright, envelops the space, swallows me up, and swiftly delivers me to a new location before blinking out of existence.

What's left behind resembles the far reaches of outer space. I float weightless, without protection. I don't think to breathe. It doesn't seem necessary any longer. Floating in the space underneath my feet a wooden floor appears, like that of an old log cabin, just before my feet touch it. There is no ceiling. The night sky is filled with what looks like a semi-permeable, indigo-colored border. Nothing seems to exist beyond it. When I turn back, I see someone walking in my direction from the corner of my field of vision.

She's a pale woman, no taller than five-foot-two, wearing a dull green apron dress over a long white tunic. She has dark brown eyes and hair that falls in curls to her shoulders. Her shoes are constructed of old leather, more akin to what I'm used to seeing in the Smithsonian Museum of History than a modern shoe store.

I don't even bother asking her name. I already know she's Zelia. The Ceraphirian who possessed my light before escaping to the human world. She died centuries before I was born.

"What am I looking at?" I ask, pointing toward the sky overhead.

"It is waiting," she says with forceful confidence.

"What is?"

"The edge."

"Edge of what?"

"All things. It's the edge of your existence. The observed one, anyhow. The place where her equations run roughshod across every sentient being as they try wildly to balance themselves."

"There is no time there?"

"There is no entropy. Time can be experienced if it makes one happy. I happen to enjoy seasons."

"What exactly am I waiting for?"

"To die. But not like before. Not stuck. Gone."

"Wait. Am I dead?"

"Not yet. You're no longer breathing, back in your world. But it takes five minutes before the brain starts to die. The only way the living can visit the dead is to die. If the indigo border crosses you, it's over."

"What about those in the Woods of Lamentation?"

"Suffering of such magnitude requires a physical reality. Past the boundary above, all of that goes away. Physical bodies are like a prison you never knew you were trapped in."

"So, I'm going to die, and you're here to talk me through it?"

"No. You're here to listen."

"Why didn't this happen last time I was here?"

"You weren't ready."

"I'm not even going to argue with you."

"Good. That makes it easier. Coming within an arm's distance of the spot where Charles died will bring you here, to me. You can stay for a short while. As long as I make the ground release you in time, you will come away unscathed."

"How can you have control over anything in my world anymore?"

"Because from here, I can share the light with you. Truthfully, you're mediocre at best when it comes to harnessing it. You could split the planet in half, quite literally, if you knew how."

"Maybe that's for the best. I have a temper."

"So I have seen. But, Naomi, anger is what fuels your abilities. That's worked in your favor. There has to come a time when you can use them with a calm heart. I don't mean forgiving, but exacting. The best you've done thus far is more akin to flailing."

"It's worked."

"Surprisingly well. Beyond fathomability, considering."

"You've spent too much time around humans. It's made you judgmental."

"Probably. But it's also taught me to see humans as more than pieces on a chessboard. Besides Theta, none of my sisters have learned this simple principle."

"Why did you leave the Ceraphirian?"

"I wanted what you have, a family and children. The price was mortality. I willingly paid it. I raised two daughters who had independent streaks of their own. You very much remind me of them."

"Was it worth it?"

"Every bit. More so, despite everything. Having a family and friends for just one human lifetime gave my consciousness meaning beyond anything in Ceraphiria. That's what I would think about when I harnessed the light while mortal, my daughters. Then, calm would come over me, and everything would become clear. You have a daughter. I imagine we're similar in that way.

"I think," I say while simultaneously thoughts of Little Milly play through my brain.

"Keep your mind right there," Zelia says.

––––––––––

My next conscious thought is to gasp for air. My chest wheezes as life-giving oxygen enters my lungs.

"What happened?" I attempt to say, but my first breath was too shallow to make the words audible. I repeat the sentence. This time a hoarse version of my voice makes its way out.

Nate replies, "You collapsed. Just before your body hit the floor, it was like an invisible cushion caught you. There, you lay on your back, floating a few inches off the ground. You stopped breathing. We tried to give you rescue breaths but the air wouldn't enter your lungs. All we could do was monitor your heart rate, hoping you came to before it stopped."

"How long was I out?"

"Two, maybe three minutes."

"That's it?"

"Yeah, that's a good thing," Nate says sarcastically, the way only my best friend could. "Did something happen?"

"I met Zelia."

"What was she like?" Rebecca asks.

"Stern but kind. Far more introspective than I would have imagined. Ceraphirians are capable of feeling all the same emotions we do. Most choose to cut themselves off from their feelings as they allow us to foolishly play out the equation. That's their biggest flaw. Their lack of judicious intervention is what winnowed the Universe down to one final sentient observer, us. Now that their own existence is at risk, they're overplaying their hand with callous indifference."

"How is their existence in peril," Rebecca asks.

Without a conscious observer, there is nothing, meaning no more Ceraphirian, and no more universe."

34

It takes a few minutes before I can stand. After which, I promptly move away from the spot where Charles died. My friends help me return to my sleeping bag. I lie on my back and focus on bringing my mind back to a state of normality. Or, rather, the reality in which my family lives.

"You didn't have to take losing at Scrabble three times in a row that hard," Herschel jokes.

"Ha, ha," I say in a raspy, sarcastic tone.

———

It's noon before I'm able to get up and move around.

While we eat, I say, "I'm going to try to send Svangi home."

"You weren't breathing a few hours ago," Nate says.

"It's been nine years. I owe him."

"What's one more day, then? Anyhow, he seems to enjoy your company."

"Well—"

"You don't have anything to prove to him."

"He's not wrong," Rebecca says. "You need to rest. Svangi seems content."

"Okay, okay. I get it. My well-being affects the entire party, so it's not just my choice to make."

"What you need to do is sleep until tomorrow morning," Herschel says. "What happens if while you're trying to open a portal, you pass out again?"

"Zelia will send me back."

"What if your body can't take it? Zelia doesn't control that."

"Fine. I'm not going anywhere or doing anything stupid until tomorrow. Are you happy?"

Unintentionally, in unison, all three say, "Yes."

For the remainder of the day, I drift in and out of sleep while they occupy themselves playing board games. I fall asleep for the last time at eight o'clock in the evening, then sleep soundly through the night.

———

The next morning is Monday, April fourth, twenty-sixteen.

At breakfast, Nate asks, "Are you going to send Svangi home today?"

"Yes. Whether I'm successful or not, we should head back to the dome, run the Hummer to charge the batteries, and call home."

As I drink my second cup of coffee, I contemplate how I felt the four times I was able to create portals before. The first was from a burst of anger, and the other three, desperation. It's different than harnessing the Earth's energy or asking organic materials to bend their shape to my will. It feels synthetic because I'm not manipulating a physical object, but reality itself.

To accomplish this, I have to concentrate all of my energy on visualizing a far-off place hard enough that somehow I'm able to defy the laws of physics. Strangely, creating a portal to another plane, like the Woods of Lamentation, is easier. I believe it's because the laws there are already so different, and the barrier is so weak. The first two doorways I created led there. The second two were to a place I knew well, my home in Virginia. But, how do I harness that raw burst of emotion?

I continue to concentrate on my breathing while sipping the warm beverage. When I open my eyes, I see Svangi still vigilantly patrolling the cavern. I haven't gone into the weapons room yet. There's enough space to allow me to walk around the spot where Charles died, but I'm still cautious not to make an inadvertent trip to visit Zelia.

When I stand to approach Svangi, everyone does the same. I meet him at the center of the cavern. He kneels, and I rub his grotesque head. His breath smells of acrid sulfur and feels like a warm desert breeze.

I look into those soul-draining eyes and say, "You've protected this holy site for so long. It's time for you to go home."

He emits a brief, high-pitched scream. But is it one of joy or melancholy?

The portal I brought Svangi through nine years ago was on the north wall, to the left of my current position. Fifteen feet in the same direction from the new mineshaft entrance. It worked before. It's best not to mess about and create new variables.

Svangi follows me as I run my hand along the stone surface. I know the spot because when I touch it, I feel a distant heat radiating off of it, much like irradiated material setting off a Geiger counter years after exposure. Instead of creating an archway in the rock wall from a distance, as I've done before, I place my left hand directly on the wall itself.

I think of the spot where I awoke inside the Woods of Lamentation. It's the most vivid representation I have. I close my eyes and imagine the gray, gnarled trees that surrounded me when I left my bubble. I cast my mind there like a fishing lure. I begin to feel the energy from the wall synchronize with the light in my chest. I feel light trickling down through my arm, out my hand, and into the granite. I open my eyes. I'm there, looking back at myself, hand pressed against the rock like clear glass. We place our hands together across the clear plane. I close my eyes momentarily. When I open them, I find my consciousness has been transported into the reflection of myself. It's the body I inhabit while I'm on the other side. Closing and opening them again brings me back to the cavern.

I watch as the archway forms. The dry air of the Woods of Lamentation wafts out. The sound of heavy footfalls in the brush echoes inside the cavern. Then come the screams.

Stepping away, I look at Svangi and say, "It's time, boy."

He looks through the portal, then at me. We stand in silence for a few seconds. It's as though Svangi is attempting to remember his former self. Out of the darkness comes the outline of a man running. His screams are high-pitched and primal, like a pig being slaughtered. This piques Svangi's predatory instincts. His head turns sharply, focusing on the man. His ocular cavities follow the familiar shape. Svangi looks back at my face. I softly say, "Yes," and he swiftly passes through the doorway and scurries off through the trees. I stand there in disbelief as I grieve the end of my relationship with a monster.

I let go of my focus and watch as the doorway dwindles down toward the floor, then vanishes. I stare blankly at the granite surface.

"I'm sorry," a voice says from behind, startling me.

It's Rebecca. She, Nate, and Herschel must have moved closer while I was off somewhere in a mild trance-like state.

"No. It's okay. He's just a—"

"Friend. He was a friend," she says.

"He was. As strange as that might seem."

"Not at all," she says before taking me by the hand and leading me back to camp.

As we pack up, I say, "We'll have to get into the weapons room once we return. We're going to start running low on food soon. There's a three-year supply in there. It's old MREs, but we can survive on it.

With our packs on, the four of us begin the five-mile trek back to the dome. I notice small specks of bioluminescent material a mile in on the walls. As we continue, they become less sparse.

"It's spreading," I say aloud to myself.

"What is?" Nate asks.

"The lichen is spreading from the dome, down through the tunnel. I didn't expect that.

"You've grown stronger than you realize."

I stop and place my hand on the wall, sending a surge from the light inside me into them to accelerate their growth. This causes a pulse of bright blue light through the length of the tunnel. It calms, growing slightly dimmer within a few seconds. However, the residual illumination is far greater than before. I turn off my headlamp to save the battery. We'll need to charge them when we get back.

Throughout the early afternoon, we keep up a healthy pace, only stopping to rest once.

We finally exit the mineshaft on the other side to everyone's relief.

35

After unloading my pack, I begin a complete walk around of the dome. I run my hand across the surface as I go. There's been no further damage to its integrity since we began sleeping at the excavation sites a month ago. Had I been more sensible, I would have returned a few times before to place calls home, but I've been single-minded.

Still on the ground level, I ask the dome to open the ceiling above the observation deck. The bright light from the mid-afternoon sun is startling to eyes that have been underground for so long. All of us hold hands over our brows and look down as we adjust. The wind entering is cool, but not freezing.

Sitting in the Hummer's driver's seat, I insert the key into the ignition. I turn it to the start position. A yellow light that looks like a roller coaster track with back-to-back loops illuminates. It's supposed to symbolize glow bulbs. They use the battery's power to heat each cylinder before starting. Diesel becomes thick when it's cold. The six-figure war machine fires up on the first try. Wasteful as the stupid thing is, it's reliable.

Herschel plugs in all of our electronic gear into chargers, most importantly the satellite phones and his laptop. It will take half an hour before one of the phones can be used. The laptop will take even longer. Once we're certain the Hummer's batteries are completely charged, I turn off the engine.

I unplug one of the phones to take with us. Everything else continues charging.

Once the exhaust from the diesel engine wafts away, we ascend the stairs to the observation deck, just below the now-open roof. Rebecca curses the least when she dials the phone, so she's our designated operator.

It takes her just over a minute from bootup to ringtone.

"Hello," Tiffany's voice says over the speakerphone.

"Tiff, it's Rebecca."

"Have you seen the news?"

"No, Herschel's laptop isn't fully charged."

"He did it. Abraham held an event in Raleigh three weeks ago to kick off his campaign. Rebecca, he can levitate. He opened a portal, letting through two false beasts of lamentation. Unlike Joseph's, they seem to have been trained. They flank him on both sides without ripping bystanders to shreds. Instead of the flamboyant indigo-stuffed robe of Joseph, Abraham hides away the fabric he wears imbued with the substance. It's all anyone can talk about."

"How did he look health-wise?"

"For a man in his late seventies, fantastic. He appears fitter. Even though he's bald, Abraham keeps a neatly manicured beard. With the distinguished appearance of an elder white man and the ability to spin Biblical myths into modern relevance, he's built a cult following. It's growing faster than I would have anticipated. He's even made the national news. Disciples are visiting every white

Evangelical church in the state to hold court with their pastors."

"It's that bad?"

"Naomi was right. But it's even worse. He's weaponizing social media and encouraging violence against queer folk and anyone who dares to dissent openly against his message. Abraham has them frothing at the mouth over slights that never existed. Counter protests have mounted, but the police, whom he dotes upon, are flagrantly beating people bloody in the street. Even worse, he now has disciples who are black."

"What?!" Rebecca says. "The Apostles are a white nationalist organization."

"He has at least two men of color who are close confidants."

"White supremacy isn't just for white people. Hatred can be internalized. Ignorant people can be conditioned to become the agents of their own destruction," Rebecca says.

"We're really scared. We've kept the TV off when Little Milly is around. I think this might spread outside of the state."

"Has President Montgomery said anything?"

"No, not a word. I can't imagine she hasn't taken notice. She likely doesn't want to give him the clout or be caught in the crosshairs of his supporters."

"You need to try and keep everyone calm," Rebecca says.

"But, if this gets worse, there will be nowhere for people like us to go. There are thousands of threads online with people lauding support for Abraham while joking about hanging and shooting people. Some are using grainy lynching photographs from the early twentieth century to create what they deem to be funny memes about 'murdering fags'.

"If I'm alive, our family will always have somewhere to go," I say.

"He's powerful. There's so much anger in people that I never knew existed. And they're mad at us for no reason."

"Baby, I'm going to put him in the ground along with anyone else who stands in my way. We can't stop how hateful people feel toward us, but we can make them afraid to act on their violent intentions."

"I know, but there are so many of them now. It happened so quickly."

"They were always there, Abraham just gave them permission."

"At least they've exposed their true selves," Tiff says defiantly.

"The only thing I can do right now is learn whatever I can from Zelia and prepare. I think the best thing for y'all is to keep living like this isn't happening. Make sure Little Milly's life is disturbed as little as possible. Maybe if we're lucky, she won't even notice."

You've never been what I'd call lucky. But you're too goddamn stubborn to lose."

"That's right. No matter how confidently he acts, know that in the back of his mind, he's haunted by a monster. That monster is the same woman who reads dinosaur books to a little girl every night."

"How do you know he's afraid?" Tiffany asks.

"He's ignored us for the most part. No more RPGs or surveillance that I can discern. His strategy is to charm consent from the most suggestable of us, instead of fighting me head-on."

"Abraham tells his followers that they're special. The feeling that gives them makes their perceived relationship with him personal. Speaking against him is seen as a slight against their own character. What do you think they are going to think of you?"

"More shitty people with more shitty thoughts. So what?" I reply.

"What if he convinces so many that even after he's gone, they refuse to let it go? They'll come after you for the rest of your life."

"That suits me. What good is a retirement where you go soft?"

"You enjoy killing horrible people, don't you?" Tiffany asks bluntly.

There's silence as my three companions stare at me.

With little thought, I say, "Yes."

There is an utter lack of surprise on everyone's faces. But, no one seems to have enough of an objection to my flawed character to provide any kind of vocal dissent.

"Sister, you're not alone," Rebecca says, assuredly.

Nate and Herschel are quiet. I know Nate is afraid his anger will consume him. Herschel has never killed anyone. He certainly doesn't want to, but would if need be.

"I know," Tiffany says. "It's understandable when your supposed lack of humanity is a part of their snide political banter."

"Yeah," I reply, as the mood begins to flatline.

"It's like all of our excited energy has suddenly been used up.

Quietly, I say, "I'm going to have to be gone for a while. The training I have to complete with Zelia is going to be physically demanding, even dangerous. But, without me here to open our observatory, there won't be much in the way of communication."

"I know," Tiff says.

"Listen, we only have so much battery left on this phone. I'm going to hand it over to Nate so he and Malcolm can talk in private. It's been a while. Tell Zeke and Diane that I love them. And hug that little gremlin for me."

"I love you, Naomi," Tiffany says."

"I love you, too."

36

I descend the stairs, leaving everyone else to their private conversations. I'm exhausted from walking five miles through the mineshaft, two days after nearly suffocating to death.

I find myself thinking about Svangi's absence far more than I believed I would. Strangely, the itch in my hand has returned after fading once we finally met up with him. I hope Svangi isn't so out of practice that he can't catch his own food. Logically, I know he doesn't require food, but I don't want him to feel uncomfortable. I reckon this must be how my neighbor across the street in Tysons Corner feels about his Weimaraners. They're all he talks about. I envy his simplicity.

I crawl into my sleeping bag, even though it's only four in the afternoon. I make sure not to drift off so I can close the roof after the phone calls and whatever research Herschel needs to do is completed. Herschel comes down to switch out phones and retrieve his laptop. I dread the images it will bring me later.

Nate was the first to wake me. I look at my watch. It's seven in the evening. I've been asleep for two hours.

"I'm sorry," I say louder than I intended.

"It's okay, nothing is wrong," Nate says in a soft tone. "We just need you to close the ceiling."

I pull my left hand out of the sleeping bag and place it over my head, arm twisted so that I may place my hand palm down. Quicker than usual, I'm able to map the dome in my mind. Granite sheaths fill the void so quickly that it creates a small tremor that passes through the granite wall and into the ground beneath us. Though slight for an earthquake, it's unsettling. I keep my hand in place, waiting to react if I sense the first hint of a cave-in. But all things remain in equilibrium.

"Do you reckon they felt that back in town?" Nate asks.

"Probably."

"Good. Abraham is staying in Burnsville tonight because he scheduled a news conference for the local mountain papers. However, reporters are coming from as far away as the Cape Hatteras Gazette."

"Do you think he'll know it was me?"

"No doubt," Nate says. "But, it won't be just him. There are dozens of religious leaders present as well. Mostly, snake handlers along with run-of-the-mill fire and brimstone preachers. They're keen on apocalyptic predictions based on geological or weather phenomena. They're likely terrified."

"That makes sense. It's easier to convert zealots first," I say.

I hear two sets of footsteps coming up behind me.

"You scared the shit out of us," Herschel says, seemingly in the early moments of relief.

"I didn't do it on purpose. I feel different since meeting with Zelia. I'm still myself, but using my abilities takes less effort. I can sense further away from my position than I ever could. Everything is accelerated."

After a pause, Rebecca asks, "You have to back there, don't you?"

"If I want to stand a chance, yes."

The following morning is Tuesday, April fifth. I'm the first to wake up. Mostly because I already had plenty of sleep after going to bed so early. Coffee in hand, I confiscate Herschel's laptop and head up to the observatory. With the roof open, I sign into the satellite service and bring up a web browser.

The controversy in the local press is palpable. The vitriol and hatred he harbors against people like me and many of my family members make his growing hordes of admirers shout mindless sayings about the prophecy. None of it is particularly coherent, which plays better than I would have figured. It's by Abraham's design. These are not intelligent people.

In some of the more recent videos, Abraham alludes to the ideas of violence. He doesn't outright call for it but jokes about how it might be used against their enemies. You know, people like two moms raising a child and minding their own goddamn business.

The Apostle's Party, as Abraham has been calling it, has yet to announce a running mate for Lieutenant Governor. Though not technically on the ticket together, the Lieutenant Governor is second in line. It's preferable to have someone in that position who has your back. The candidate will be announced in the near future. I get to the point that I can no longer take the vapid grandiosity of it all and am forced to shut the screen for my sanity.

It's bad. I know it's bad. I can't wallow in it, though, I think.

I lie back and watch what remains of the night sky as the crisp air dances off my neck and face. Not long after sunrise, I hear stirring below. After closing the ceiling, I head down to join my crew.

When I reach the bottom with the laptop in my hand, Herschel says, "You saw?"

"Yes," I say with an angry grumble. "But there's nothing we can do at the moment. For now, I have to go back.

"Zelia is that important?" Rebecca asks.

"We have an intense connection because we've shared the same light. There is no one else who can help me to become strong enough to defeat Abraham. She's passed on. Despite having no more claim here, she's reached out anyway. That has to mean something."

"Maybe she wants you to join her?" Rebecca says.

"If she wanted that, I'd already be dead."

The walk back to the cavern takes less time because we've rested. The bioluminescent glow of lichen now shimmers through the entirety of the mineshaft, even brighter than before. Upon our arrival at the cavern, we find that lichen from the cave is now sending tendril out of the mineshaft and up the walls. The lichen runs in veins, which spread out until bumping into one another. At this point, the organism's hive mind sends out even more tendrils.

After setting up camp, I say to Nate, "I want you to begin the process of making indigo. I've told you everything I know. Once it's all setup, you're going to need my blood. You can collect it on days between my sessions with Zelia."

"Do you think you can withstand all of that?" Nate asks with a worried look in his eyes.

The mood is shared by everyone. The three of them watched me put myself on the line last time and nearly pay with my life.

Looking at them, I say, "Little Milly needs a safe world to grow up in. For that, I would walk directly into death's horrendous maw with a smile on my face."

Settled in, we begin preparing lunch.

As we eat, I say, "I need one of you to go investigate the weapons room. I don't want to get too close to the spot until I'm ready to visit Zelia, just in case."

"When do you reckon you'll put yourself through that wretched experience again?" Nate asks.

"Tomorrow afternoon. Directly after, I want you and Herschel to head back to the dome and set up that bizarre upside-down, martini glass-looking thing we had made."

"There isn't a point where we can tie the rope off to."

"Shit. You're right. I wish I had thought of that before leaving."

"You'll have to make one, which means coming back with us," Herschel says.

"Goddamn it," I say.

After going back to my meal, I have a sudden urge. "What if?" I say aloud.

"If what?" Rebecca asks, intrigued.

"This," I say, as I reach down and place my left hand on the cavern floor.

Closing my eyes, I send my consciousness through the rock. The clarity of my vision is much crisper than ever before. The lichen in the cave communicates with electrical signals, not that different from our neurons reaching out toward one another. Because of that, when my mind reaches them, everything accelerates because of the compatibility.

My mind is whisked down the glowing hallway until arriving at the dome floor. I wind my way up the stairs about six feet and cause a very thick spur of rock to shoot forth from the staircase toward the center of the cave. It's three feet in length and one-and-one-half in diameter.

"Sturdy enough," I mumble to myself, eyes still closed.

When I'm satisfied, I release my consciousness. The returning snap into my body is abrupt. I had never pulled the rubber band of consciousness back that far before. A stinging, electrical pain pulses through me for a moment.

"Ugh," I say, shuttering, eyes open.

They stare at me in silence, not like a sideshow, but in curiosity at their friend's growth.

"Popping back so fast from that far smarted," I say.

"From where?" Nate asks.

"The dome. I changed the structure of the staircase, giving you a point where you can hang the glass condenser. After you get everything set up, return for my blood.

37

The next morning is Wednesday, April sixth. Breakfast is quiet. Everyone is on edge about me visiting Zelia again.

"You know the body can go for five minutes without oxygen before the neurons begin to die?" I say, breaking the silence.

It feels like I just walked into a party and accidentally caused the needle to skip off a record.

"That's not helping," Herschel says.

"Thank you all for caring about me."

"Yeah, whatever, Naomi," Herschel replies, jokingly.

"No. I mean it, all of you. Some people have no one. But here I am with three friends who are willing to live underground with me for months."

Everyone looks at me with soft eyes, knowing for a moment that I let my guard down and said something unfiltered by my abrasive personality. Instead of ruining it by saying anything further, there's quiet for most of the remainder of breakfast.

After my second cup of coffee, I stand and announce, "I'm ready," quietly, and with a bit more reverence than usual.

Last time I wasn't aware of what would happen. Now it's daunting. I don't want to die. I have a daughter to raise. But, I need to ensure she is safe and this is the only way to accomplish that.

As we head toward the sacred ground where Charles died, Herschel and Rebecca walk on either side of me. Nate follows at my back. All with one task, to catch me if I fall and there's no Zelia-created force field to cushion my body's impact onto the granite floor.

My field of vision flashes between our worlds in slow succession. Then there is darkness, except for one point of light. In the back-and-forth, darkness wins, but just for a moment. I wait as the light rushes toward me like a train. I wake again, floating in empty space waiting for the wooden floor to materialize beneath my dangling boots. I take notice of the indigo band, demarking my existence and the beyond, creeping toward me one small tick at a time.

"It's not an illusion. It's getting closer," Zelia says, materializing behind me.

"And beyond, I die?"

"Yes."

"But you're here."

"Because of the light, we are connected. This makes it so the Universe sees me as both dead and alive at the same time. I can slip across but can't stray far. The longer I'm dead, the less your world concerns me. But things there are dire."

"What do you want?"

"For you to commune with the Earth properly. You're barely speaking her language. What you're doing is akin to pointing and grunting."

"Why haven't I mastered it?"

"You, like so many humans, have forgotten that they are from the Earth and not a separate entity. All your atoms, down to the electrons that orbit their nuclei, originated in her oceans, soil, and atmosphere. Before that, in the hearts of embryonic stars. You are no different than the mountain or winter wren who live in their high forests."

"I have a doctorate in Marine Biology. I've got a pretty good grasp on the subject of evolution."

"It's much like the way we share the light. It lived inside me for millennia before you existed. You had to accept that before we could speak. That's why you walked over that spot years ago without a blip. Today it's different."

"The elements inside your body are rather similar. Borrowed for a finite period of time. When you see that you share the same stuff in the dirt you trod upon and the water you swim in, then you'll be ready."

"I understand."

"Yes, but you do not believe."

"I'm not big on the concept."

"The Earth doesn't care what you think, Naomi, even if you do possess the light that commands it."

"So, what?" I say. "Am I supposed to go sit in a corner and try to will myself into believing something?"

"You cannot will yourself. You either accept or you do not."

I awaken, taking a giant gasp of air. My chest is tight, and my lungs don't feel like they can take in as much air as they need. Nate holds my hand as I slowly regain control of my respiratory system. As I sit up, the cavern spins slowly, like a merry-go-round ending a cycle and discharging passengers.

Thirty minutes later, I'm in my sleeping bag, exhausted from the experience.

Knowing that I'll be asleep soon, I say to Nate and Herschel, "Take the small pebbles from the ground near the sacred point and the water we've collected back to the dome. Get to work setting up the glass condenser so you can begin manufacturing your first batch of indigo. When you're done, come back with the blood collection tubes and needles."

Nate replies, "We'll return tomorrow. Get rest. We love you and have it under control from here."

"You always have. I just wish I had realized it sooner."

The blinds of reality slap closed with me behind them.

When I wake, the time on my watch says eight in the evening. I turn to my left to see Rebecca sitting on her sleeping bag reading a book using the low light setting on her headlamp.

"What are you reading?" I ask.

"*The Man Who Folded Himself*," by David Gerrold. It's about a young man who inherits a TIMEBELT from his uncle, which allows him to place winning bets on horse races, making him very wealthy. But, with each travel forward or back, a new version of himself appears. That's the tricky part."

"That sounds exhausting for him."

"It is. Tiff gave it to me, and several other books when we left."

"She's still trying to start her family book club?"

"I think you'd like that more than you let on."

"Probably," I say with a sigh.

"Can you sit up?"

"Yeah. Everything is working, just at a delayed pace."

Rebecca puts her book down and we share a dehydrated chili mac. After, I play a round of Scrabble and lose horribly. Two more rounds yield the same result. By midnight, we both begin to doze off. With our headlamps off, the only light remaining is the faint hue of lichen. The cavern is being overrun with a tendril of the more aggressive strain I inadvertently created. They're not just blue, but also green and indigo. They twinkle almost like stars fluctuating between three spectrums. It makes me think about watching the night sky with Tiff as children. When the world was ahead of us.

The next morning is Thursday, April seventh.

The first words out of my mouth are, "I want to go again this morning."

"To where?" a yawning Rebecca replies, innocently.

"Zelia."

Instantly, her groggy-headedness vanishes, and Rebecca firmly replies, "Oh, hell no, Naomi Pace. We're here alone."

"It doesn't matter if they're here or not, y'all can't save me. You don't have the equipment to restart my heart. All you could do would be to give me CPR until you collapsed and I die anyway."

"Did it ever occur to you that maybe Herschel and Nate might want to see you one last time?"

"No, I just—"

"Were getting ahead of yourself. You're not strong enough at the moment. You have to give blood later today. You are only allowed to do one horrible thing to yourself per day."

"Why do I all of a sudden feel like Little Milly?"

"Because this is the same voice I used when she's pushing herself too far and is liable to get hurt."

There's really not much else I can say to Rebecca after that. Her aunty skills reign supreme.

38

I barely moved off of my sleeping bag all morning. Mostly, I dozed lightly as Rebecca read quietly.

Through that thin cerebral veil, I hear the sound of footsteps coming through the tunnel. Rebecca lays down her book and picks up the shotgun she has at her side. There's always a shell in the chamber. That way, she never has to rack the slide. Instead, all she has to do is wait quietly, click off the safety, and pull the trigger.

"It's us!" Herschel shouts from inside the tunnel, still out of sight.

"Just to be sure, answer a question."

"Come on, Rebecca," he says irritated.

"What was your mom's nickname for you when you were little?"

Herschel grumbles, "What does that have to do with anything?"

"I reckon me not shooting you."

After a moment of hesitation, he says, "It was Bunny. There, are you happy?"

I hear Nate's laughter echo loudly.

"It's because he liked wiggling his nose," I say. "His mom told me that less than a month after I met Herschel. She tells everyone."

"I guess it's really you," Rebecca announces.

The look on Herschel's face as he enters the cavern, is contrasted by the sheer glee on Nate's. Rebecca gets under Herschel's skin. He loves it but is afraid to let on how much.

Both place their packs down at the edge of our little camp and come in closer to talk. Rebecca sits down beside me as we face Nate and Herschel like we're in circle time back in Kindergarten.

Shaking it off, Herschel says, "We got that giant chunk of glass suspended about two feet off the ground. We looped the rope around the large spur you had the Earth grow out of the staircase. We attached the other end to the Hummer's J-hooks. Everything is in place. Now, all we need is a blood sample."

"When?"

"After Nate and I eat. We have to get back as soon as possible so we can be done with the first batch before returning tomorrow."

"So you don't miss my date with Zelia?" I ask.

"Yes, exactly."

"Thank you," I say with a genuine tone.

Herschel lets down his guard, replying, "We love you."

"Me too," I say teary-eyed.

A few drops fall but we have to keep moving forward. There is no other choice.

After finishing lunch, Nate brings a sterile collection set to my left side. I feel the cooling evaporation of the alcohol, followed by a sharp sting as the needle pierces one of the veins running along the inside of my elbow. He attaches a vial to the end of the unit. It's quickly filled with deep red blood.

"Done," Nate says as he places a gauze on the tiny wound.

He has me take over holding it so that he can have both hands free to store the vial away. Task completed, Nate places a small Band-Aid on the site.

"I feel weak having y'all carry the load like this."

"Naomi, you've signed up to die over and over. I think we can manage," Nate replies softly.

"It comes naturally."

"Meaning what?"

"Dying is so easy. The moment you accept it, there is a sense of relief. What a burden this flesh is."

"You better keep putting that flesh of yours back on every goddamn time, Naomi," Rebecca says, "For Little Milly."

"Always."

I'm exhausted. The last thing I remember is Nate holding my hand.

I wake up with rail ties digging into my back. I rise quickly to my feet, unsure if I'll have to defend myself. A wisp of wind tickles the skin of my cheek. This escalates into a brief wind surge, followed by a seven-foot-tall tornado, kicking up snow and dirt. It stops in the middle of the tracks and transforms into Theta.

"I have horrible news," Theta says abruptly. "Frieda has escaped."

"Keeping her was your job, Theta!" I shout.

The Woods of Lamentation shudder with my angry words. The beasts have taken notice.

"I know, but I had business to tend to in Ceraphiria. I couldn't open the timeline back up to return directly after leaving. There was a two-day gap because this era is obscured to me, making travel between our times imprecise. When I returned, she was gone. The chain and collar around her neck had turned to dust."

"And how do I know that you didn't purposefully let her go? I trusted one of y'all before. Perhaps I've made another mistake?"

"No. I would never," Theta says as a lantern appears on the horizon.

"She's here," Theta says, pointing behind me.

Theta walks around me and stands on the tracks, shielding me with her body.

Theta begins gathering wind, driving it in Frieda's direction. Frieda is knocked off her feet and lands on her back. As she rises, Theta prepares another round. Suddenly, she drops her hands to her side. Then I hear the train heading in our direction. Theta slowly turns to face me. Her eyes are white, crackling with indigo lightning. The train is bearing down behind me. I step off the track, but Theta stands her ground, staring blankly at the locomotive.

"Theta!" I scream.

She doesn't answer.

As the train grows louder, I feel the ground begin to vibrate. I run in Theta's direction. Swiftly, I cause a stone archway to appear behind her, just before tackling Theta into it, leaving it to slam shut in Frieda's face.

We land on the hard stone of the island where Frieda was previously held prisoner. When I open my eyes, I look to my left to see the chain's remnants turned to dust, still retaining a shadow of their former shape. How could she have done this on her own?

"What happened?" Theta asks from underneath me.

"She took over your mind and nearly had you killed by the oncoming train she summoned."

"You shouldn't be able to create a portal leading here. How did you do it?"

"I wanted to."

"You've met Zelia, haven't you?"

"Yes."

"I should have known. She was never completely in or out with the Ceraphirian. She thought we were too extreme, treating sentient creatures like expendable things, never accepting them as equals. So, it doesn't surprise me that she reached out."

"You once felt like them."

"Yes. I knew nothing else. My experience with Frederick Severe changed all of that. I kept him prisoner here for one hundred eighty-one years, but I never entered this space until you stumbled through the entrance. I had the shadow man, who I would inevitably use to torture Frederick, shackle him after he ventured inside. It's less of a cave than it is a trap."

"His hammer. Would it have a kind of naturally occurring indigo in it because it was created by a Ceraphirian?"

"Yes," Theta says in disbelief that she missed this fact. "I once controlled what mind he had, but let it go dormant after releasing Frederick."

"Could she have woken him?"

"Absolutely."

"Then she would have had him dash the chain to bits."

On our feet, I point to the door, saying, "I can't leave that way. We're too far from the dome."

"I can send you back. I created the rules of this space. Though, you seem to have broken a few."

"Only out of necessity."

"No. I'm impressed. You have done something no Ceraphirian could, breach this place's defenses."

We fall silent for a moment. Commingling with the sound of water dripping from above, I hear a scraping noise underneath us. I approach the edge of the flat-top, rock island. Peering over, I ignite my hand so that I can cast light down into the deep, clear blue water. I hold steady for a while. Then I see it, a figure slowly scaling the side of the island, under the water. It's Frieda.

Cautiously, the two of us step back and wait for her to surface. "How?"

"She learned through watching you and absorbing your thoughts as you manipulated the physics of this place. She's likely been doing so since you first met her. She's extraordinarily manipulative, even if she's not physically powerful."

"She doesn't need to breathe?"

"No. She isn't mortal."

I think to boil her, but realize it would collapse the island. She's too close now, anyway.

Frieda crawls over the edge of the island and stands to face us. To my surprise, her face still carries the two knife-blade-shaped scars I gave her on either cheek.

"Hello, sister," Theta says, greeting her.

Frieda stares at the two of us without speaking, seething with anger.

I hear Frieda's voice in my head. It's just garbled noise glancing off of my consciousness, having no effect. Aware of her failure, Frieda turns her attention to Theta. Under her control, Frieda forces Theta to reach down and grabs me up by my collar, lifting me to her blank face. I can see the indigo lighting crashing through the sticky, white surfaces of her otherwise dead eyes.

With no hesitation, I turn my left hand toward Frieda and cause a brief gust of hurricane-force wind to blow in her direction. Her body is thrown off the island, over the water, and onto the ground near the cave entrance.

She tries fruitlessly to enter my mind again. I look up to see Theta blinking, her eyes back to normal. Just as she regains her bearing, her eyes begin to deaden again as Frieda reignites her psychological attack. But, before they go completely white, her pupils begin to reappear. Slowly at first, then they flash back to normal.

"That won't work any longer, Frieda. And that's the only ability you have," Theta says, defiantly.

"I can't defeat you, but I can control them," Frieda says, pointing to the cave entrance. They, in turn, can destroy her," she says pointing in my direction, "ending this pointless delay."

"It won't work on all of them," Theta says.

"It works on a large minority. Honestly, I expected more from you, Theta. But, you're only a Ceraphirian of the physical realm. You don't understand the conscious mind."

"I understand something you do not, sister. Empathy."

"What do you want?" I question Frieda.

"For you to surrender to Abraham."

"As a demigod, you're probably not used to being spoken to this way, but fuck you."

Unphased by my insult, Frieda says, "If you don't, then nothing will be off the table."

"It's already that way."

Pausing, Frieda says, "You'll see."

Furious at her threat, I begin to pull heat from the earth underneath Frieda. She begins backing away, attempting to find her way around, but I keep pushing it toward her. As she begins to run down the narrow cave, I cause a wave of lava to run behind her. I wait to hear her screams, but instead, I watch as Frieda dives through the cave entrance and out into the human world.

"Run little rabbit," I whisper under my breath.

"She's more dangerous than ever, now," Theta says in disbelief.

I force the ground to cool, leaving a black floor made of volcanic glass.

"I'm going after her," I say.

"No!" You're needed back with the others.

I hesitate.

"A cat will instinctively chase almost any small, fast-moving object without understanding why. The stimuli are all it takes. You are a bit like that," Theta says.

I calm myself.

"The scars on her face?"

"It seems that Ceraphirians are as susceptible to lamentation blades as the beasts are."

"Those scars are permanent?"

"As is her acrimony," Theta says, just before taping me lightly on the forehead. Seconds later, I wake up in my sleeping bag.

It's Friday, April eighth. Rebecca and I spent most of the morning waiting for Herschel and Nate to return from their first indigo production run.

Upon their arrival, Herschel shouts from out of sight to alert us of their presence. This time, Rebecca doesn't bust his balls and tells them to come straight in.

"Well?" Rebecca says to Herschel.

"It worked," Nate replies, putting words into Herschel's mouth.

"It made a lot," Herschel says. "I mean a whole lot," he continues, holding his arms wide, as to add a flourish to his statement.

"Running more would be gratuitous," Nate says. "I have never seen anything like it. The Petrie dish inside the cone overflowed. We have pounds and pounds of the stuff. It's all stored in the thick, black, commercial-grade trash bags we brought for waste. There was no point in attempting to store them in the one-gallon freezer bags."

"Your blood is extremely potent," Herschel says. "Probably more so than when Joseph was using it."

"Zelia?" Rebecca asks.

"Without a doubt," I reply.

"The four of us settle in for lunch while we contemplate our next move.

After a few moments of silence, I say, "I'm going to go back to see her after I digest."

"Are you sure?" Nate questions.

"Very."

By mid-afternoon, I've gathered the nerve required to approach the spot and begin my journey to see Zelia. The transition is no less jarring the third time around.

"Persistent," Zelia says when I arrive.

"Stubborn," I reply.

Zelia says nothing, but the look in her eyes shows a level of respect not present before. Zelia draws a ball of light into existence, larger than either of us. It pulses with an electric hum, like the intensity of a star rotating quickly.

"The way you're able to weave your consciousness through the Earth, you can do the same with reality itself."

"How am I supposed to do that?"

"Step inside."

"Inside the light?"

"Yes."

Time on the other side is always at a premium. I don't waste it and do what she asks. There is a hot-white flash. I feel myself floating in a bright, comfortable, warm embrace. It's as though each of my cells detaches from its neighbors and I disintegrate. I'm scattered in every direction, like rice at a wedding.

As I begin to reassemble, I feel the universe come along with me, indelibly touching every fragment of my being. After, there is a peaceful silence.

I take a substantial gasping breath as I wake up in Nate's arms.

"You were gone for nearly five minutes. This can't go on any longer or you are going to die."

"I had to," I reply, coughing.

Nate pauses for a moment as he studies my face.

"Your eyes," he gasps.

"They're not green anymore, they're indigo," Rebecca articulates what Nate cannot.

"Can you see okay," Herschel asks, standing further away than the others.

"I can see you just fine. In fact, my vision is sharper than ever."

"How do you feel?" Rebecca asks.

"A lot lighter and can hear everything, down to the tiny droplets of water falling thirty feet away. I already feel like I can stand."

Without assistance, I rise to my feet.

"It feels like any limb of my body touching the ground creates a connection. My consciousness spreads out of them like mycelium expanding through the soil. I can map the cavern, mineshaft, and dome in my mind like a bat with echolocation. I can even extend it above ground into the mega-church. I only sense three people moving inside of it, likely a cleaning crew before Sunday's big service."

The three of them smile.

"It worked?" Rebecca asks.

"I think so. I really do."

"Watch," I say, as I reach out with my mind and grab one of the boulders at the top of the cave-in with my mind. It's the size of a Volkswagen Beetle. I cause it to roll down the stack. Just as it reaches the halfway point, I force it to crumble into dust.

"I think we should head back to the dome and place a phone call," Nate says.

"But beforehand, we need to visit the weapons room. I've been avoiding it, but I think I'm ready," I say.

I open the familiar, solid metal door. Inside the blue-tinted fluorescent bulbs still burn, one flickering every few seconds. There's a substantial amount of dried blood on the wall near the ladder to the manhole cover.

"From the look of things, they must have sent down dozens of young men over the years," I say.

"They don't even care about their own," Herschel says, shaking his head.

We gather up as many MREs as we can manage and leave everything else as it was. As we approach the mineshaft, I stop. With the map of the physical space in my mind, I cause an archway to form on the wall to the left of the mineshaft entrance. It leads directly to the inside of the dome. The three of them follow me through with no questions asked.

On the other side, we immediately put down our gear and head directly up to the observation platform. There, I open the rock dome and Rebecca places the call.

There's a puzzled look on her face. "They're not answering."

Rebecca tries several more times, alternating between Tiff, Diane, Malcolm, and Zeke's phone numbers. Nothing.

"Let me tap into the internet," Herschel says, motioning for the phone.

"The tracking app is showing all four of their phones on the side of the road in Upper Marlboro, east of Washington D.C.," Herschel says.

"What?" I reply with fearful anger in my voice.

"What the fuck? Herschel gasps. I received an anonymous email yesterday.

"What does it say?"

"It says, *Open the Video.*"

Herschel clicks. Then we wait an agonizing ten minutes for it to load over the slow satellite bandwidth.

A still image from the video finally materialized right before it was ready to play. In the center is Little Milly. On her left stands Abraham, and on her right...

I scream. I want to claw my brain out through my skull for forcing me to be a conscious lifeform.

But, when the video begins to play, his voice is unmistakable, "Hello, girlie," Vernon Proffit says.

40

The Earth rumbles underneath us, caused by my outburst of emotion. I collect myself before I collapse the entirety of Yancey County into the bowels of Hell. Herschel hits the pause button on the video playback. Everyone braces themselves. Another wave of tectonic movement washes over us.

"They know you got the email now," Rebecca says with emotional exhaustion.

Tears roll down my face as I reach over to restart the video.

Little Milly is shaking conspicuously. Her eyes are red as though she's been crying. There's a thick black sheet behind them, obscuring any distinguishable characteristics about their surroundings.

"Things would have been simpler if you'd died when you were supposed to. But, you've never been one for doing what they're told by their betters. I underestimated that tendency before, and it cost me dearly. But this time, I've got something you cherish more than your own life. This little brat right here," Vernon says, snatching Little Milly's wrist up over her head, as though she were raising her hand in class.

Little Milly begins to cry uncontrollably, screaming, "Momma,

Daddy, Momma-Naomi!"

In her six-and-half-year-old mind, we're the only people who can make it all stop. But we're not there to answer her cries. That fact guts me.

Pointing at the screen, Vernon says, "Girlie, you have two options for how this is all going to end. Hand yourself over to us. If you don't, I will do everything I did to you, to her. But this time, I'll finish the job."

"You brought this on yourself," Abraham says in a deep voice. The tip of his nose moves as he talks. "Not everyone gets a happy ending. That doesn't have to be the case for the little girl. She's inconsequential. Come in and we'll let her go."

Another figure walks into the screen from the right.

It's a scarred face and voice I recognize. Frieda. She's mortal now. Her word from Theta's cave came back to me. She said, "Nothing will be off the table." Now, I know what she meant.

"You will meet us eight days from now, on Friday, April fifteenth," Frieda says. "At noon, you will climb up the ladder to the chapel. We know you've been skulking around under there. We'll be waiting."

Afterward, the screen goes blank. I tuck my head between my knees and release a series of involuntary guttural noises, followed by more screaming.

Somewhere in the middle of my fit, the phone in Rebecca's hand rings.

"Hello," she says, answering it on speakerphone.

"Rebecca?" a voice I recognize responds. It's Diane.

"Where are you? Is everyone okay?"

"No. They have Little Milly."

"We know. They sent us a video."

"How does she look?"

"Frightened, but she doesn't look physically hurt. Where are you?"

"A hotel in downtown Baltimore. We figured it was best to go somewhere with a lot of eyes."

"How did they…?"

"Getting off the bus yesterday. Three men with their faces covered with black balaclavas swooped in and snatched her away. Zeke heard me scream and followed after me as I began to chase them down. He had his sidearm but couldn't take a shot without risking hitting Little Milly. We didn't call the police. We were afraid that if they were pursued, they might kill her."

While they talk, Nate moves toward me and wraps his skinny arms around my torso.

"My baby girl," I hear my bride cry in the background.

That hurts so much. If I'd known, I would have turned myself in without hesitation when Frieda told me to. But there are no do-overs in this reality.

I motion to Rebecca, and she hands me the phone.

I turn off the speakerphone function.

"Hey, Diane. Would you mind If I spoke to Tiff?"

"Of course not. Give her a second."

I hear Tiffany loudly blowing her nose.

A cracked version of Tiffany's high-pitched voice answers, "Hi, baby."

"They sent us a video. Little Milly's on it. She doesn't seem to be hurt, but the only way they'll release her is if I turn myself into them."

A pained wail comes through the speaker.

"There's no choice. I won't leave her to them. All they want is my blood."

"Which they'll use to make indigo and build an indestructible army of beasts and hateful rubes."

"I know. You'll have to live a life in hiding. It won't be easy, but you can make it through with our little girl.

"Don't let them do this."

"What choice do I have? I'll always choose our daughter, no matter the consequences."

"I know. But it's all up to you now."

There's silence on the line while I take in Tiffany's statement.

"I'll take care of it. Once you have her back, get as far away from here as you can. Leave the country. The Apostle's doctrine will take a long time to reach Southeast Asia. Maybe you can whittle out a peaceful lifespan for her somewhere like Thailand?"

"Our plans went from growing old together to living off the grid in another country?"

"I don't have a better solution."

"Are they going to set up a time and place to hand her back over?"

"I don't know. All I can do right now is trust the most dishonest man I've ever met. Motherhood demands it."

Tiffany lets out a bittersweet laugh at my candidness.

"I suppose," she says, voice straining.

"Can I talk to Nate? He's her father, after all."

"Of course. He's right next to me."

After Nate takes hold of the phone, I get up and walk down the stairs, unable to deal with the current situation emotionally. I trek around the interior of the dome three times, gliding my left hand along her surfaces. Once my mind is centered, I head back up. By then, Nate is speaking to Malcolm.

When they get close to the end of their conversation, I say, "When you're done, put it back on speakerphone."

After a few seconds, Nate clicks it back over to speaker mode and lays the handset between us all.

"I need to get y'all out of there. But I can only create a portal to a place that I know well. The nearest point to y'all is the house in Tysons Corner."

"Their men are probably crawling all over it," Tiffany says.

"That's what roaches do. Stay where you are tonight. What car are you driving?"

"The Subaru," Diane replies.

"Good. I want you to stuff it full of non-perishable foods, toiletries, medicine, bandages, plastic storage bags, sewing kits, spare fabric, and anything else you can think of you'll need for long-term survival. Then meet us at our house at two in the morning on Sunday the tenth. By then, all of them will be gone."

"How are you going to get here?" Tiffany replies.

"I'll make a doorway."

"Are you sure?"

"Very."

"Then what?"

"Y'all will come through the portal to be here with us until it's time."

"But—"

"If they catch you, you're going to become another bargaining chip for them. There's no place safer than behind five feet of Appalachian granite. We'll figure it out in a few days. But I'd like to spend what time I have left with you all, as a family."

"We can do that."

"I have to go, the battery is fixing to die."

"We love y'all."

"We love you, too."

When the phone line goes dead, my insides feel drained. The

four of us stare at each other for a few seconds before I begin to close the roof above us. Besides preparing dinner, the remainder of the night is filled with quiet reflection and internalized what-ifs. All the while knowing that within thirty-six hours, we will be murdering every Apostle guarding our house in Tysons Corner. I'm looking forward to it.

I have a fleeting worry that they'll retaliate. Then I remember the copious blood stains around the ladder leading from the chapel down into the weapons room. I realize that their goals are only for those at the very top of their internal hierarchy. Everyone else is a tool to be used, stored, or discarded. They will pay their losses with little mind.

41

I wake up the next morning, Saturday, April ninth after a sleep filled with roiling nightmares. In them, I saw the love of my life, Tiffany, and our daughter's bodies ripped to pieces by gunfire. Their faces were gone from extensive damage. Limbs were severed, lying in jumbled piles on the ground.

What could they be doing to Little Milly? I've wondered to myself every few minutes after seeing the video.

The biggest question is, how did Vernon Proffit return? At the moment, it doesn't matter. The consequences are the same. Still, I was certain he was doomed. I left him many miles offshore, sitting on a whale carcass. The sharks circling him would have finished whatever job exposure started.

I think back to the video and realize what was off. His right eye. I blinded him with shrapnel during my escape. But it appeared normal. It didn't have the sheen of glass. No one would make a prosthetic eye that appears to be extremely bloodshot. This was the real thing. That means he was delivered from the Woods of Lamentation.

Mordecai, you fucking bastard, I say to myself.

"I want to go back and visit Zelia," I say at breakfast.

"Absolutely not," Nate replies. "If you're incapacitated, you will be sending our family into a trap. What if I can't get through to their burner phone? There are too many things that could go wrong. Put it out of your mind, Naomi."

"Nate's right. You keep your ass right here," Rebecca says.

I find myself feeling like Little Milly again, but they're right.

Herschel looks at his food, saying nothing. Though, I know he agrees with them.

"I'll go after," I reply to Rebecca.

"Do you really want to let Tiff watch you die?"

"No. She can stay here in the dome."

"Why are you being so obtuse? I think one person dying three times in a week is enough," Rebecca says.

I can't manifest an answer, so I sit in silence, sipping coffee, while eating another awful meal.

The remainder of our day is quiet. We try to relax and save our energy. Luckily, I've been retired to the spectator section for their inane games. We watch the clock tick by, waiting for our red light to turn green.

———

As midnight rolls into view on the temporal horizon, we begin preparing. I wield the Lamentation gun Zeke made. Nate and Rebecca carry pump-action shotguns and sidearms. Nate only carries a Glock Nineteen, nine-millimeter.

"I'll broadcast the doorway inside of Zeke's shed at our Tysons Corner house," I say. "Your weapons are options of last resort. This ain't the country. Wealthy white folks will call the cops if their neighbor's cat barfs on their lawn. Gunfire will bring them in fewer than three minutes. They won't be like the Burnsville Police or Yancey Sheriff's Department, on the take for the Apostles. These will be real police officers. I don't have any interest in engaging them. If the cops come, we retreat."

I easily cause a doorway to appear underneath the dome stairs. On the other side is a night just cool enough to cause someone's breath to condense into mist as they exhale. Rebecca goes first, followed by Herschel, Nate, and then myself. Shortly after appearing on the other side, I release my hold on the fabric of reality. The doorway dwindles to a point and then vanishes.

"I thought Frieda said you wouldn't be able to travel through your own doorways until you loved yourself?" Nate asks.

"When you have a child, you have to care for your own well-being, so you can take care of theirs."

Nate gives me a glance that lets me know he understands exactly what I mean.

"They won't have anyone conspicuous stationed outside because of the dense population. But, there's likely a lookout posted in a car nearby. He's there as a warning system for our home invaders."

I place my left hand on the concrete shed foundation and say, "I see three men in the house, and one sitting in a sedan across the street. There's something else. A Beast of Lamentation similar to those Joseph created. They're all wearing body armor, likely laced with indigo."

"How have they made this much indigo?" Herschel asks.

"My little girl," Nate says. "They're bleeding her."

"I'm like a sunlamp. If you're around me long enough, the glow from the light in my chest will wear off on you. Who better to collect from that the little girl who crawls all over me every day?"

"It's not your fault," Nate says.

"It's theirs. I'm going to see that the local coffin maker can afford to send their kids to college."

"How are you planning on doing that?" Herschel asks.

"Wait here. I'll show you," I say while forming a smaller archway inside the workshop.

I use an image of my running path with Herschel and Rebecca to create the exit doorway. It comes up right behind the car. Without warning to my companions, I run through.

As I do so, I reach down into my lefthand pocket and unclip my green-handled auto knife. I press the button to extend the blade, then flip the handle so that it's positioned backhanded.

The car is a white Crown Victoria. Despite the vehicle's age, it could easily have been misidentified as an undercover police cruiser.

I run on the right-hand side of the empty road. The stationary car is coming up on my right, directly across from our house on the left. When I'm close enough to read the North Carolina plates on the back, I dart off to the right and up onto the grass. To my right is a tall, weathered privacy fence.

I ignite the knife into a lamentation blade, then jab its point into the front passenger side window. This causes it to crumble into indigo-colored dust.

I dive through the window head-first and immediately slash the driver's right wrist, nearly severing his hand. This causes him to drop the smartphone he was holding. It was one command away from placing a call to his coconspirators. It lands screen-side down, causing the interior of the car to go dark.

He's a plump white man in his mid-forties wearing a flak jacket. There is utter shock painted across his red face as he looks me in the eye, my long legs still hanging out of the passenger side window.

He says, "Abraham promised nothing could hurt us," just as I jammed the blade into his throat. The man attempts to scream. Instead, all that can be heard is wet gasping noises as breaths through the gaping slit in his windpipe. Seconds later, he begins to spasm as his soul is shaken off and cast into the Woods of Lamentation.

With the lookout removed from the picture, I create another archway. This one leads back into Zeke's workshop where Rebecca, Nate, and Herschel wait.

The blood on your coveralls tells me all I need to know," Nate says, deadpan.

"Stay behind me," I say to the three of them as I open the workshop's front door.

We crouch down as we make our way to the back porch. Here, we've celebrated many birthdays and enjoyed warm afternoons. It feels bizarre to now be treating these innocent wood planks like a battlefield.

The French doors are locked. I put my left hand on the door and feel through the floors and walls. One man is asleep in Diane's bedroom, which is to our left. Another is in my and Tiff's, on our right. The third is in Malcolm and Nate's bedroom upstairs. All seem to be relaxed.

"They're not moving," I whisper. "I can't say for certain, but they're likely asleep. What isn't sleeping is the beast I sense walking through the foyer."

On my new lamentation gun is a slide button that can be pushed upward or downward by the shooter's thumb. When the switch goes up, a six-inch bayonet extends quickly out the front of the blued steel, rectangular box underneath the muzzle of the gun.

Zeke had to make it this way so the Hummer could accommodate the driver's side holster he created for the weapon. Otherwise, it would have been too long and posed a risk to the driver's right leg. Pushing the slide button down retracts the blade.

Still crouching, I extend and ignite the bayonet. I use it to slice through the deadbolt between the frame and the righthand door. I slowly open it and peek inside just in time to see the beast charging me from across the house.

42

The creature is similar in form to those that Joseph created nine years ago. They're dogs that the Apostles force-feed indigo to. The transformation is traumatic and painful. The resulting creature has no volition of its own. They're simple killing machines.

These false Beasts of Lamentation have brown leathery skin, and long gray, conical beaks. They part horizontally down the center, revealing two rows of pointy teeth. There's a pair on top and another on the bottom. The four upper canines are so long that there are corresponding holes for them to protrude through in the lower beak. Their front-facing eyes are indigo like mine are now.

Am I a beast?

Jagged, black obsidian forms a row of cutting glass down the back like a mohawk, extending atop a long, lizard-like tail. Its whipping motion could easily deal a fatal blow.

From nose to tail, the monster is about six feet long. Its rear legs are hinged backward. The black claws on all four feet are sharp and about a foot in length. There are only two ways to kill them, a lamentation blade or full immersion in water. I'll have to kill it with either my knife or bayonet charged as a lamentation blade if I want to stay covert.

The Lamentation gun fires custom, long 4.10 shells containing six-inch stainless-steel spears. Each is linked back to the gun temporarily with a thin braided wire. For the time it is linked, I can keep the projectile charged as a modified lamentation blade, destroying them when piercing their body's center mass. The sound of the blast, however, would turn everything to shit.

I raise the bayonet at the end of the lamentation gun, expecting a mindless beast like I've encountered before. Unsettlingly, the beast stops mid-stride. It sees and understands the trap I've set.

"It's thinking," I whisper to my companions.

"How?" Rebecca whispers.

"Frieda can influence minds. She's the Ceraphirian who oversees the development of conscious thought. I imagine it wouldn't be difficult for her to do."

The beast then does the worst thing possible. He screams. I sense the vibration of feet hitting the floor. There's a jostling as the men equip themselves. That gives me a moment to snatch a six-foot sheath of granite from the ground underneath the house and through the floor. It's in front of us just as they begin firing in our direction. Each round pings off the stone surface. In the melee, I lose track of the beast.

Gunfire deafening us, I turn to see it no less than ten feet from our backs, preparing to pounce. I draw the lamentation gun and fire off a round, striking it in the chest while it's in mid-leap. It falls to dust at my feet.

"This has gone sideways. Now the gloves are off," I say.

Guns are still being fired through my house like it's a goddamn range. I reach down into the ground and begin shifting plates below us. The Earth starts to shake. This earthquake isn't like the ones I've released in Yancey County. The ongoing tremor causes car and house alarms to blare a symphony of chaos. sound. Soon, it's mixed with sirens zig-zagging across town.

The firing stops. They're retreating. As I lower our stone shield, I see their back as they file out the front door in a rush.

"Stay behind me," I shout, moving forward through the house in pursuit.

Terrified, and likely empty, they don't fire back. All they want is to be as far from me as possible. Once they reach the Caprice Classic sitting outside, they work together to jerk the dead body of their lookout onto the residential road in front of my house and load up.

I hold my left hand out and blast their car with a strong gust of wind just as they begin to drive away. It flips onto its right side, exposing the belly of the automotive behemoth. I spy the metal fuel intake in the rear between the dual exhausts. Leveling my lamentation gun, I let off a round, piercing it. Without an ignition source, the fuel doesn't ignite, so I surge a lamentation current down the wire, causing the car to become instantly engulfed in flames.

The men scream as they burn alive. One is able to get his charred husk out of the rear passenger window before expiring face down on the blacktop, next to his recently exsanguinated accomplice.

The electricity blinks out as we retreat back into the house, leaving the burning car across the street as the only exterior light source.

"This isn't going to work anymore," Herschel says. We need to move the rendezvous point or at least get out of here."

"You're right," I say, causing an archway to appear.

It leads to Herschel and Rebecca's backyard, half a mile down the road.

On the other side, I feel the ground.

"There are two inside. No beasts," I say.

Foolishly, they left the back door unlocked. There are cigarette butts all over the pace.

"At least they had the courtesy to smoke outdoors," Rebecca comments.

"Stay out here," I say.

The first of the intruders is in their half bath on the right side of the hallway. From the odor, I'd surmise his dinner isn't agreeing with him. The other is asleep in Herschel and Rebecca's bed. I approach him first, slowly opening the closed-over door.

The thirty-something, bearded man is sleeping soundly with an indigo flak jacket around his torso. I raise the bayonet and thrust it into his exposed right underarm. With one lung pierced, he screams silently as he drowns in his own blood.

I catch the toilet man just as he turns off the bathroom light.

The last thing he sees is the glowing eyes of a woman taller than himself, whose hands are jabbing a crackling lamentation bayonet into his throat.

"Are you going to do anything with the bodies?" Herschel asks.

"No. I want them to be found. They should be afraid. Their fear of what will happen if they harm Little Milly might be the only thing that gets her out of this unscathed."

Rebecca and Herschel still have a landline, so instead of stepping outside to use the satellite phone, I use it to call Tiffany's cellphone.

"Naomi?" Tiffany answers.

"Yes."

"Did you cause the earthquake?"

"Um, yeah. Four dead men are burning in an upended car across from our front lawn."

"Oh, no. I hope Ted's Weimaraners are okay. Their fence wasn't on fire when you left, was it?"

"Not when I left, no," I answer very diplomatically. How strong was it?"

"According to the radio, it was a magnitude five point nine. It's the largest on record."

"I hope I didn't hurt anyone that didn't have it coming."

"I think it's more startling than anything. It caused branches to fall across power lines. Mostly, folks are just unsettled. We aren't used to this on the east coast. Luckily, there are no injuries or deaths reported."

"Can you get to Rebecca and Herschel's house? It's time to go."

"We're heading your way. We should get there in ten minutes."

"Alright. I love you. See you in a few."

"Love you, too," Tiff says before the line goes dead.

The four of us stand on guard in Herschel and Rebecca's dark living room waiting for our family to arrive. That, or Apostle reinforcements.

Eight minutes later, the phone rings. It's Tiff and she's panicked.

"Someone in a white van is following us. At first, they kept their distance. Now, they have their high beams on and are on our tail blaring their horn."

"Head this way. When you drive past the house, tell Diane to press the accelerator to the floor to put some distance between y'all and the van. I'll handle the rest."

With that, I hang up and run out the front door.

There, I see headlights coming through the trees. Diane revs the Subaru's engine and it comes to life. This allows them to pull away from the van's intrusion into their space. I heat the Earth underneath the van. Its tires begin to melt, then their wheels and rotors, until they're sliding across the asphalt, spinning, on what remains of their frame.

While it does, I open an archway large enough for their car. Diane drives through.

43

I close the archway Diane just drove the Subaru through with Tiffany, Malcolm, and Zeke as passengers. The white van carrying the Apostles continues careening, throwing sparks as its differential is ground up into metal shards by the blacktop. It comes to a stop directly in front of Rebecca and Herschel's house, putting us all in their line of sight. Dizzy from spiraling through the street like a pinball, the passengers fall out of the stationary van. Despite this, the three we see have guns in their hands and indigo-infused body armor around their chests.

I fire a charged round into the chest of the first man attempting to stand on his feet, mortally wounding him. I pull the trigger again, hitting the man next to him in the head. This kills him instantly. Now, two shells remain in my lamentation gun.

I fire off the next to last shell into the neck of the most affected man. What catches me off guard is the fourth Apostle. He exits the other side, running around the front of the vehicle and opening fire with a pistol. The rounds ping wide off of the concrete of the walkway in front of the house. They miss us, only to fly randomly toward the house of an annoying but innocent neighbor.

I pull a large sheath of granite up from the ground between us as a shield from a follow-up volley. Like prophecy, we hear the pistol rounds striking the stone protecting us.

I can feel where he's standing. With every step he takes towards us, my mental image of his location sharpens. I picture the scene directly behind the approaching figure and open an archway. I step through and immediately shoot him between the shoulder blades. It's fatal. The spear drives itself through his heart. After exiting the front of his chest, it glances off the granite shield I pulled in front of us moments earlier.

With my magazine empty, I cock open the six-shot cylinder, using the oversized spindle on the lefthand side of the custom firearm. Six empty, ten-inch long .410 shotgun shell casings fall onto the concrete with slight hollow plastic resonances. I snap one of my speed loaders off of my belt and reload the empty cylinder, just in case.

I lower the granite I pulled from the Earth minutes before, allowing it to drag the empty casings with it. This exposes Rebecca, Nate, and Herschel who were still taking cover behind it.

"That's all of them. Let's get back home."

"This used to be home," Herschel says with melancholy.

"It will be again," I reply.

"I know," Herschel says, with obvious doubt.

We retreat into the house. I open an archway in the living room. It leads to the dome wall under the observation deck's stone staircase. The indigo illumination of the portal lights up the opposite wall, projecting our figures as four shadows before quickly closing.

Diane had come to a screeching halt inside the dome. She pulled her Subaru to the right of the Hummer. This left the two vehicles parked front to back, driver's side doors opposite to one another.

Tiffany emerges from behind the vehicles first, then runs to me full force. She lunges her tiny body in my direction. I pick her up off the ground as she cries on my shoulder. Her tears flow like a storm surge of unyielding sorrow.

"I don't want to lose you, too," she says in my ear.

"You aren't going to lose anyone. My freedom will only be delayed."

"Your eyes."

"Zelia," I say without explanation.

Diane wraps her arms around Herschel, as Malcolm does Nate. I look over Tiffany's shoulder to see Rebecca somewhat sullen. She never knew her parents, though Diane has been a wonderful substitute. As she has been for Nate and me, who our own biological families rejected. Eventually, Rebecca walks over to Diane and slides in for her own hug.

Tears drying, Tiffany says, "So this is what you've been doing?" Referring to the dome.

"There's more," I reply.

I catch a glimpse of overwhelming awe on Zeke's face as he looks up at the quickly spreading bioluminescent lichen.

He says, "I've taken many heroic doses of psilocybin mushrooms, but it was never this real."

"It's all real, even though it was made only using my mind."

Zeke is a difficult man to impress, but I see him silently mouth, *wow*.

The tour is minimal since it's mostly empty space. Eventually, we all end up sitting on the observation deck. I open it to demonstrate how we make calls and access the internet.

"I think about her every single second," Tiff says aloud, to herself, here with us, but not entirely.

"She's still alive," I say.

"But won't he—"

"No. Only girls who've reached menses. It's part of the prophecy."

"Not all of them abide by the rules."

"They wouldn't dare. In their eyes, she belongs to Vernon. Assaulting her would mean death and certain damnation afterward."

"That makes me nauseated," Malcolm says, visibly uncomfortable.

"It's about to get worse," Herschel says to Malcolm. "I'm going to check the news and email. Vernon has likely sent us something by now."

"I can't," Diane says. "I'm going to go back downstairs. I want to know the truth, but I just can't look any longer."

Tiff makes a face that lets me know she feels the same. She catches up to Diane and begins holding her hand as they make their way to the bottom of the stairs. Malcolm kisses Nate on the cheek and follows suit. Zeke doesn't budge. There's a seething anger building up inside of him with crosshairs directly aimed at the Apostles of the Cloven Hand. That is something I understand better than anyone.

Just as everyone who has opted out reaches the bottom, I cause the mossy patch where we've been sleeping to double in size, making way for more sleeping bags.

As they begin to unpack, Herschel boots up the laptop.

After a brief search, Herschel says, "The authorities have descended on our houses. The media has dubbed it *The Earthquake Double Massacre*. The speculation over how so many murders could have taken place in two scenes, nearly simultaneously while an earthquake raged is unending. However, being that all the dead were heavily armed and dressed in tactical armor, detectives are hypothesizing that they were likely killed in self-defense."

"Were there any witnesses?" I ask.

"No. It all happened so fast. Everyone was still cowering in their doorways because of the quake and it was dark from the ensuing power outage. There's no video, either. Detectives aren't sure about our identities yet."

"It won't take long before journalists put it all together. My guess is we'll be considered victims of kidnapping," I reply.

"There's an email from Abraham," Herschel says. "It states, *Next time, blood will be met with blood.*"

"I can only imagine he means Little Milly," Zeke says, breaking his furious silence.

There's a campaign video called *Proffit for Lieutenant Governor*, attached. It features Vernon, showing a fabricated life where Little Milly is his adopted granddaughter. He calls her Mildred Proffit, which makes me ill. Frighteningly, the rallies pictured in the video are disturbingly large. Their fervor isn't about policies. Belonging to the Apostles has quickly become a personal identity and excuse to claim authority over the lives of their fellow citizens. They even seem obliged to circumvent the law itself when it becomes inconvenient. All while touting the virtues of the Constitution and law enforcement.

"I'm worried that he's going to try to take her to one of these rallies as a prop. What lies he must be filling her mind with," I say.

"She's extremely smart. It won't take," Zeke says.

"Pain is funny like that. It swiftly deconstructs intelligence."

44

It's nearly four in the morning by the time the emotional tsunamis churned up by what we saw on the recording die down. It's at that point that we force ourselves to attempt to sleep out of necessity.

I wake first, at ten in the morning. Everyone but Nate sleeps past noon. Partially it's exhaustion, but also depression.

Little is eaten. Less is said.

We trudge through the week getting ready. Rebecca, Nate, Herschel, Zeke, and I empty what remains inside the old Solid Rock weapons room. I create an archway between the room and our dome to expedite the chore.

We have reclaimed a year-and-a-half worth of food, one-hundred-twelve M-16s, two-hundred-three Glock nineteens, seventy-one tactical vests, and a shit ton of ammo.

There are hundreds of gallons of water. We leave it. It's extra weight for nothing since we have our own spring.

Diane teaches Tifanny and Malcolm to sew. Their task is to stitch fabric pouches containing indigo inside enough vests to keep all of us safe. They're rolled up in sealable sandwich bags about the diameter of a cigar, sewn into thick fabric, and then stitched into place inside the vests. In theory, the jackets should protect the wearer from anything but a lamentation blade. That's how they work for the Apostles.

When they're finished, everyone but myself tries theirs on. Indigo has the opposite effect on me. It voids my abilities. I've been wearing an unmodified tactical vest and will continue to do so.

I test an extra indigo vest with a nine-millimeter round. It doesn't work. The vest absorbs the round, of course, but there was no shielding as we've witnessed with the Apostle's armor and indigo-lined clothing. I believe it has to be worn by a person to work. But I'm not firing a live round at any of my family members. I don't even mention it because Nate would likely volunteer. No one else seemed to acquire abilities like Abraham or Joseph did. Regardless, the vests as they are could still save their lives.

On the afternoon of Thursday, the fourteenth, two-thousand-sixteen, I ask Herschel to let me use the laptop so that I can personally respond to Abraham. The log-on time is excruciatingly long, but once the window is open on the document, it operates just like any word processor.

I type,

Abraham. This is Naomi Pace.

I am going to willingly turn myself in tomorrow on the condition that you allow Little Milly to climb down the ladder and back to her family. Then, you will let them leave unharmed. If not, I will collapse the cavern below. Without the water and rock, your ability to make more indigo will have a severe terminal limit. The Ceraphirian consider this a holy place. Despite that, I would burn it, and the entire world, to the ground for her. Take caution that

I spend the next few hours with my family, reminiscing about the times gone by. Much of it, I have no memory of. I still feel as though I were as much a part of it, even though I was trapped unconscious in the Woods of Lamentation for seven years. I could be gone for good this time. I don't care as long as Little Milly gets back home.

Out of nowhere, Herschel asks, "What's your plan?"

I pause for a moment.

"You, Rebecca, Nate, And Zeke will come with me. I'll keep the portal open between the dome and cavern. Once you have Little Milly back, all of you will pass through it and load up into the Hummer. I'll open a door for y'all to drive through. Likely, somewhere in Raleigh since there's an airport close by. I figure the abandoned K-Mart parking lot on Western Boulevard. After escaping, I lived in the complex behind it. I walked in and out of there hundreds of times when the store was still open, so I should have no problem visualizing it. If you can't get out for some reason, there are two-and-a-half year's worth of food in here. They'll leave you undisturbed in the dome as a bargaining chip so that I'll be compliant. They know no matter how brilliantly crafted the device meant to keep me imprisoned is, it will have weaknesses, like all things. In the worst-case scenario, I have two-and-a-half years to free myself. I've done it before."

"And, if we get out, we just flee the country?" Herschel asks.

"Exactly that. Cults often begin by infiltrating other religions. There's no shortage of those in the United States. That's how the Apostles come into power in the first place. Their cerebral virus has begun spreading beyond the snake handlers and into the mainstream Evangelical churches. The world is changing around them, which has stoked their fear. The Apostles are selling them an antidote with promises of violence against those whose existence makes them uncomfortable."

"But, you're going to collapse the cavern anyway, aren't you?"

"You're goddamn right. Don't worry, all of you will be out in time."

We head to bed around midnight. I lie with my eyes closed, pretending to sleep until I'm certain everyone has dozed off. I can tell because I'm familiar with each person's breathing patterns. Once I'm to my feet, I make my way to the far wall, near the mineshaft. I open an archway leading to the dome. Once on the other side, I step onto the spot where Charles died and begin my final journey to Zelia.

I calmly accept the transition to temporary death, letting the light absorb me and deposit my consciousness at Zelia's celestial doorstep.

"Time is closing in on you," Zelia says from behind me.

"No two ways about it."

"The last time you were here, the motherlight disintegrated you."

"God?"

"A piece of her, yes."

"It felt like the process reorganized me somehow. My blood feels like it's charged. My eyes used to be green."

"They certainly aren't anymore," Zelia says, leaning in to take a closer look. "They're indigo."

"But why?"

"You've been drinking water from the cavern and inhaling the dust. Your blood is now producing its own indigo."

"The veins in my forearms are becoming indigo-tinted. They remind me of Svangi."

Just after saying this, I wince and look at the point on my hand that twinged when I first left Svangi here nine years ago.

"That's not far off from the truth. The Beasts of Lamentation are built out of indigo, and animated with basic instincts."

"Like a golem?"

"Exactly," Zelia says, looking me over.

"What's wrong?"

"When I see you, I recognize Naomi, but my intuition senses a Beast of Lamentation."

"But my body is made of water. Indigo can't get wet. I should be disintegrating, like when Joseph pelted me with indigo during Tropical Storm Gabrielle on top of the Frying Pan Tower."

"Yours exists before the vaporization stage. It needs to exit your body and come into contact with fresh air before it can become the dry indigo you're accustomed to."

"So, I'll mist when I bust my knuckle working on a car?"

"Yes. If it's not condensed and captured, the indigo in your blood will disperse harmlessly into the atmosphere."

"When you harness it, you'll become as powerful as one of them, combined with the abilities you already possess."

"How have I acquired some of Theta's?"

"Only a select few of the most determined and pernicious will develop abilities when wearing indigo. Those without the intellectual capacity or ones lacking the desire to subjugate and control others do not. Even then, it takes stamina to push one's self hard enough to develop them. Joseph was such a person and, to a smaller degree, so is Abraham. Vernon Proffit is a lazy man whose only talent is to convince others to do for him. The few who develop abilities reflect those of one of the twelve Ceraphirians. Joseph's reflection is that of Theta. When he died, some of him disintegrated with you and was pulled into the Woods of Lamentation. Those particles reformed in tandem with your body. Now, that part of him is inside of you."

"And who is Abraham's reflection?"

"Alodia. She is the Ceraphirian tasked with the regulation of gravitational fields."

"Now what?"

"You make choices and the rest of us clutch hope and our belief in you close to our exhausted hearts."

My body surges into consciousness, involuntarily gasping for air. I look at my phone. Just before I disappeared it was two-o-three in the morning. I came back at two-o-seven. I've been gone four to five minutes. *Just in time*, I say quietly to myself.

It doesn't take long for me to get my breath back, unlike the first two trips. The third was less so. This one, the fourth, has barely affected me.

I have to get back before anyone realizes I'm gone. I open an archway in the cavern wall leading to the dome. I enter. On the other side, I come face-to-face with my wife, Tiffany.

"What did you do?" she asks.

"I went to see Zelia one last time."

"Died, you mean?"

"That's one way of looking at it."

"I know you stop breathing when you go to her."

"Yes. But it was important.

"I understand," Tiffany says, surprising me. She sighs, "I know you did it for Little Milly out of desperation. I won't allow our last few hours together to be an argument."

"To be fair, I'm compulsive and did stuff like this when it wasn't desperate."

"You said it. I didn't."

"No. Just in case I never see you again, I wanted you to know you were right."

"About what?"

"Basically, everything since the day we met in first grade. Anytime we argued, it was because you were afraid my rashness would get me hurt. I know that now. It's taken too many years for me to realize it."

"Don't worry, we'll have many more to come. I believe in you."

45

Tiff and I unzip our sleeping bags, doubling their surface area. We lay on top of mine and pull Tiffany's atop ourselves. I wrap my arms around her.

Whispering, I say, "This reminds me of our last night together as children. We arranged our blankets the same way on the island while we watched the Perseid meteor shower."

"A day hasn't gone by in the past twenty-three years where I haven't thought about that night. It was one of the best of my life," Tiffany says.

"Until it wasn't."

"I try to think about the first part and imagine what should have happened."

"We went home and finished having childhoods while falling madly in love?"

"I was already there. So were you. But you were so clueless. I spent the week before that night flirting with you."

"Rubbing your foot on mine under the library table? I recall you smelling my head while we sat out on our boulder."

"I like how you smell."

"Thanks?" I say, jokingly. "But, you said I smelled bad."

"You'd been trudging through the woods and creek all day. So, objectively, you did. Either way, you kissed me when I chickened out."

"I've never regretted it."

We both go quiet.

Sleep comes in shallow waves. I'm in and out every few minutes. Eventually, we both slip away.

It's nine in the morning, on Friday, April fifteenth, twenty-sixteen. I have three hours until I'm supposed to turn myself over to the Apostles of the Cloven Hand.

Tiffany inadvertently wakes me when she gets up to visit the bathroom. Everyone else is already milling around. The trepidation in my stomach is sharp and acidic, but I console myself knowing that I'll get to see Little Milly, at least momentarily.

I don't eat, though I drink three cups of coffee.

We're all nervous and quiet like we're reluctantly attending a stranger's funeral.

"We should go check the news and email before you visit upstairs," Herschel says.

"Yeah," I reply in a quiet voice.

Apparently, the earthquake only knocked out the power. A few of my smug neighbors' homes were damaged. Good. I created a lot of work hours for folks who likely need the extra money.

They've identified all of us. I'm named as Hannah Sillman, not Naomi Pace.

Their email read simply,

The Holy Spirit is all the protection we need. When you arrive, Mildred may leave. Know, that afterward, you belong to me until the end of your days.

Pastor, Vernon Proffit.

Those three sentences cause my circulatory system to sizzle.

"Your veins," Nate points out, astonished.

I look down at the inside of my forearm to see my veins illuminated with indigo.

"Your eyes. They're glowing," Rebecca says.

"Zelia said my body is making its own indigo. Becoming angry must have set off some kind of reaction."

As I cool down, the glow recedes. My eyes remain indigo-colored. Just without the backlighting.

"Tiff told us you visited," Nate says.

"I had to. I'll never see her again once the cavern is leveled."

Everyone is quiet after my response.

"I understand. But, if you had died, you wouldn't be here to get Little Milly away from those people," Nate says.

"I trust Zelia. I think she helped me."

"It's just that I'm afraid for my daughter."

"So am I. You have every right to be angry with me."

With no argument to be had, the conversation recedes back into a fearful quiet.

————

Before I close the ceiling, we run the Hummer for half an hour to make sure it's warmed up and ready to start when everyone gets back to it. Nate will drive. Diane is his backup. With the ceiling closed, it's just a matter of two short hours.

————

An hour passes and we begin to prepare. Indigo-laced tactical vests are fitted onto everyone but myself. I don the unaltered flak jacket I've been using since we departed on this journey.

Herschel and Rebecca arm themselves with pump-action shotguns and holstered Glock nineteens. Nate is armed with an identical pistol and nothing else. Zeke has taken one of Solid Rock's old M16s and has his Sig Sauer nine-millimeter. I take the lamentation gun in case they release their false Beasts of Lamentation down the manhole cover. Other than that, I have my left-handed, green auto knife.

The Hummer is going to be packed with bodies, so they're only taking a few days' worth of food and the duffle bag stuff with cash from the safe in the Tysons Corner house. Diane was brilliant enough to grab everyone's passports and cram them into the bag as well. Herschel will launder the money out of the country, through our still-open Vanuatu accounts from our illicit cannabis days.

Diane, Malcolm, and Tiffany will remain in the dome while we're gone. Once my family has Little Milly, I will open a portal big enough to drive through. Afterward, they board a jetliner at Raleigh-Durham International, headed far from here.

The time ticks down until it's ten minutes until noon. I embrace Tiffany. Our tactical vests make it stiff and unnatural. Above them, I'm able to lean down and give her one last kiss. She begins to sob as I create the archway to the cavern. Once through, I turn to take one last glimpse. It makes me feel like Lot's wife. But instead of salt, I'm animated indigo.

I walk wide around the spot where Charles died and am the first one inside the nearly empty weapon's room. The metal ladder embedded into the wall leads to a still-closed manhole cover overhead.

"Well, this is it," I say, as I remove my lamentation gun and hand it to Nate.

The only weapon I keep is the knife in my left pocket, just in case.

At the top of the ladder, I place my hand against the granite wall. I can sense two men standing above me on either side of the manhole cover. There's a cavernous interior above. North, about sixty feet, are several adults and one small human, likely Little Milly.

All the while, I'm keeping the doorway back to the dome open for Rebecca, Zeke, Nate, and Herschel. They're standing directly below, waiting for Little Milly to be handed over so she can be spirited away. I use my left palm to push upward on the heavy lid of the manhole cover. I slide it forward slowly until suddenly its movement accelerates without my effort. I step up into the world above.

The men on either side of me attempt to take me down. Each grabs one of my arms. I light their hands on fire, which spreads to the entirety of their bodies. Both scream as they fall backward into pews on either side. They flail and roll under them until the wood of the pews themselves ignites. Men rush to retrieve fire extinguishers and subdue the blaze while I look on. It's too late for their comrades. The two men lay charred under the smoking pews.

I'm in the center aisle of a mega-church that likely seats five thousand people. The safe and Vernon Proffit's house are long gone. Instead, the manhole was hidden under a piece of carpet that they pulled back.

On stage stands Abraham at the podium. Vernon Proffit sits on his right. Each loves to present themselves elevated so they can speak down to others.

To his left sits a woman with Little Milly on her lap. I don't recognize her at first. After a few seconds, her identity is clear. It's my mother, Dotty Pace. This almost sickens me more than Vernon's presence. Two false Beasts of Lamentation prowl back and forth behind Abraham as he begins to speak.

"You, ma'am, are trouble incarnate."

"No shit?" I answer rhetorically, my voice echoing. "Allow her to leave and I'll let your men cuff me."

I sense four people walking up behind me. They stop ten feet from my location, waiting for commands.

"Are y'all still making those nineteenth-century indigo handcuffs, or have you advanced since Joseph?"

One of the men behind me ratchets a modern set of cuffs forward, creating a familiar audible click.

"That's up to Mildred," Abraham says.

There's a stepstool at the podium for her to stand on so she can reach the microphone.

She walks hand in hand with my mother up to the podium, climbs the two steps, and says, "I want to stay with Mema. You are not my real mother."

Her head is tilted down. I can tell her statement is coerced and conflicted. Years of calm, purposeful parenting on my family's behalf have collided with the shock and awe of bombastic propaganda and hate.

Frieda, I think. She has her tentacles in Little Milly's head. Suddenly, one of the men behind me lunges forward, releasing a hand grenade down into the manhole.

I turn and push the four men with a powerful gust of wind. It throws them back. Pews are upended as the wind lifts them, breaking their bolts loose from the floor. The wood and bodies land in jumbled, broken piles. All are dead.

The grenade releases a fast thud. I keep the portal open as long as I can. The resonance through the rock from the blast is shielding my senses to my family's fate below.

Through the mic, I hear Abraham say, "Show Mommy what we practiced."

Little Milly walks back toward my mother. Dotty reaches into her purse pulls out a small .38 pistol and hands it to Little Milly. Small feet carry her to the front of the stage. She places the muzzle to her head.

"If I ask her to, she'll do it. I can't thank you enough for forcing Frieda into the mortal world," Abraham's voice says, resonating through the cathedral-like space.

I fall to my knees and place my hands on my head. Little Milly returns the gun to my mother as I'm restrained behind my back with indigo cuffs. I sense nothing. My abilities are extinguished.

I'm led out the back. Chief Ray's police cruiser is there waiting for me. He grins while waiting to receive his prisoner.

"I've been dying to get cuffs on you," he says, grinning.

46

Chief Ray pats me down and confiscates my knife. He drives me in alone, though we're flanked by four additional squad cars. Two in front, and two behind. I expected to be beaten mercilessly after being cuffed. By the time he's pushing my head under the door of the patrol car, I realize why I haven't been. I'm more valuable healthy and easy to bleed. The same goes for Little Milly. Unscathed, she's leverage and a propaganda tool.

I'm so angry, the thought that my friends may be dead has just registered. Then, in horror, I realize the cavern is unprotected. And worse, the mineshaft will lead them to the rest of my family who are now trapped. They can put up a fight against traditional weapons, but Abraham's beasts may be able to get through their armor. It won't be long before everyone I love will be dead, except Little Milly. Frieda and them tooling around in her head is akin to vandals rubbing sandpaper across a Monet. Her poor, gorgeous mind.

Mental images of my loved ones being torn apart and eaten flow through my head like venom injected into my psyche. If it wasn't for Little Milly, I believe I'd try to find a way to end my life. If I can just get her out of here, we could escape to somewhere far away. She's still young and could adjust. This has to be my sole focus now, to give my daughter the best life in a world I damned.

"I didn't know Vernon was trying to burn you alive in that barn back in ninety-seven," Chief Ray says from the driver's seat of the moving cruiser.

"But you knew he was burning down an innocent man's house after breaking in and shooting him?"

"I serve the one true prophecy of Abraham. It was God's will."

"Your God gives you permission to kill people?"

"Yes, that's right," Chief Ray says with the cold assuredness of a man whose mind is devoid of logic.

"You feel no remorse?"

"If I knew you'ins were in that barn, I would have brought Vernon two gasoline cans."

I have nothing more to say to this stupid man and choose to ride quietly, unaware of where I'm headed.

To my surprise, Chief Ray brings me to the Yancey County Sheriff's Department. The town is so small that the county and city share an office and jail. But it's all the same organization, Apostles of the Cloven Hand.

When I exit the car, two officers greet me on either side. They put their arms under mine and drag me forward so quickly that I stumble. I feel like they scoured the holler for the tallest boys they could muster. One is my height, six feet, and the other two inches taller. That's rare in these parts.

I'm hauled into the bright office area with a receptionist behind bulletproof glass. A door buzzes and I'm paraded in front of three rows of empty cells. We stop at the fourth and final cell on my left. This one is different. The entire ten-by-ten space is comprised of three-quarter plate steel, sparkling with indigo flecks. The bars appear to be new and have an identical shimmer. One officer opens the barred door while the other clips something else metal to each of my wrists.

"Step inside," the tallest commands.

I do as I'm told because they have my daughter.

Once inside, he says, "Back up to the bars."

When I do, he uncuffs me. I pull my hands up to see heavy, smooth steel bracelets on either of my wrists. Each has a tubular, pin-style mechanism. Their shiny metal glistens with indigo. Abraham spared no expense. And it appears no detail was left unconsidered. I turn to see the backs of the two men as they walk away. They say nothing. Obviously, we're well outside of the legal system. They don't even bother with a mugshot. The seven other cells remain empty. This is my private wing.

There's a bunk on the left. It's an elevated concrete slab with a thin, blue, waterproof mattress. The toilet and sink are the same fixture. Water from the sink flows into the toilet tank, preserving it for flushing. On the right, there's a small desk area built into the wall. It consists of a minuscule round desk and a circular seat. There's nothing else inside the cramped space but cold, damp air.

I think to run water onto the restraining bracelets but realize quickly that it will only lead to my wrists being dissolved, severing my hands. If I use water to damage the bars, they may kill Little Milly. So I refrain.

It's not long before footsteps approach from down the hall. It's Vernon Proffit. He looks the same age he did when I left him to rot on the whale carcass. It's as though the Woods of Lamentation are a form of suspended animation. Because of my time there, I'm biologically seven years younger than I am chronologically.

"I fed you to the sharks," I say sharply.

"Perhaps, but the Lord willed that I should rise up from that evil place and return to finish his divine prophecy. God allowed me to experience hell, so I could more accurately describe it to the masses."

"Mordechai," I say, gritting my teeth.

"Yes, I understand you met Brother Mordechai. He's the one that led them to me. Abraham was able to open up a passageway from the church to that awful place. Men in indigo-reinforced armor went in after me. The creatures didn't see them as prey. It took weeks but they were finally able to pull me to safety. I have a new church and growing flock thanks to you."

"How is that little shit?"

"I don't know. Abraham stripped him of his armor and threw him through the gateway and let it shut behind him. Mordecai was too ambitious. He was insistent on being named an elder, despite his lack of qualifications. Vanity is a terrible sin."

"You're one to talk," I say dismissively. "So, what now?"

"We bleed a vial of blood from you once a week."

"And if I refuse?"

"I'll have them bring up parts from your loved ones to rot in front of your cell. Do you really want to see Tiffany's eyes spilling over with maggots, or would you rather be a good girl?"

I'm too mortified to speak. Is he confirming that they're dead? His men couldn't have gotten through the mineshaft by now. My heart flutters as I realize that their beasts could have. The ones Joseph created had no volition of their own. Basic instincts prevented them from attacking someone wearing indigo-lined clothing because it caused them to see the wearer as another beast. But Frieda's intervention means they won't be subject to the same prohibition. Even so, they eat the entire carcass, leaving no body parts to rot in front of my cell.

"I'll make you a deal. When they come in to draw your blood, I'll let your Dotty bring Mildred to visit. That way, you get something out of it."

He's never tried this hard to keep me docile. Then I realize, it's because there are still combatants from my side on the board and he doesn't want me to know it. Not only that, but he views them as a legitimate threat. This gives me hope, like a slight blip on an EKG after a broken heart flatlines.

———

A week goes by and no stray body parts make their way into my cellblock. Ironically, the food I'm served is much better than what I've been reluctantly downing for the past few months while in the dome and cavern.

Since Vernon's appearance, the only other person I've seen is the officer who brings me those trays three times a day. He's a tall, thin, dark-haired young man, in his mid-twenties. He's always dressed in a Yancey County Deputies' uniform. Though, he doesn't have a nametag. However, he does wear an ACH patch like the officers from the SWAT team I dispatched at the Register of Deeds office. He never speaks. I've tried saying hello, but get nothing but silence and a scowl in return.

Not once in that week has someone come to collect my blood. The Apostles' stagnation compounds my hope. They must be running low on crushed rock and water from the cavern. Otherwise, they would come and take what belongs to them, my blood. What's blocking their advancement?

———

Inside the weapons room, one week earlier.
Rebecca, Nate, Herschel, and Zeke stand despondent at the bottom of the ladder, while simultaneously hopeful for their

reunification with Little Milly.

Their first hint of trouble is the echoes of men screaming and the smell of smoke. Then comes the sound of the grenade's spoon striking the edge of the exposed manhole. There's a thud as the heavy body of the grenade lands on the concrete floor. Its five-second delay fuse isn't long enough to escape the blast-radius. Lethal amounts of shrapnel are propelled at their fleeing bodies. All four come to rest at the exact spot where Charles died twenty years before.

The concussion of the blast is deafening, especially in such small confines. It makes their ears ring horribly. Otherwise, they're unscathed. Each was cradled momentarily in a soft, shimmering, indigo aura, absorbing the effects of the shrapnel hurled in their direction.

They dive through the archway Naomi was holding open. As they look back, they can see men rushing into the cavern from the manhole above. Just then the portal closes, leaving them staring at granite cast in shades of bioluminescent light.

With tears in his eyes, Nate says, "We have to brace the mineshaft door using the Hummer!"

Each of them realizes neither Naomi nor Little Milly is coming back. But, there are still people to protect. There's no time to mourn their lost family members. It is time to keep safe the ones they have left.

Nate backs the Hummer up to the mineshaft entrance, allowing the bumper to just kiss the rock around it. He leaves it there as a barrier. Nate takes the keys out and stows them in his pocket. The four make their way to Tiffany, Diane, and Malcolm. They look to Nate as their de facto leader. He shakes his head, letting the others know that their mission failed.

All seven of them amass themselves at the top of the observation platform for their final stand.

47

The news crushes Tiffany's already delicate heart. To hear that her child and spouse will live out their days as captives is incapacitating.

She stares off into a non-existent distance, completely blank, mind on lockdown mode to save itself from crashing. That can't be dealt with right now. In a matter of hours, men will attempt to break into the dome. Hopefully, the heft of the expensive war machine will hold them at bay. Pushing its nine-thousand-pound bulk forward will be impossible without specialized equipment. Explosives would cave in the mineshaft. They'll have to use something pneumatic anchored into the walls. The logistics will take days if not weeks.

Herschel, Rebecca, Nate, and Zeke prepare the firearms stolen from Solid Rock's old weapons room. Diane and Malcolm attempt to console Tiffany. But they can't even be sure if their words are making it through.

To their surprise, Tiffany stands up. For a moment, this seems like a positive development. Then, she begins running toward the side, which leads to a three-story drop. Malcolm rises to his knees and dives toward Tiffany. His hands just catch her ankles.

She stumbles but catches herself and slips free of Malcolm's grip. He shouts to Nate who drops the box of ammo he's holding and runs in her direction. Tiffany's left foot is on the edge when Nate catches the back of her tactical jacket with his right hand. He yanks Tiff backward hard enough that she falls onto her bottom.

"Ow," she says, suddenly ejected from her fugue state.

"Ow!?" You were trying to kill yourself!" Nate yells, furious. "You're the mother of my child and my friend. There's no way in hell I'm letting that happen."

"Knowing that they're alive, but in the hands of those monsters is more than I can bear. My brain wants to turn itself off but there's no switch."

"Don't you dare do that," Rebecca says sternly at Tiffany. "I know what it's like to be one of those left behind by suicide. I won't have you putting those same scars on them," she says, pointing at everyone else.

"I can't exist like this any longer," Tiffany says, wild-eyed.

After hearing this, Nate motions to Malcolm, "You're on Tiffany-watch."

Malcolm begins to hold the back of her flak jacket to prevent Tiff from getting up.

"This isn't over," Nate continues. "They're alive. Abraham needs both of them healthy. Naomi for her blood and Little Milly for propaganda. I know Naomi. She's already developing a plan."

Malcolm sits down next to Tiff, still holding tight to his dear friend's life. Nate returns to loading magazines and preparing for the inevitable onslaught.

———

Five hours after Rebecca, Herschel, Nate, and Zeke returned from the cavern, the first men from the Apostles reach the mineshaft exit to the dome, still blocked by the Hummer.

It proves to be a significant impediment. They shoot at it with automatic weapons, which create the sounds of high-pitched ricochets. Realizing they're only wasting bullets, the Apostles cease their fire.

Another hour passes before any more noises stir near the entrance of the mineshaft. There are more footsteps than before. Eventually, one of those figures begins to shimmy out from underneath the Hummer. Rebecca fires a round from Naomi's rifle into the back of the intruder's head, killing him instantly.

"They don't have indigo-lined armor, or any, for that matter," Rebecca says.

"These are the people they value least. The Apostles don't have a lot of indigo left. The ones wearing it will show up soon enough."

Two hours later, that is exactly what happens. Several more men arrive. Eventually, a skinny man with an indigo-laced vest climbs under the Hummer and exits beside his dead comrade. Rebecca fires a round at him. It lands true but is absorbed by an indigo field around the intruder. He points a machine gun up at them and begins firing.

"They know that after not finding our bodies at the blast site bullets will do no good. They haven't brought in beasts to kill us. They plan to take us prisoner," Rebecca says.

Split logs appear piece by piece, delivered by a disembodied hand reaching out from underneath the Hummer. Eventually, there's a handsome-sized pile. The skinny man lights a match onto dry, fine wood shavings. Eventually, he uses it to ignite kindling, then the split logs. The dome is sizable, so the smoke isn't overwhelming at first.

Moments later, an unusual rhythmic scratching noise echoes out from inside the tunnel. It's closing in quickly.

"Heavy machinery?" Herschel asks.

"Probably," Rebecca replies.

The hope in their eyes dims as it comes in at a roaring pace. Then they hear the men scream. The errant noise becomes more erratic. The men are silenced one by one. Something begins pushing the Hummer. It gives way, sliding six feet away from the wall. Out of the gap, a large clawed appendage appears. Svangi wriggles through the hole like a tarantula exiting its tunnel.

He makes short work of eating the body of the first Apostle to enter the dome whole. The man who set the fire begins running, despite having nowhere to go. After the boots of the deceased man disappear into Svanvis's flappy gullet, he's on the hunt. Within seconds, Svangi traps him against a wall and pierces his chest with his front-right spear-like appendage. Promptly, the scrawny man finds his new home inside Svangi's gut.

Tiffany let out an audible gasp at his presence.

"Stay here," Rebecca says to everyone else as she heads down to greet Svangi.

At the bottom, Rebecca uses her heavy boot to kick apart the burning logs.

Approached by Svangi, she nervously says, "I don't have the light, boy."

Svangi responds with a shriek.

"You haven't eaten me yet, so that's a good sign."

Svangi paces around the bottom level of the dome looking for something; somebody. For his friend, Naomi.

———————

Inside the cavern below the mega-church, ten minutes earlier.

Apostle members begin to chip away at the granite floor using a jackhammer. The pneumatic line snakes to the surface, through the manhole cover.

They don't hear it over the noise at first. It's not until one of the men, in shock, begins pointing at the wall to the left of the mineshaft. There appears to be a jagged, flickering veneer across the rock. Black claws are the first thing they see, followed by two spear-like legs.

Svangi.

It's the same spot where he had entered and exited through Naomi's archways. The barrier between realities still remains weak there.

Svangi's portal isn't complete like the ones Naomi creates. Crossing over, he shatters the surface off of the granite wall as he forces his body through. The two men closest to the weapons room escape. The rest are consumed in fewer than two minutes. Their attempt to harvest new ingredients for indigo has failed.

Svangi senses the men attempting to gain access to the dome on the other side of Naomi's mineshaft, five miles away. He gives chase. Svangi blasts through the tunnel at highway speeds, using all six appendages against the floor, ceiling, and walls, keeping his small plump body suspended in the center. The question now is, does he remember them?

When Svangi's search for Naomi fails, he returns to Rebecca. He's so close to her that she can smell the dry, hot sulfur wafting from his innards. She doesn't budge, even though everything inside of her says to run. Svangi does something unexpected. He kneels, lowering himself to the floor like he does for Naomi. Rebecca raises her hand and gently places it on the monster's head. He leans into the pet like a loving cat rubbing its face on their human's hand.

"Herschel, come here," Rebecca shouts up at the observation deck.

"Why is it always me?" he says, distraught.

Rebecca says nothing while staring in her husband's direction.

More fearful of her wrath than the beast, he heads down the stairs.

At the bottom, Herschel is greeted by a prone Svangi who is still showing reverence to Rebecca. He doesn't react to Herschel's presence. In fact, he's able to pet him. Nate comes down next and receives the same reaction. Zeke volunteers to be the first person to approach Svangi who had never done so before.

With Zeke fifteen feet away, Rebecca points and says, "Don't eat him. Protect him," mirroring Naomi's words.

Svangi reacts to Zeke in the same non-threatening manner. Diane and Malcolm are given the same treatment from the beast.

Tiffany is the most resistant of them all. After several hours of cajoling, she slowly begins to make her way down. Tiffany is still being followed by her escort Malcolm, whose Tiffany-watch duties were taken over briefly by Diane when he first greeted Svangi.

Before being given the command not to eat Tiffany, he breaks past them. She screams and impotently tries to flee. Svangi is on her in milliseconds. But she isn't devoured. Instead, he places his head against hers as a greeting.

"It's like he can smell her love for Naomi," Rebecca comments.

———————

Because of the speed at which Svangi can travel, the Apostles are forced to suspend their attempts to harvest stone and water to manufacture indigo. However, they have reserves from years past, and Naomi's blood is more powerful than ever.

Everything goes silent for months. Naomi's family enters an information void, surviving on their food stores, knowing Naomi is up there plotting her next move.

48

I go a month before seeing anyone besides the guard who brings me food and toiletries.

Until you've been confined alone, it's difficult to understand or contemplate the monotony fully. Humans thrive on social interaction and physical movement. This is akin to killing someone.

When visitors finally come, it's three of the last people I ever want to see escorting the one I want to see most: Vernon Proffit, Frieda, Dotty Pace, and my sweet baby girl, Little Milly.

Vernon walks up to the bars, unafraid that I'll reach through and grab him. He knows the kind of leverage he has over me. Everyone else stands behind him, roughly ten feet away, in front of one of the four unused mirror-image cells opposite my position.

Little Milly looks healthy but unaware of what's happening, just staring forward, seemingly hypnotized. My mother reaches into her purse and rematerializes the snub-nosed revolver from before. She hands it to Little Milly. My daughter doesn't put it to her head this time. Instead, she just holds it.

"Naomi—" Vernon begins to say.

Interrupting, and speaking around him, I say, "Frieda, what are you doing to my child's mind?"

"Keeping her calm," she responds.

"When I get my hands on you, I'm going to do more than leave you with more scars. I'm going to remove things you'll miss."

"As I was saying," Vernon continues, purposefully clearing his throat, "You are so frightening that we have been unable to hire a phlebotomist to take your blood. I didn't want to damage valuable livestock, like yourself. So, we had Frieda train. Well enough, anyway. Every time she comes down to collect, Frieda will be accompanied by Little Milly, with Dotty as her chaperone. She won't be able to interact, but you can at least lay eyes on her."

"I understand," I say with defiance in my voice but submission on my tongue.

Compliance is all I can do right now. Their cell design is flawless. Even if it weren't, the indigo bracelets they have me wear are solid and professionally crafted. It seems that political donations made for retribution are lucrative. Even if I could escape, I couldn't get to Little Milly before they knew. Would Vernon actually kill her? She's a PR prop to help him build a political empire. One day, she'll lose her value. The longer I wait, the more powerful they become. And, the more apt they are to throw her away. I need to make my break at the first opportunity.

The following day, Frieda returns with Dotty, who has Little Milly in tow like some kind of pet.

"Put your arm out," Frieda commands.

Dotty places the revolver in Little Milly's hand.

In fear for my daughter's life, I do as I'm told. Frieda is a far better phlebotomist than I would have guessed. She hits a vein in my right arm immediately. Frieda collects only one test tube, ten milliliters at best.

"Is that all," I say. "Joseph was collecting pints."

"We don't want to exhaust the supply," she says, flatly.

"Why not collect your own?"

"It doesn't work," Frieda says, almost appearing ashamed.

"But, if your blood is as strong as Abraham thinks, we won't need much rock or water from the cavern."

"I didn't damage the cavern. It shouldn't matter, unless…"

Frieda doesn't say anything, slashing her eyes toward my daughter, letting me know she could kill her at any moment. All because she got hurt feelings. It's difficult coming down from the platform of a demigod to trudge through the mud with the rest of us. She's not accustomed to secrecy yet. When she was a Ceraphirian, threats were all Frieda needed. It seems that's still her default.

This ritual repeats itself one week later. I say nothing this time, not wanting to risk Little Milly's life. To get her out of here, I'll have to neutralize Frieda first.

They've begun collecting two vials a week. Each time it's the same dance as before.

After asking for books, Vernon Proffit personally had them deliver a television instead. It's turned on each time there is a rally or news coverage of their campaign. His legion of frenzied devotees is obviously Frieda's handiwork. Not everyone is under her influence. Sometimes protestors stand up at Abraham's rallies and unfurl signs. Abraham encourages the audience to beat them. And they do, to cheers.

As they become more powerful, the TV stays on longer and longer. Abraham is always flanked by two false Beasts of Lamentation and several armed guards wearing tactical vests with

ACH patches on them. He levitates over the crowd while preaching narcissistic re-imaginings of the gospels.

By early November twenty-sixteen, Abraham and Vernon's poll numbers were very competitive. On November eighth, they were elected Governor and Lieutenant Governor, respectively.

The news I'm allowed to see on television shows protests put down by heavy-handed cops. The newscasters on the station are sympathetic to the Apostle Party. They make jokes during the replay of videos of protestors being brutalized, snarkily blaming the victims for being traitors.

———

By December twenty-sixteen, Abraham had become the de facto, unquestioned Lord of North Carolina, even though he hasn't even been sworn in as governor yet. Technicalities don't matter if laws don't get enforced.

The outgoing administration has all been arrested and is being held without bond. Anyone else who has spoken out against them has met the same fate. Abraham boasts that on inauguration day, he's going to have them all hanged publicly.

———

It's Saturday, December tenth. Inauguration day is the first of January, twenty-seventeen. Today, during a broadcast, Abraham threatened to take a convoy of semi-trucks and trailers loaded with false Beasts of Lamentation to Washington D.C. He promises to set them loose into the streets of the Capitol until everyone is devoured if he's not given unilateral control over the federal government.

If they refuse, Abraham promises to do the same in each major city up the Northeastern seaboard. Leaders from the two major parties are now faced with an unimaginable dilemma. They can hand over democracy on a platter to save millions or let them die and lose it anyway.

Regardless, the closer Frieda physically gets to those regions on the convoy, the easier it will be to influence the local simpletons to join the Apostles' cause.

In response, the Virginia National Guard has blocked off the border with its southern neighbor, North Carolina. The federal government is assessing its non-existent options. The South Carolina, Tennessee, and Georgia borders remain open. Enthusiastically so.

The Apostle Party has grown exponentially across the Southeast and Midwest. However, there are headquarters in all fifty states.

When the television is turned off and the lights are out, I lie on my right side, overlooking the cell. Just before falling asleep, I see something glimmering faintly in the crease between the wall and floor. It's so infinitesimal, that I initially believe myself to be dreaming. But I'm not.

As far as I can tell, they don't have a camera system in my private prison wing. I assume it's in case their enterprise goes awry, there's no evidence. I've been exercising every night without repercussions. So, I don't think much of it to go investigate this anomaly.

The wing is dimly lit, but not completely dark. The closer I get, the more distinctly I believe I can identify this phenomenon. It's the lichen. On closer inspection, the substance sparkles blue, green, and indigo. It's not like any other organism that I've ever seen. It can seemingly grow anywhere, regardless of light exposure, or substrate. In this case, it's growing on metal infused with indigo.

I created my first colony almost ten years ago. But this one is different. Almost sentient. When I slide my fingertips across the small growth, they sparkle. It provides me with a feeling of familiarity that I find comforting. I stare at it for a while up close. But eventually, fatigue gets the better of me and I crawl back onto my mattress pad.

49

I knew immediately who I'd see when I woke up outside, staring at the false night sky.

Theta.

I use the metal railroad tracks to lift myself into a seated position, and then onto my feet. Even in this world, I'm exhausted.

After a wisp of wind blows gently through my hair, she appears.

Despite the dreariness of this place, it is wonderful to be outside.

"Why didn't you take me to your in-between space?" I ask.

"With the indigo surrounding you, I can't pull your physical body through. Here, only your mind is needed. I just needed a way to connect."

"The lichen?"

"It fills the spaces you tell it to, but also follows you wherever you go. It will grow on and through anything in its pursuit to be near you. More importantly, you've neglected what Zelia told you."

"What's that?"

"That you're a Beast of Lamentation."

"I'm just a woman."

"You may not look like what human sensibilities would call a monster. However, you can do as they do. But you lost focus. Even in this place, you can feel it coursing through your veins. Blood laced with indigo, charged up with nowhere to go but through Frieda's needles."

"They have Little Milly," I say.

"Have you not noticed that Frieda is never at his rallies? The Apostles won't risk exposing a woman mutilated with severe facial scars, with no verifiable background to the public. But Little Milly is almost always at Abraham's side."

"She's a trophy. It's equal parts show and to rub his prize in my face. Why else have a television set up across from my cell? When I don't see her with my mother, holding a revolver in her tiny hand, she's being plastered across the screen. He holds her up as a victim of same-sex parents, saved by the blood of Christ and his one true prophecy. Even if I could get out of here, I'd never find Frieda quickly enough to prevent her from causing mortal harm to my little girl. She has total control over Little Milly's mind."

"It's easy to do to someone so young."

"Even if I were to take Frieda out, the rally would have to be somewhere I've been to many times before so that I could form an archway leading there. That's if I can even get out of the cell. The lichen acts like a neural network, allowing me to speak with you. I can't use it to tap back into the Earth to harness my abilities."

"You don't need to. Everything required is already within you."

"All that I have left inside me is despair."

"I mean literally."

"The indigo being formed in my bloodstream?"

"If accessed, you can do anything. Because you won't just be a Beast of Lamentation, but a beast across all planes."

"Why do you say, *if?*"

"Because what happens next is up to you."

"Will I ever see you again?"

"I don't know." Frieda pauses in thought. "I don't think I've ever used that phrase before."

"Distressing, isn't it?"

"Very much, my dear friend, Naomi," Theta says.

I wake up back in my cell in Yancey County.

Days tick by. Abraham continues to have televised rallies even though he won the election weeks ago.

I expect that after his inauguration, Abraham and his minions of slack-jawed dipshits will make good on their promise and clash with the Virginia National Guard on their way north to Washington D.C.

As inept as the Apostles are, they'll be flanked by droves of false Beasts of Lamentation created with my blood. Their men will be wearing indigo-laced armor, protecting them from conventional firepower. It will be a slaughter. Then will come the fall of our country, resulting in millions of deaths. All for the ego of a single insubstantial man and those who enable him.

I trudge through on a loop. Lots of sleeping, regular blood collections, wretched news broadcasts, and three generous meals each day.

North Carolina's gubernatorial inauguration will be held at noon on January the first, twenty-seventeen.

The television comes on at five in the morning on inauguration day so that I can watch the festivities in downtown Raleigh, the state's capital. They didn't let the coincidence that it was Sunday pass them by. There's a sunrise service being held in front of the

Archives Building. It's a large, austere, gray structure with wide steps. A preacher I don't recognize gives a homily about retribution against their enemies.

Behind him, a large wooden structure is being assembled as he speaks. It's a platform with a heavy beam overhead intended to hold a rope. Below, there is no trapdoor. It's designed for short-drop hangings. The intended victim will have a stool kicked out from under them. Its function is not to break the condemned's neck, resulting in instant death. This method is purposefully crafted to leave the victim kicking and in horrific pain for up to half an hour. It's murder by torture.

At the end of his rambling sermon, the pastor explains the former governor, Winstead Wallance, will be first to the gallows. He's a milquetoast centrist who looks like he drives his kids to soccer practice in a minivan. Governor Wallace is by no means an ally, but he certainly isn't deserving of a brutal public hanging, either.

Other Apostle leaders come on throughout the morning until Abraham begins the main sermon at ten o'clock. He likely intends to talk right up until the inauguration at noon. Abraham does love the sound of his own voice.

Just then, Frieda walks down the hallway to my cell carrying a blood collection kit. Neither my mother nor Little Milly is anywhere to be seen.

She stands at my cell, staring at me as I lie on my bunk, as though she expects me to say something. I rarely do. Nowadays, I just look at Little Milly and long for our past life.

"I thought I'd come today so I could watch you finally understand that it's over."

In my mind, I think about what Frieda said to me when we first met, *"Oh Naomi, whose rage has served her well."*

She was right. Months in the cave had given me time to calmly approach my abilities. In my complacency, I had forgotten the strength of my rage. Now as a mother, it is stronger than ever.

Frieda snidely turns around to watch the festivities on television, leaving her back toward me.

Raw, old anger, hard like cured maplewood, wells up inside me. I feel warm blood rushing to my face. Soon it flows throughout the entirety of my body. It's then that I look down at my hands and arms to see them glowing indigo. I stand slowly, unbeknownst to Frieda. I look into the shiny, indigo-flecked metal surface that passes for a mirror over my cell's sink to see my face glowing. All of my skin is sparkling with hues of indigo. My eyes glow like a predator's illuminated by the moonlight.

After Zelia put me through the motherlight, I felt the same surge, but until now I hadn't been able to access it. Intuitively, I know exactly how to use it.

"Frieda," I say, startling her.

She turns to see me directly behind her, still on the other side of the bars. Terror bathes the depths of her cognizance like a corpse's final wash before placement in its casket. As she attempts to step backward, I lightly touch the bars. They crumble into indigo dust. Before she can move, I have my right hand around Frieda's neck, pushing her against the empty bars of the cell opposite mine.

Frieda's face turns red as I whisper, "Get the fuck out of my daughter's head, right now!"

I loosen my grip and she says, "No," in a raspy voice.

I reach down and grab her right wrist with my left hand and send a surge of blistering heat into the fingers encircling it, burning off the appendage while simultaneously cauterizing the wound. She tries to scream, but the air can't escape her mouth because my right hand is around her contemptuous throat.

I raise her dead, severed hand in Frieda's face saying, "How about now, bitch?"

She loses consciousness. I lower her small, limp body to the floor. Frieda's breathing is shallow, but she's still alive. Before rising to my feet, I place my left hand on the floor and send out a small electromagnetic pulse, shutting down all the electrical devices in the building and damaging the semiconductors, making them inoperable. I keep it small, not wanting to disable the entire town. That would garner attention.

The lights blink and the television goes dark. There's shuffling in the office down the hall. The cell wouldn't automatically open after an outage. Regardless, it's their protocol to check afterward.

Their singular guard, more annoyed than concerned, unlocks the gate at the end of the hall with a physical key. I stare back into my former cell, peering into the same metallic mirror. I see two bright indigo eyes looking out through the darkness, facing forward, like a beast on the hunt.

I wonder if thoughts like these fill the guard's mind when those same eyes meet his seconds later.

50

I sprint toward him, still fit from evenings of jumping jacks, pushups, and various calisthenics performed in my cell at night.

Regardless, he's able to get off a shot. Well-trained, his bullet finds the center of my chest before it's deflected by the indigo aura outlining my body. His hollow point clacks as it hits the floor. More shots ring off in quick succession. Each finds their mark with expert precision until the magazine is empty. I keep moving forward, unimpeded by his lethal intervention.

"This isn't fair," the stupid young man says as I close in. I decapitate him using the heat of my left hand the same way I did Frieda's hand. I lift his head off the ground by the hair and dump it into the toilet of my cell, face up. The dead man's eyes and mouth are still open, his dismay preserved in death. I toss Frieda's hand in with it for good measure.

I return to Frieda's limp but living body. I grab her by the collar. While holding her up, I open an archway back to the dome, where I hope to find my family still alive. I back through while dragging Frieda along with me.

On the other side, I'm greeted with a familiar, yet unexpected high-pitched scream.

"Svangi?" I say, confused.

As he bounds my way, I hear another shriek from a very different creature, Tiffany.

Svangi arrives quickly and immediately kneels at my feet. I touch his head, and for the first time, I notice he's vibrating. Kind of the way a cat purrs, only sustained and without audible sound.

Tiff makes it to me a distant second, running into my open arms.

"Our little girl?" she asks.

"I know where she is. I'm going to get her."

"What happened?" Tiffany asks, pointing at an unconscious Frieda.

"Comeuppance."

"Is that…?"

"Frieda? Yes."

"The Ceraphirian that was responsible for my baby being taken?"

"She's human now. And when she wakes, is going to be in excruciating pain."

"Her hand?"

"It was that or let Frieda use her abilities to force Little Milly to end her own life."

Tiffany rears back and kicks Frieda's unconscious body. I don't stop her. She does so several more times but exhausts quickly. Considering everything, I doubt Frieda will even notice the extra bruises. A few moments later, everyone in my family, besides Little Milly, is present.

"I'm going after her and it has to be right now. I need my lamentation gun, coveralls, a hat, and boots."

"We're coming," Herschel says.

"No. Not this time."

"You're just one person," Nate says.

I look down to see that the indigo glow has faded from my body. I focus on the anger I have for Abraham and Vernon for kidnapping my child. The heat returns to my face, then I ignite like an indigo neon sign. The seven of them stare.

"This just deflected an entire magazine of hollow points," I say referring to the indigo aura around my body.

"Our vests worked," Rebecca says.

"Yes, but you can't hurt them. Only I can. And their beasts are different now, conscious. Even if they can't hurt you, they'll try to separate us. Once I have Little Milly, the only escape will be through a portal. If that happens, some of us will likely be left behind."

"What are you doing with her?" Nate says, pointing at Frieda's unconscious body.

"I'm trading Frieda for our daughter. After, we'll have to run, but at least we'll be together."

"Svangi?" Tiff says.

"If he comes with me, the Apostles will quickly realize he's not down here. They'll be on top of you in no time."

They've been locked away from media coverage for months. Their disbelief over Abraham winning the Governorship rivaled meeting Svangi for the first time.

"That's impossible," Nate says.

"Nothing horrifying is impossible if masses of stupid humans work together."

After dressing and getting the lamentation gun back from Zeke, I ask Nate for his black auto knife.

He hands it to me, asking, "Are you sure we shouldn't come?"

"I need him to focus directly on me. This is a negotiation, not a battle. If we go in numbers, it will make it appear to be the latter."

"Where are you headed?"

"I spent a lot of time at the Natural Science Museum back in college. It's diagonally across the street from the stairs of the Archives Building, where the inauguration ceremony is occurring."

As Frieda begins to wake, I press the button on Nate's knife, initiating the side release of the drop point blade. A conventional blade will do now that Frieda is mortal.

I kneel and hold it to her throat saying, "You know I'll do it. If we get there and my daughter is dead, I'm going to take you somewhere quiet and carve you up, slowly."

"My hand," she cries.

"My child," I respond. "Do you know what happens to humans like yourself? Those who aid and abet butchers, rapists, and authoritarians?"

"I'm not human."

"You still haven't accepted your mortality? The process you've gone through is no different than that of Zelia centuries ago. Though, instead of for love, it was the result of your short-sighted hubris. You took the path of least resistance that you believed would serve your needs, having Joseph and I eliminate one another nine years ago. When that failed, you stubbornly continued down this foolish path, exacerbating the harm you already caused, until I forced you out into this world with fire."

"They go to the Woods of Lamentation," Frieda says, teeth chattering.

"And you're still willing to risk it all to prove you're right?"

"God is on my side. I know she wouldn't. I've been a loyal servant."

"Calling God's name aloud isn't serving her. It's only serving you. None of us exist to be servants. We're alive to enjoy sentience, to be kind, to care, laugh, grow in our experiences, and eventually pass away when we've exhausted our physical selves. Our experience is the gift. Zelia saw that. As do I, finally."

Frieda doesn't respond further.

Addressing Svangi, I say, "If she tries to escape, eat her."

I embrace each member of my family in case this is the last time ever see them. When I reach Tiffany, I give her a long kiss goodbye.

After, I say, "I'll be back with our daughter shortly."

I concentrate on a specific spot, the lobby of the North Carolina Museum of Natural Sciences. The light is dim on the other side. The museum must be closed because of the ceremony. I pull an injured Frieda to her feet by the collar. I continue holding it like a leash as I force her through.

On the other side, I find myself in the lobby of a building that held my imagination so intently during my undergraduate years. But now, all the exhibits are covered with tarps. The windows are blacked out.

"They want to hide it all," I say to myself aloud.

I ignite my skin indigo again, just before touching the door to the outside. It crumbled into powdered rust.

The crowd is huge. It spreads across an empty municipal parking lot in front of the steps of the Archives Building, expanding beyond it for blocks.

I'm not taken note of at first. When I start bumping into people, glowing indigo, with a knife to a woman's throat, the spectators move.

The Red Sea of humanity parts. They're scared at first. Then they begin cursing at me, some hissing and booing. As I make it to the center of the audience, Abraham and Vernon both begin to take notice from the stage. My mother and Little Milly are together with him as well.

She still looks hypnotized and stiff, not the curious, happy little girl I knew. There are threats of violence being hurled at me by the increasingly antagonistic crowd. None are brave enough to act, knowing it would be certain death.

Abraham is so shocked upon seeing me that he steps back, dropping the microphone in his hand onto the podium, resulting in a thudding echo over the PA system.

Vernon stays seated like a deacon. He remains calm on the surface. The way his eyes shift back and forth gives away his internal state. Fear. He doesn't want to go back to the Woods of Lamentation.

In a voice that booms unnaturally through the air, I say, "Give me my daughter and I won't cut this rancid witch's head off! Without her, this all ends."

Picking the microphone back up, he says, "No, we never yield. Cut her damned head off for all I care. Most of my followers would have come to me without Frieda. She just made getting their attention easier. But now that they're awake, it doesn't matter."

His statement is met with thunderous applause.

Abraham gives a signal to his two beasts. They charge in our direction. Keeping my right arm around Frieda's throat, I'm able to pull the lamentation gun up from my hip, firing it one-handed twice, killing both of Abraham's unnatural sentinels.

Frieda, knowing that she's about to die, begins to enact a policy of maximum pain. She influences my mother to reach into her purse for the snub-nosed revolver. As she begins to hand it to Little Milly, I drop the knife and lamentation gun to the ground. Holding Frieda with my right hand, I reach my left into her chest. I grasp Frieda's light and rip it from her body. This breaks her hold, causing Little Milly to drop the gun.

My grip on Frieda's disembodied light gives way and is pulled from my hand and drawn into Little Milly's chest.

51

Frieda drops to the ground, stunned but not injured further than she already was. Terrified, she curls up into a fetal position. Not having ever actually understood what it was to be human, Frieda never learned how to be resilient and adaptive.

"Some demigod you are. So certain for eternity, now unmoored and shivering in terror," I say, glaring down at her.

I look around the crowd. Frieda's hold on them has been severed. Many are stunned, staring out into oblivion. However, about half are still jacked up on three-times distilled zealotry. My mother is one of those.

She reaches down for the revolver that Little Milly dropped. Assuming that my daughter is still under Frieda's influence, Dotty tries placing the gun back in her hand.

Little Milly screams, "Stop! Don't touch me!" in a high-pitched voice.

Her words, picked up by the microphone send a shockwave of compliance rippling across the crowd, including those on the inauguration stage. Each takes the command literally and is forced to freeze in their tracks. Despite not moving, they're all still very aware.

I look deeply into Vernon Proffit's eyes.

"Joseph once quoted to me the entire prophecy Abraham made about you. I memorized it."

"He said, *The witch shall call forth the one who will bring the end. She will be sired by Vernon Proffit through a virgin girl, less than one year since her first menstruation. The child will present with a cloven left hand that will cause the world to tremble.*"

"I've come to believe that Abraham is indeed a prophet. And these words are true. Just not in the way you'd hoped. The Apostles said I stole the prophecy from its intended, who you expected to be born of one of your rape victims. But that is a lie. I meet all the criteria."

"I'm here with a witch who called me forth and back onto this path. I present with a cloven left hand. When you tore me apart, I was a virgin who'd had her first monthly half a year before. You were technically my adoptive father. Unfortunately, what I'm doing will make the world tremble. Things people don't understand usually do. And, I'm here to bring the end. But not to the entire world, as you'd hoped. Just to the lot of you."

I hear my seven-year-old daughter's chaotic thoughts tapping gently at the door of my mind. Instead of ignoring them the way I did Frieda, I absorb hers.

It's going to be okay, baby, I say to her in my head. Little Milly remains still, but a smirk paints itself across her tiny face.

Tell them to take off their jackets, I silently transmit to her consciousness.

Once the sentence exits Little Milly's lips, Vernon, Abraham, and Dotty throw their coats and dress jackets onto the stage. Each is lined heavily with indigo, which imbued them with protection.

I bring forth a large archway on the stage behind them. Through the passage is a gray landscape filled with bare trees.

Screams and other horrifying sounds project out across the petrified forest of an audience.

Tell them where to go, Little Milly, I say to her with my mind.

Little Milly points to the archway and says, "Leave us alone!"

Sweating and shaking, Vernon rises from his chair. He's in disbelief, betrayed by his own legs, which are involuntarily returning him to an eternity of punishment.

Abraham is far more stoic, never letting the enemy see his fear. Closest, he's the first one through. He's followed by my mother, whose gaudy jewelry rattles as she shakes with fear until reaching the threshold. Vernon is the final person on stage to enter. He keeps his head turned as far as he can manage, to keep eye contact with me as a last act of defiance.

Frieda rises to her feet to do the same. I close the portal.

"No. Your punishment is to live as a mortal woman for a lifetime. In the end, perhaps you will have redeemed yourself. Consider it a sisterly gift. Now go."

Frieda dashes through the opening we created in the crowd. The people, still under Little Milly's control, do nothing.

I holster my weapons and run up onto the stage. I pick my baby girl up off her feet and hold her close to my glowing indigo chest. Just then, I feel Frieda's light shift from Little Milly's chest into mine.

"Thank you, Mama Naomi, that thing hurts."

"I'll hold onto it for now. But, you might want it back someday."

Exhausted from the weight of carrying Frieda's light, she falls asleep in my arms.

I pick up the errant snub-nosed revolver from the stage because it's covered in Little Milly's fingerprints, and stash it in my pocket.

Behind me, I create a small archway leading back to the dome and our family. As I pass through, I watch the eyes of the audience. It's as though their mental software has encountered a fatal error. Even though they have been released from Little Milly's hold, they still stare off, trying to comprehend it all.

With the doorway closed, we're safely inside the dome.

I hear Tiffany's voice scream, "My baby! Is she okay?"

"She's asleep, not hurt," I assure Tiffy.

She embraces us both, kisses me on the lips, then takes our daughter across her shoulder. Nate is not far behind, gently kissing his beloved daughter's forehead. I'm inundated with the embraces of my many family members, even Zeke.

Svangi's deep, dark eye voids look in my direction as he instinctively begins following Tiff and Nate.

He takes on protecting Little Milly as his primary objective. As I told him so many years ago, "Protect what is sacred."

Little Milly naps for most of the afternoon, while I dissect exactly what happened with my family. I open the ceiling over the observatory so that Herschel can access the internet with his laptop. The incident is the entirety of the day's news coverage and occupies most of the internet's speculation hubs. They're calling the footage, *The New Zapruder Film*.

Facial recognition IDs me as Hannah Sillman through my North Carolina license photo. It doesn't take long for them to connect me as a missing person from *The Earthquake Double Massacre*. That revelation only hypes up the conspiratorial game of Twister, which every know-nothing online bloviator wants to participate in.

Little Milly wakes up to eat, then quickly falls back asleep.

That night, as I occupy my sleeping bag next to Tiffany, Little Milly sneaks over and wraps her arms around me. I try to savor it.

One day she'll be too cool to hug her mama.

———

At seven the next morning, I sense heavy equipment outside.

With Svangi behind me, I flash my skin to indigo and open a doorway in the granite toward the road. There are half a dozen black SUVs and two armored trucks in front of the property. I shut the opening with thick granite as a precaution.

In front of the group is a fit, dark-skinned man in his early fifties, with a full head of short-cropped hair. He's dressed in a nice, but not too nice, suit. An obvious public servant.

The men don't move, but they tense up at the sight of Svangi.

"Hold your fire," the man shouts.

He approaches me, seemingly unafraid.

"I'm Special Agent Postlewait from the Charlotte FBI satellite office."

"You're not sufficiently afraid," I say. "You can see my companion, yes?"

"I know you won't let him hurt me. Every incident we could link to you, Naomi, shows that you only kill murderers, rapists, and their enablers. Not once have you harmed a legitimate officer of the law. You have a code, just like we do."

"Your code protects a country and is thus bound by laws. Mine protects a family, and I will do so by any means, regardless of the law."

"Right now, we're worried about families."

"Whose?"

"Everyone's. In the aftermath of the Apostle's abrupt dissolution, we're left with suspects on the run and tractor-trailers full of fucking monsters. Tracking down their human counterparts; we excel at that. The question remaining is, how do we dispose of those creatures?"

"Toss them all into the sea. Submerging them in water is the only way for humans to kill Beasts of Lamentation."

"But, you can kill them another way. We'd like to see how you do it."

"I'm not available. And, Special Agent Postlewait, stay away from my family."

"Or?" he says with the bluster of a man who's used to being in charge.

"I'll begin to see you as a threat to their safety, and let him eat you all whole," I say, pointing behind me to Svangi.

Hearing this, Svangi screams in anticipatory excitement. The high-pitched sound echoes through the valley.

Each of them quietly begins moving back toward their vehicles.

"Oh, and Special Agent Postlewait," I say as he walks away, "if you ever want to speak with me again, there's a price."

"What's that?" he says annoyed.

"Put a set of cuffs on Chief Ray."

He smiles, "I've already got a bead on him."

———

Drone footage, days later, shows the federal government doing exactly what I suggested, using barges to dump the large enclosed trailers into the Atlantic Ocean, one-hundred-twenty miles offshore. Home to fish now, instead of horror.

With monsters of all types tucked away where they belong, I begin the process of rebuilding my family's world. The venue doesn't matter, only those in it. And for that, I couldn't be happier.

Epilogue

It's November twenty-fourth, twenty-twenty-two, Thanksgiving. I'm watching Malcolm and Diane execute their plans for the big dinner in a spacious log cabin home we had built on Al and Milly's old land in twenty-eighteen.

Most of the valley now belongs to me, including the old Solid Rock Campus and mega-church. Frieda's abilities allowed me to pay substantially lower prices to former Apostle members and sympathizers, practically free.

I flooded the remaining caverns below Solid Rock with lava. Cooled, it filled the entirety with obsidian, preventing any further collection of rock or water.

Using a substantial portion of Herschel's tech fortune, we created the *Al and Milly Sillman Foundation*. It serves the needs of homeless teens at the former Solid Rock Compound.

In the subsequent years, Special Agent Postlewait became someone I consider a friend. His testimony put Chief Ray in Supermax prison for life.

He assisted with having Charles's body exhumed and autopsied. I had him re-interred next to where Milly and Hannah were once buried. I planted a young Oak tree on the site to replace the one the Apostles burned.

His tombstone reads, *"A friend is never really lost, only away on sabbatical. The lesson of their love continues in perpetuity."*

On a winter's night in twenty-nineteen, Rebecca, Nate, Herschel, and I took my dive boat out to the site of my former home in Wrightsville. Unexplainably, at least to the state of North Carolina, the land had returned by the next morning. I had a new home of the same modest size built there. There's a new larger dock with two lifts. One for my dive boat and the other for the tugboat Camille, which I couldn't bring myself to part with. It's fantastic for taking Little Milly stargazing on calm nights. She saw the Perseids out at sea for the first time aboard her this summer.

The world is slowly returning to a tolerable state. However, I keep my ear to the ground for possible sightings of indigo stolen from the Apostles' supplies. According to Special Agent Postlewait, most of it was confiscated by the FBI, though not destroyed. That doesn't sit well with me, but there's nothing I can do about it. At least it's locked away for now.

Little Milly's recovery has not been simple or perfect and is still ongoing. Her abduction will lurk like a beast in her mind for a long time, perhaps forever.

During our time here, I've taught Little Milly the way Al and Milly did me, on paper with a stack of books. She's utterly brilliant.

At twelve, she needs to reintegrate back into the social structure with her peers. She returned to school this fall, just not locally. Instead, she catches the bus from our Tysons Corner house after I take her there through an archway each morning. Every evening, we return to the cabin and the serene quiet of the Appalachians.

I placed a speck of Frieda's light inside her. Only enough to let me track her whereabouts. Just in case.

Svangi walks the perimeter of the mountain property without ceasing. The tinge in my hand from his hunger pangs disappeared upon his return. When he began to think, his primary drive turned from food to companionship and protection of his family. He seems content.

This year, Zeke returned to his home in Asheville, and Rebecca and Herschel to Tysons Corner.

The cabin has more than enough room for myself, Tiffany, Nate, Malcolm, and Diane. Each night, everyone returns for family dinner through the archways I create. That way, we're never really apart.

I no longer have an active sense of restlessness. Instead, I've settled into the role of wife and mother. Most nights I sleep well. But occasionally, I wake up screaming only to be comforted in the arms of my loving wife.

Me and Tiffany are more in love today than when we were teenagers. Our shared life and history have brought complexity and depth to our relationship that my younger mind couldn't have foreseen or understood. Tiff probably did, but she's always been the smarter one.

After all these years, I can say with certainty that everything I ever did, I did for her.

Acknowledgments

Dear reader,

One tends to imagine the art of writing as a solo affair; one person at the page, inking it up with ideas. There's plenty of that, to be sure. But, writers aren't made in a vacuum; therefore, neither are books. At the end of a trilogy, I feel it necessary to take a moment to thank them.

To my mother, who always read to me and sparked my love of the written word.

To Mrs. Ellis, my first-grade teacher who allowed me to check out library books beyond my grade when I became bored.

To Mr. Joyner, my high school English teacher. He would have hated every last word I've written here but would have been proud of me for doing so.

To my Freshman American Literature One professor, who said that I should not pursue writing. You were wrong.

To Dr. Dale Russell, my Dinosaurian World Professor at NC State. You opened my eyes to a wider world and an understanding of deep geologic time that has influenced my work greatly.

To my wife, Juliana, who puts up with the bullshit that living with a professional writer entails. She's been there with me at the darkest and never once faltered.

To Kisstopher Musick, who gave me my first chance as a writer. I will forever be grateful.